The Stone
Cathedral

The Stone Cathedral

by

Todd L. Schachter

iUniverse, Inc.

New York   Bloomington

The Stone Cathedral

Copyright © 2009 by Todd L. Schachter

iUniverse books may be ordered through booksellers or by contacting:

iUniverse
1663 Liberty Drive
Bloomington, IN 47403
www.iuniverse.com
1-800-Authors (1-800-288-4677)

Because of the dynamic nature of the Internet, any Web addresses or links contained in this book may have changed since publication and may no longer be valid.
This is a work of fiction. All of the characters, names, and events as well as the city of Pittsburgh and all other places, incidents, organizations, and dialogue in this novel are either the products of the author's imagination or are used fictitiously.

ISBN: 978-1-4401-6268-8 (pbk)
ISBN: 978-1-4401-6267-1 (ebk)
ISBN: 978-1-4401-6266-4 (cloth)

Printed in the United States of America
iUniverse rev. date: 08/17/2009

Prologue

Tim Murphy had been out walking his dog after leaving his wife, Doris, to watch "I Love Lucy" on the new thirteen inch black and white television set. For two years Doris had wanted a television for the living room. Finally this past year Tim was able to purchase a new 1955 General Electric table top model for their home.

Tim had walked over to the college campus several blocks from his home. The night had been cooler than usual for spring time in Pittsburgh and the students were hurrying back to their dorms to avoid the chill. He watched as the students laughed and carried on all the way back to their dormitories. Some said hello, while others even stopped to pet Dizzy, Tim's German shepherd.

The air was crisp and getting cooler. A full moon was out and there wasn't a cloud in the sky. Tim loved nights like this. He pulled his jacket tight around his chest, and blew his warm breath into his hands. They warmed easily enough. Then he slipped them into his jacket pockets. Content and relaxed, Tim was left alone, unless you counted the dog, but he tried not to.

In the distance, glass shattered, a long high-pitched noise rang out. Tim looked toward the Cathedral where he thought the sound came from just in time to see a large blob falling to the ground at the base of the tower. It landed with a low squishy thud. He looked around for the German Sheppard but didn't see Dizzy anywhere. Tim moved closer to the dark blob's point of impact while searching around for his dog at the same time.

Taking baby steps, he walked among the trees, finally reaching a clearing. He crept closer to the tower to get a complete visual of the situation and then suddenly gasped in horror. Tim's jaw dropped when he realized the full extent of what he saw. He knew what the blob was before he actually saw the mess. Tim looked around anxiously, wanting -- no desperately needing -- to find a friendly face, someone to help him through the next few moments of his life. He stumbled back, staggering away from the dead bloody mess.

Dizzy quickly trotted over, sniffing around the dead body. For a moment Tim was paralyzed. He had never seen anything like this. The poor soul lay there, his entire body limp in death. His head was cracked open, and blood oozed everywhere onto the pavement. Tim had seen lifeless bodies in movies, at a couple of funerals over the years, but this was different. This was foul; it was cruel. This was a violent death. Tim could actually see the blood draining from the man's wounds, especially at the crack in his skull. He fell to his knees and latched onto Dizzy's collar. He had to find a phone as fast as possible. His house was several blocks away, but if there was a phone in the Cathedral than it would save him time.

Tim tugged at Dizzy's leash, pulling her away from the nightmare at his feet. Tim began to run towards the Cathedral with the dog in tow. He wasn't sure if dogs were allowed in the building, but if not, they'd have to make an exception this time.

Through the Cathedral's revolving doors, Tim noticed a man in a long grey trench coat and matching fedora coming out toward him. He tried to get the man's attention, waving his hands, but didn't have any luck. The man had seen him, but didn't bother to stop. The man in grey suit was probably a professor at the college with much more on his mind than helping another person find a phone. As the man in the grey suit moved away from the revolving doors Tim noticed the man had glanced back, but still ignored his pleas of help.

Tim redirected his energy to the task at hand, continuing his search for a pay phone. If the man in grey found the body in the meantime, maybe there would be more than one call to the police tonight. No matter, he wouldn't stop until he found a phone.

Defenestrate (*dee-FEN-uh-strayt*) - the act of throwing someone or something out of a window.

Chapter 1

I'm a hero, a patriotic hero, but one no one wants to talk to. Most people avoid me, trying not to make eye contact. Some simply hope I will go away, never to enter their life again. People love their heroes. Like Superman or Captain America. A hero gives hope to those who need it, but only if the illusion of the hero's persona stays intact. As soon as people get to know their hero, the illusion of superiority shatters and the hero, their idol, disappears. Most people are aware of this predicament, and those are always the most disappointed ones.

I received a Purple Heart for my unsteady limp, well not the actual limp, but for taking a bullet in the thigh. The government gave me a medal for getting shot in Korea, fighting for this country. I can't remember much of what happened. Hell, I didn't even know I was shot until I woke up in the hospital. I was surrounded by hundreds of other guys, most of whom were much worse off. Thankfully, the bullet only hit my thigh just under my right ass cheek. Any closer to the left and I think it would have gone right through my crotch. Can't say I would have been happy about that.

While I was in the hospital, I met a guy from Texas, named Wilson. We didn't call him *Tex* like they do in the movies. Not everyone got a nickname for shit like that. During a routine exercise, this poor bastard was hit in the balls by some friendly fire. A new recruit tripped on a tree root firing his rifle at close range. I couldn't even begin to imagine the pain Wilson experienced that day. He was one lucky bastard though, because he only lost one testicle. Everything else was fine. The bullet just went right through clean out the other side, only giving him a small burn on his ass, and taking a nut.

At least he could still screw and reproduce. It's the small things in life that matter the most. I only lost the ability to feel in my upper leg and a developed a funny looking limp, while others lost a limb or the ability to walk all together.

Overall, a lot of guys were grateful that they were only wounded. There were more men than I care to remember who lost so much more in battle. Giving your right hand to the enemy didn't seem so bad if the only alternative was death.

The only part I really disliked about the hospital was listening to the damned clergy reading the dying their last rights. The death of a friend didn't bother me nearly as much as what they did after he died. There's a character from the film *Red River*, named

Simms. He says, "Fill a man full of lead, stick him in the ground and then read words at him. When you killed a man, why try to bring the lord in as a partner on the job?" I couldn't agree more Simms. I couldn't agree more.

Those who found God after the war needed him the most. He wasn't there for me, or for the friends that I lost, but maybe he could still help those he forgot along the way. Unfortunately, once you found God on the battlefield you were most likely going to see him soon after that. There's a saying that goes "There's no such thing as an atheist in a fox hole." Being scared shitless will make the most devout atheist a believer for at least a second or two. It seemed as if God was always present when death was just around the corner.

I wish I could say the way people stare doesn't bother me, and the way people avoid making eye contact with me doesn't hurt. But that just wouldn't ever be true. It bothers the hell out of me. No one wants to be reminded of the pain and suffering they feel.

We didn't think our freedom was at stake ever during the war, but our government did. That was the biggest problem for us—not believing in the cause. Just because someone told you to be afraid of communism didn't mean the message was going to stick. I think it was easier for me because I didn't have to listen to McCarthy all the time over there. No one would dare accuse the American military of being communists over in Korea. Even if they did, it wouldn't have mattered much. We saw what communism was all about, and at the end of the day, it wasn't that bad. It wasn't my cup of tea, but I could see why so many believed in it. Blaming the communists for all of our problems wouldn't solve anything.

I can recall a friend, Barry Samaranch, whose father had built a fallout shelter in the backyard of their house. Barry's dad had it ordered from *Sports Illustrated* magazine advertisement. It was a *Kiddle Kokoon* fallout shelter advertised to fit a family of five, providing a safe and secure place to live after a nuclear explosion until the radiation faded away. There was even a picture in the magazine that showed everyone climbing out of the shelter after the radiation levels dropped. The idea was to stockpile canned foods, HAZMAT suits, and ammunition in the shelter for when the communists dropped the bombs over our heads.

These last two years at home have given me some time to adjust to the life I left behind, well, it least what was left of it. I've tried not to let the changes create a problem for me; and for the most part I've been successful. A war lets a man understand his own pain. For me, it let me get over my parents' deaths and heal any other open wounds that were left from the war. I traded my innocence and a piece of my morality for closure. Overall, I thought it a fair trade.

A middle-aged woman, wearing a black wool skirt, white top and black heels stood by the trolley stop with her kid as I limped past. The woman looked like money and her kid stared wide-eyed in a stupid looking yellow sweater, red suspenders and grey wool shorts. The kid bore a resemblance to a youthful Hitler. Paint a small black mustache over the kid's upper lip and you would have the Fuhrer's look down pat. The boy was excited, walking too close to the curb causing his mother to repeatedly and angrily pull the boy back away from the street.

"Billy, stop it," she kept saying under her breath. "Just wait until you father gets a hold of you."

I leaned against the railing behind them, setting my cane between my legs. I'd sit down on the bench, but I didn't want to struggle to get back up in front of the kid. Sometimes I'd experience shooting pains down my leg and I'd lose my balance, which would be embarrassing as hell. The cane helped but could never relieve the pressure off my leg completely.

The trolley was late, as usual. It should have been here by now. Some days it was on time, but for the most part the rail cars ran late. Couldn't do anything about it, why bother getting upset. But it made me wonder why the Port Authority didn't push the schedules a head if all the cars ran late anyway. They could change the whole schedule by thirty minutes. If they didn't tell anyone, the trolleys would actually appear to be coming on time.

I shouldn't really have called what happened in Korea a war. I think the brass wanted to call it a conflict, yeah right, the "Korean Conflict". We weren't at war at all, we were just experiencing a small series of "misunderstandings" overseas. *Nothing to see here, please keep moving along. Please keep all hands and feet inside the moving conflict.*

After World War II, the American people were tired of guns, fighting and war. They didn't want to hear that we were in another one. This time, we were sent to keep the peace. The government could tell us anything and we'd buy it. It didn't matter what it was. The people didn't want to know, and the government kept to itself. But call it what you want, it was a war. One day sooner or later we were all going to wake up and wouldn't believe any of the government's bullshit any longer. Sooner or later we would see through the propaganda, see through the thick smoke screen and discover the truth for ourselves. When that day came they could take back the medals they gave me and then go to hell. I bet by then, I will have pawned all of them off for nothing more than a pack of smokes.

The little brat got even more excited as the trolley made its approach. I remember getting excited too when I was a kid and saw the rail car coming. The kid was making little spastic movements with his hands, while inching closer to the street. I watched, wondering if his mother would pull him back this time if he got too close. She didn't seem to care as the trolley pulled up only a foot away from her son. I told myself I would have pulled him back if there was any real danger, but most likely I would have just watched as he became trapped under the wheels, turning to mere pulp on the pavement. Maybe the military didn't train me that well after all. I wouldn't even bother saving a snot-nosed kid. On second thought, maybe the army trained me a little *too* well.

Mrs. "Rich" and her son climbed onto the trolley car. I noticed the driver giving me a sigh as he looked in my direction. I was wondering what gave it away. Could it have been the cane in my hand or my limp? The drivers could get impatient waiting for anyone, especially a gimp like me. I think even if I wore my medals right on my lapel they would still get angry.

Just for the hell of it, I decided to walk a little slower than I needed to. Might as well milk it for all it's worth at this point.

The kid and his mother moved to the back of the car, but I tried to stay close to the front. I didn't want to make the lady nervous. People tend not to like it when you seem to be following them around. They get edgy. Last thing anyone wants is to get into a fight for no reason.

Even during the war I didn't meet many men who wanted to stay and fight with a complete stranger. It's one thing when you can size someone up, make some observations about his personality, but it's a whole other story if you're led into a blind fight with a complete stranger. It was hard fighting a stranger and that's what war is all about. Even in boxing you get to square up your opponent. You get to do some research about the other guy before entering the ring. The fighters who went into the ring without anything on the other guy were usually the ones who were unprepared and beaten in the first or second round.

My time in Korea was like that for me. I didn't understand the enemy. Half the time, I didn't even know who the enemy was. Most of the time, I had the feeling that no one knew any more than I did either. It was hard telling the North Koreans from the South Koreans, mainly because there weren't any real distinctions. The North Koreans were supposed to be the communists, but the truth was much harder to grasp. It was all relative. Even after the British cut a line right through Korea, the North and South were made up of a mix of different philosophies. It wasn't the civilians with the opposing views, but the military from each side. When the Chinese joined the fight, the easiest way to tell the North from South Koreans was that the North Koreans were given better weapons by the Chinese. Just look for the Oriental with better firepower and it was a good bet he was a Northerner.

Growing up, I was always a fan of Superman, but after World War II it became hard to identify with what the character really represented. If I had to pick a superhero to identify with the Korean Conflict, I wouldn't choose a character like Superman or Captain Marvel. I would choose The Spectre, a character who could see the grey areas in the world. It was a skill that the other muscle-bound superheroes didn't have. The Spectre would have fit into Korea well. Captain Marvel could only function in a world where there was a difference between good and evil. World Wars I and II were the wars of Superman, The Flash, Captain Marvel, and the Green Lantern, but Korea was left to the anti-heroes like The Spectre, a character who would identify with the good and evil in every man.

The rail car made its way down Forbes Avenue, passing Craig Street and the Carnegie Institute. As soon as we hit Bellefield Avenue, there it was, through a thick film of dirt and grime, the greatest piece of Gothic architecture in the city of Pittsburgh, The Cathedral of Learning. The massive tower rose 525 feet and had a total of 42 floors. As one of the tallest buildings in the city, it could be seen from miles away. I had lived in Pittsburgh all my life and the Cathedral still gave me chills.

The trolley stopped at the corner of Bigelow and Fifth. The driver waited for me as he tapped at his steering wheel, expecting each tap to make me walk faster. He knew my story. He didn't stare. He just said, "Bye" and "Have a nice day."

I took a look at my watch. I was good on time, but liked to get to class early.

I only had a handful of friends, a couple of people I could truly depend on. I wasn't a very social person, not what anyone would call a social butterfly. I was even worse when it came to girls. Even before the war, I never knew how to talk to members of the opposite sex. You could call me awkward, but that wouldn't even come close. I would like to consider myself Errol Flynn, but realistically I was more like Bogart without the charm. A friend of mine once compared me to Vincent Price in *The Mad Magician*.

"A nice guy, but kind of creepy," he said. I thought "creepy" was a little harsh, maybe shy was more accurate. Even a little bit emotionally distant would have been okay, but not creepy.

I walked closer to the Cathedral. The massive stone structure gave me the chills once again as I approached. The upper classmen called the Cathedral the *Beacon of Hope*. If you ever were lost around campus, you could see the tower from almost anywhere in the area. Once you saw it, you regained hope and realized where you were. I thought that was clever. It really helped the freshman find their way back to their dorms. Even after a few drinks, it was hard to become lost around campus because of the Cathedral.

I was able to make out yellow ribbon close to the far east entrance. As I moved closer, I could make out a handful of Pittsburgh's finest congregating close to the base of the building. The yellow ribbon, I realized, was police tape, marking off a crime scene. The boys in blue took in the scene, following the tower from the sky down to the ground. It was like they were trying to figure out a trajectory of a fallen object.

The crime scene was moderate in size, not near that of a circus, as a half dozen cops stood around. It seemed most of the police work was done earlier in the wee hours of the morning. They looked bored, must have been there all night.

One of the uniforms was talking to a skinny looking blue-collar guy, gripping a dog leash. Looking around, I didn't see a pup anywhere in sight. The man was pale and appeared tense. He was middle aged and looked as if his whole world was spinning out of control. He could have been a witness seeing the whole show as it happened. Must be hard to see a body hit the ground like that, a heavy object falling at a speed that was unnatural for a human being to be moving at, hitting a surface that was not sympathetic to human bone. Then he'd see if there was anything he could do, knowing it was probably too late when he got there.

I've seen men die. It was never pleasant when it happened. But to see a man mutilated right in front of your eyes was an experience unto itself. Hundreds of different images flashed through my head, making the moment all too real. I didn't want to think about the war any longer, but sometimes it was almost impossible to escape from it.

There was no sign of the body anywhere, but a white chalk outline revealed the gory details along the pavement. The body fell from somewhere up in the Cathedral from a height high enough to kill on impact. White numbered evidence tags covered the pavement and along the grass where green and brown patches of grass shown through with faded red stains. There was a three-foot circle of dark red color, which had seeped into the grass several feet away from the chalk lines. It was dry and would take days to vanish. The rain would speed the process, but a faint spot would remain for days, maybe weeks to come.

As I walked along, I met the eyes of a plain-clothed cop. He was middle aged, resembling Friday from the TV show *Dragnet*, but carrying a few extra pounds around his gut.

My attention quickly switched gears when I saw Sara, the woman of my dreams, standing by the Cathedral's revolving doors. I gave a big dopey wave forgetting my age as I drifted toward her. I've been in love with Sara since the moment I met her two years ago. I was in battle, fighting for my life, but that didn't compare to the dread I felt every time I was close to her. I would rather fight over seas than experience the failure that would follow if such a pretty, sweet girl rejected me. It was Sara who originally broke the ice and started to talk to me the second week of class. We've been friends since, but only friends. One day I might tell her how I really feel, but I'm not planning on doing that any time soon.

She wore a blue pleated skirt that came down her to calves and a white blouse tight around her chest. A brown leather satchel hung from her shoulder. I could remember the purple and green notebooks and personal brown leather diary she always kept in it. I didn't think there was a day she didn't write something in that journal of hers.

As I stared in wonderment, my focus shifted from her body to her face as I realized something seemed wrong. Sara's features were more red than usual and she had tears running down her cheeks. The skin under her eyes was puffy and her eyes were bloodshot.

I was hoping she didn't see the body being taken away. When the men from the morgue came to retrieve a body, they had to be careful not to disturb any potential evidence. These men made sure the body wasn't disturbed from the time of discovery to the autopsy. Unfortunately, the actual coroner isn't the one who moves the body from a crime scene. Instead, the morgue men often referred to as *hearse jockeys,* rolled the body in a white sheet, often dropping it once or twice out of clumsiness. I can't imagine how family members would feel if their loved one's corpse was tossed around by two incompetent jackasses.

Without another word, Sara started to cry again. My heart began to break with each sob she made. Tears rolled down her cheeks, following their predetermined course made by the previous drops of salt water.

Sara lunged for my shoulder sending me off balance. We almost toppled over as she burrowed her face into my neck. Her tears dripped onto my pressed shirt. I wouldn't have minded if a tidal wave flowed from her eyes. I would be happy as long as she was there. It was not often I got a woman to rest her head on my shoulder, even if she was crying.

"It's okay Sara. It's okay," I said, trying to comfort her, but accomplishing little at all.

Sara looked up. I had the chance to stare into her deep blues, as she mumbled something softly that I couldn't hear.

I whispered back, "Speak up, honey." As my words came out of my mouth, I realized what she must have said. I tightened my grip, pulling her a little closer, but really wanting to push her away. I wanted to run, far way, far from Sara, far from the police, and the blood splattered grass behind me.

She repeated what she said a little more clearly, a little louder this time. I could hear the words as they echoed inside my head. I saw her mouth move, opening and closing, making each separate syllable. I could hear each sound as she said his name.

"Alex," she said.

"What about Alex?" I asked with care, knowing what was about to happen, knowing it deep down inside, but not letting it out. Sara choked, briefly looking over at the boys in blue and the dried red stain on the pavement. I wanted to move my legs, get them working, but nothing happened. My feet wouldn't move. My body became tight, and I could hear Sara grunt, in pain from my grip.

I shook my head, directing my gaze at the stained grass. That couldn't have been his blood. Sara was wrong. She had to be. But I slowly began to believe that she wasn't. Alex should be in his office engrossed in work, but I knew he wouldn't be. I looked up, but couldn't see the office window from where we stood.

I broke away, running over to the yellow tape towards the plain-clothes detective as he wrote in a small hand-held notepad. Sara followed right behind as I tried to get the detective's attention.

The officer stopped taking notes and focused on the odd gimp in front of him. He was an older, clean-shaven, straight edged kind of guy. He was sporting a grey fedora hat and a brown trench coat covering a brown sport coat, which might or might not be straight out of a bad Spillane novel. He gave me a once over and then turned to Sara.

"Can I help you?" The officer asked in a jaded tone.

I moved to get his attention. "Could you tell me what happened here, please?" I asked.

"You got a name?"

"Jamie Schmidt," I responded, "I work for Dr. Alex Gerlach as a research assistant." I tried to choke back the words that slipped out next. I had to ask the question, yet still fought back the words. "Who was that?" I pointed towards the stain.

The detective looked back toward the patchy ground, then flipped his notepad back a page.

"Alexander Gerlach," the detective said. "Sorry son." He looked back at his notepad. "Couldn't find a suicide note, but that's what it looks like."

I was speechless. My mouth wouldn't move. No sound was produced. I nodded in comprehension, and then my whole world began to spin out of control. Everything was wrong. Nothing seemed right. I heard what he said, but I just couldn't believe it.

"You say you knew the victim?" I nodded in agreement. "How about the girl?"

I nodded again, still unable to form the words. "I'm Detective Lawrence Bloom. Stick around and one of my men will be with you as soon as they can."

I heard the words, but couldn't connect their meanings. My mind started to explore connections, but couldn't find reason. I turned around nauseated, leaving Detective Bloom with Sara, and staggered to the closest tree I could find. This time it was different. The death of my friends was bad. The death of my parents was worse, but this was something completely different. This was too much to deal with. After everything and now this, it was too much. I couldn't keep it down any longer. The liquid started to come up through my esophagus, exploding out of my mouth.

I leaned over trying to breathe through the gagging. Sara stepped behind me, comforting me by rubbing my back. Gasping for breath, I tried hard not to get any vomit on my shoes, but there was no use. I would have to have them cleaned later. I liked to keep my shoes clean, but sometimes there were worse things than a little puke on polished leather. Too bad I couldn't think of much else.

Dr. Alex Gerlach had practically adopted me after my parents' accident. In 1946, I was sixteen and my parents went away for the weekend celebrating their anniversary. My pop surprised my mom with a weekend in Atlantic City, leaving me with Alex while they enjoyed their time alone. They went to the casinos, where they gambled, and at night walked the boardwalk. They went down to the beach and enjoyed the carnival as if they were kids once again. After twenty years of marriage, they still loved each other like newlyweds.

We weren't a wealthy family, but we managed. My father taught in the English department at the university and my mother stayed at home taking care of me. Pop did well enough so she didn't have to work, and I never heard her complain. After I was born, my mother had complications and couldn't have any more children. The doctors said that she was lucky to have me in the first place.

My dad died instantly, but my mom suffered for a week before she passed away from internal bleeding. She couldn't speak, and the burns covered the majority of her body. Even the morphine couldn't hide the pain in her eyes during the last days of her life.

It was after my mother finally died that I decided to join the army, but it was Alex who made me finish college first. He took me in, pushed me to finish my bachelor's degree. I fought with him every step of the way, but he wouldn't give up. It was his idea to take me on as his research assistant when I got back from Korea. By then I was ready to move on with my life. I had survived my self-destructive tendencies with only a limp and a lifetime of nightmares.

At the time, graduate school seemed like the best idea of my life. I had always been fond of history. As a child, I would read the stories of ancient civilizations and pretend my life could one day be as exciting. I would wrap myself up in my bed sheets, toga style, and battle with Caesar, marry Cleopatra, and conquer Rome, all before dinner. I respected my father's chosen field, but Alex had opened my eyes to how history could explain the present and, at the same time, prepare us for the future.

I tried to regain my composure while whipping the vomit from my shoes in a men's room on the second floor of the Cathedral. I splashed some cold water on my face to remind me that I was still alive, that it was Alex who had died, not me. There was an unpleasant taste in my mouth, which I tried to gurgle out with water. After five minutes, the taste was still there. I would have to locate some Altoids when I had the chance.

I gave my statement to the police and waited for Sara to do the same. The questions were mundane. Where were we last night? Did we know what Alex was working on? Did he seem sad recently? All the questions led right back to suicide as the suspected cause of death. It seemed if as the case was being closed long before it was even opened. The police cleared the scene taking all their white evidence cards. They removed their lines of yellow tape, but left the white chalk outline of Alex's body.

Sara and I sat away from the scene under a tree. The police were about to leave when Detective Bloom walked over to Sara and me. The sun backlit the detective, making it hard to look up at his face. I squinted as he spoke.

"We're done here. It doesn't look like homicide, but don't take a vacation any time soon. We might still have some questions for you in the near future if anything pops up."

I nodded at the dark figure and said, "I still have work in the office I need to . . ."

Detective Bloom cut me off. "It's still an open crime scene in the office. I'm keeping the tape up for a little bit longer. It's standard procedure. You understand. If I were you, I'd take a break from work. Take some time to mourn the loss of your friend."

Sara thanked the officer and Bloom left without another word. We sat there watching the police load into their cars and drive away. We sat in silence for what could have been an hour. Sara turned towards me as she wiped her wet eyes for the hundredth time.

"I could go for a cup of coffee, Jamie."

"Yeah, me too," I responded with little emotion.

Again we sat in silence as we drank our coffee in the diner's booth. The only sounds were the clinks and clanks of our cups as we picked them up and set them down on their saucers.

The police had basically closed Alex's case, calling it a suicide without a note. I wondered what made them point to a suicide in the first place. Was it the lack of evidence of anything else? I knew the police weren't incompetent. They had probably done a thorough job investigating, but would they know what to look for? They didn't know Alex like I did. I knew he was not unhappy. Maybe he was lonely sometimes, but sad? I decided I wanted to do some detective work of my own. Maybe I could find something in Alex's office that they couldn't. I knew Alex better than anyone. There was a chance I could make sense out of the chaos where the police had failed. I couldn't believe that Alex's death was a suicide — not yet anyway. I would take time to examine the scene. The police wouldn't have searched as well as they should have if they assumed it was a suicide. I would read into every piece of paper and comb over every item, every clue before I gave up.

I didn't want to leave Sara alone. She was scared, vulnerable even. I had to keep an eye on her, make sure she didn't break. I asked her to come along. Maybe we could keep each other company playing private eye. She was an academic after all. A little research would distract from the sadness she felt for a while. Real research was like detective work. Using a hypothesis to start would direct you in terms of data collection. I felt that the cops were using the wrong hypothesis. They believed that Alex committed suicide and so they probably focused on that, finding evidence to back up their theory. I had to base my research on the belief that Alex did not commit suicide, that he died by another means. Now I just had to find the evidence to back up my hypothesis.

Chapter 2

We stepped out of the elevator onto the yellow tiled floor. For a building with as much character and prestige the Cathedral had on the outside, it looked like someone smeared baby shit all over the interior.

We walked down the hall; I wondered what I was going to find when we went inside. Would I discover a secret only I could decipher? Maybe I'd find a hidden note left somewhere among his library of books. I needed to find something, anything that made sense of Alex's death. I was in a state of denial about Alex's death and I knew it, but I couldn't move on until I examined every conceivable reason he was gone. The police gave up too quickly. I wouldn't. I would examine the evidence and try to prove my hypothesis.

The door to Alex's office was left open, yellow police tape warned of a crime scene. I knew I shouldn't enter, that I would be breaking the law, but I wondered if the means outweighed the consequences. I stopped at the doorway and closed my eyes. To hell with the law right now, my blood was pumping harder than it had since the war. I needed to know the truth.

Was Alex really dead? I knew he was. Would I find him sitting at his desk? No, of course not. What did I think I was going to accomplish by this? I wasn't sure. Did I really want to drag Sara into my crazy delusions? Well, it was too late to worry about that now.

"As I contemplated walking into Alex's office as a memory at my mother's funeral surfaced to the forefront of my mind. As the Rabbi stood over the open grave of my mother, and the fresh grave of my father, he spoke about the cycle of life and death. The words meant nothing, but the way his shadow fell over my mother's casket made me cry harder than anything. I cried so hard and for so long that I didn't have any tears left afterward. I wouldn't say that I became a cold person; it was more like I became emotionally unavailable.

The truth was that I couldn't even shed a tear for a fallen comrade in the war. Now, Alex, a dear friend, someone I considered family, had just died and I couldn't cry. For some reason it seemed okay though. Sara had enough tears for the both of us.

Jamie?" I opened my eyes. I had forgotten that Sara was waiting behind me.

I thought the hell with it and pulled the tape off the entrance, and stepped into Alex's office, I was surprised. Everything looked to be in its place. If the police were in the office at all, they were not here for long. It didn't look like they were looking for anything besides a suicide note. It made me wonder if they put any effort into the investigation at all. They had made their decision before the body was even cold.

The office was small, yet cozy to say the least. Two desks were positioned in the middle of the room. The one closer to the door was mine. It was a simple and modern oak that Alex pulled out of the school's storage room. His desk was modern metal with a green trim. A number of different sized filing cabinets stood against the left wall. Each time one would fill up, we'd grab another, no matter its color or size. The far wall was covered with completely filled built-in shelves. Thousands of books took up space along the shelves, most of which, once placed on those shelves, were never picked up again. Literally every day, I found a new book that I hadn't seen the day before. It occurred to me a while ago that even Alex couldn't read that fast. He would purchase books with no intention of reading them. He was an informational materialist. Alex lived for research. That was his true passion. The topics of interest were often an afterthought.

I went through some of the titles, running my hand along the spines. The police were not focused on the books, as only several were removed from the shelves. They could have been left by Alex the night before. Nothing looked unusual. One book on ancient Rome, *Tiberius and the Roman Empire* and two others I have never seen, *The Lame, the Halt, and the Blind,* and *The Journal of Diseases and Vaccines,* were spread out on the desk. I had used the book on ancient Rome once before, but the other two were completely new to me. Although it was common to see a new book in the office, why would Alex have books on medicine? I couldn't recall any research he had done on the subject.

The books caught Sara's attention for a moment, but she decided to move on once she was content with their irrelevance. She turned to the window, following the yellow police tape that tried hopelessly to cover the shattered glass. She was cautious not to get too close to the edge, but the thought of falling out was the last thing on her mind. She was only thinking of one thing, the same question running through my head. Would Alex have jumped to his death? She ran her hand over the broken pane of yellow and orange glass. She cried in pain pulling her hand to her mouth.

"Damn it!" Sara yelled as she sucked on her thumb.

A gust of wind rushed into the office, blowing her hair away from her face. Papers flew, scattering around the room. I tried to move quickly, picking them up and setting them under a small silver elephant. It was actually a lighter in the shape of an elephant, a present I brought back for Alex from Thailand, when I was on leave. The elephant was small, but very detailed, and had real ivory tusks.

"I didn't know Alex was interested in the history of medicine," Sara said.

I took the bigger of the two new books and flipped through it. Pencil marks underlined and filled the margins. I started to read the writing, while Sara stayed miles away in her own thoughts, pacing the small room.

"I can't believe it," she cried. "He was so happy." My eyes fell back on to her blood shot eyes. The little makeup she wore around her eyes had dripped down her cheeks. Even in the emotional state she was in, she was still the most beautiful woman I had ever seen. I wanted to go to her, hold her, make everything okay again, but I couldn't. I returned my attention to the book in my hands, but couldn't read the words Alex had written on the page.

Sara's eyes rested on Alex's desk as she walked around it, pulled out and then sat on his brown leather chair. The chair was worn. The leather had started to crease and crack along the sides of the seat. Sara looked small in the leather chair, the frame towering over her small body.

She wasn't wrong. Alex was a happy man. Since the day I met him, he was always smiling and joking. He had a terrific sense of humor, never wanting to give away a punch line until just the right time. If Alex ever appeared lonely, it was only an illusion — – the picture of a middle-aged single man who had disregarded society's standards a long time ago. He liked living alone, had for as long as I knew him. He wasn't unhappy. Perhaps he was merely content, but he never came across as sad. In fact, the only time I ever saw Dr. Alex Gerlach shed a tear was on the days at my parents' funerals. While my parents' caskets were lowered into the ground, I looked over and there on Alex's thin left cheeks were tears.

Alex and my father were like brothers since first meeting at their faculty orientation. He had been named my godfather and was always there since the day of my birth.

I walked over to the window. The cool breeze felt good as it whipped my hair around. The sharp gust of wind felt good against my skin. I didn't want to move. I wanted to stand there until the cold stung my bones. I welcomed the pain with open arms.

I was taller than Alex and at about five foot nine I had to duck down through the hole his body had made in the glass. I looked over the ledge, down to the pavement below. From my prospective, the people seemed so small, like children. The red stain was less noticeable form here, seeming only a shade or two darker than the rest of the pavement. The grass around the pavement held the off color of auburn next to the greens and browns. If I had not known that a body had splattered against the ground just hours earlier, I would think it was simply a shadow or a figment of my imagination. I began to move further out into the broken window. I wanted to know what it felt like to fly through the air, knowing that any second would be your last.

My reflection reminded me to pull my head back in. Having my own eyes looking back at me I could no longer able to stand those morbid thoughts. My light green eyes were crystal clear in my double's image. I had gained some weight over the last couple of years, rebuilding a frame that was to thin from the army. My hair was a mess and needed cut, but that would have to wait.

My attention shifted to the shattered stained glass window before me. The broken edges came together in sharp points able to tear apart the roughest of men. Why hadn't he opened the window before he jumped? If he wanted to end his life so quickly, why go through so much pain? The glass would have ripped into his fragile body as if he were a rag doll.

The window frame was still intact, only the glass was damaged. I tried the handle. It turned, and I pushed what was left of the window slowly out and up.

Sara picked up a small ashtray from the desk and held it in her hands. She studied it for several moments before sighing and putting it back down.

"It looks like he smoked a whole pack last night," Sara murmured.

I worked the handle again, turning it smoothly on its axel. The window definitely worked. If anything, the impact to the window would have made the handle stick, but it still worked perfectly.

I looked back over at Sara. "What was that?" I asked, not having paid attention before.

"It's odd. Alex must have smoked a whole pack of cigarettes last night. Look at this." Sara lifted the ashtray. It was overflowing with cigarette butts. "Have you ever seen anything like it?"

She was right. There must have been over twenty smoked butts put out at their filters. What was it about the ashtray and the window that bothered me so much? And just like that, something in my brain clicked. I felt two puzzle pieces reorganize themselves in my head.

"He didn't smoke those," I said pointing at the finished cigarette butts. "Alex didn't smoke filtered cigarettes!" I didn't know why I was excited.

Sara frowned in skepticism, "Then if he didn't smoke them, who did?"

I wasn't sure. If he didn't smoke them, then obviously someone else did. Someone else was in the office last night before or after his death, or perhaps that person was there at the time of Alex's death — maybe his murderer.

I looked back at the window. It all seemed so wrong. Alex wasn't sad. As far as I was concerned, it wasn't even a possibility that he committed suicide. He was a religious man for God's sake. He hated even the idea of someone committing suicide. I began to think out loud.

"Let's say Alex did want to commit suicide," I began, "he wasn't that strong. He'd have to take a running start to break through that window. But look." I walked across the room. "There are only a couple of feet between the desk and the window. It would be nearly impossible for a man of his age to gain that much momentum and strength to break through the window like that and land where his body was found." "What's your point, Jamie?" Sara leaned over the desk and slid her arms under her chin. "What else could have happened?"

"My point is that I don't think that he jumped out of this window," I said.

In fact, I was certain that he didn't do it. The evidence may have seemed minimal, but to me it was overwhelming. Why hadn't the police seen this? Sara couldn't understand. How could she? Sara didn't know or even understand Alex as well as I did. How would she know the truth?

I walked over to the tallest filling cabinet in the corner of the room. Sara waited as I combed through the first drawer, then the second. There were too many damned files. I couldn't tell if anything was out of place or missing.

"What are you doing?" she asked.

"Someone was here last night besides the professor. The cigarettes point to it. Help me figure out if anything is missing."

"Maybe he switched his brand."

I moved to the next drawer, and then the next, finding nothing out of place. I moved over to the desk. I didn't know what I was looking for, but there had to be something.

"A man doesn't just switch the type of cigarettes he's been smoking for the last twenty years like that." I returned my attention to the filing drawer.

Sara waited patiently behind me. I flipped through file after file looking for something that would give me a clue to what Alex was doing last night. I scanned everything, but couldn't find a clue.

"Damn it!" I shouted causing Sara to jump out of Alex's chair. She looked at me questioningly. She just didn't understand. I moved forward grabbing her shoulders. "Did you see the police take anything?" She was shaking and began to turn pale. I knew before she spoke that I had crossed a line.

"No," she mumbled, "They didn't . . . take . . . anything," Sara said in broken sobs. I was pushing her over the edge, but I couldn't stop myself. She pulled away, slipped out of my grip. Her legs buckled and she almost fell backwards. She regained her balance as she stumbled out of the office, slamming the door behind herself.

I stood in the office silent, not wanting to move. Sara was at her breaking point and I was pushing her too far. She really liked Alex, losing him took its toll on her. Fearing that he was murdered and having to deal with this while she was still in shock over his death was more than she could handle. It wouldn't do either of us any good to push her when she was so emotionally troubled already. Her crying echoed through the halls, then turned into a light whimper.

When I walked out, I saw Sara on the floor in the corner, curled up into a fetal ball. I felt ashamed for the way I had treated her. Although I was angry, I was not angry at her. I could never be angry at her. I closed the door behind me, hearing the lock click into place.

"I'm sorry Sara," I said as I dropped to the ground as I got closer. I wanted to hold her, but didn't know if I should. She made the decision for the both of us as she leaned over laying her head on my chest. Putting my arms around her shoulders, I felt her whimpering slow small sighs and hiccups.

"You probably don't want to hear this." She looked up into my eyes wanting me to continue although it tormented her to think about Alex's death. "I'm not convinced Alex would kill himself."

Sara silently nodded, wiping away her tears. Her eyes were already becoming puffy again. She sniffed and started to giggle. I looked down and realized my shirt was wet all around my chest. When I started to laugh, Sara's laugher grew into a steady chuckle.

"How about if I walk you home?"

Sara looked up at me and nodded in agreement. "Thanks, Jamie."

We didn't say much as I walked her back to her house. What did you say after something like that?

During the war, there wasn't really much to say after a platoon member was killed. Dead soldiers were common and the others didn't want to talk about their fallen comrades. They were gone and there was nothing you could do about it.

When my parents died I didn't talk to anyone. Alex thought I was mute for the better part of a month. There really weren't any words that truly comforted me while I grieved — not my own and not the words of others. I didn't even try to talk about my feelings. Words only made the feelings worse. Everyone has a different way of dealing with death. Some people fought the pain until the day they die, but others let the pain go, coming to terms with the loss of their loved one.

As for Alex, there was no way I could believe that he killed himself. There were just too many reasons why he wouldn't. People like Alex didn't take their own lives. They fought to the end and tried to cheat death when the time came. He wouldn't beg for his life or grovel at the feet of Death. I could only imagine that when his time would come, Alex would have a rational conversation with the Angel of Death. He would make two cups of hot cocoa, and then go on to convince the Angel that there were better things to do with his life than die. Too bad he never got the chance to make the cocoa.

Sara had been renting a room on Atwood, close to campus, from an old widow who cooked almost every night for her boarders. The widow was a traditional old lady. She didn't allow men in the house after dark and all that kind of crap. I was under the assumption that her husband had fought in the Great War. She was old. She looked as if she could have a husband who fought in the Civil War.

Sara led me to the small three-story townhouse where she lived, stopping in front. The city was filled with hundreds of streets filled with three-story town homes. The house was long and skinny, rising up the three floors, coming with a full basement. The stairs were usually steep and would tire out the unfit by the third set. The ceilings were higher and better-suited for the claustrophobic than their suburban counterparts. Compared to the houses in the suburbs, the city's homes had character and a historical richness that the cul-de-sac could never convey.

She gave me a hug and then kissed me on the cheek. "I'm sorry Jamie. I know how much he meant to you."

"Thank you," I quietly responded.

She let go of my arm and walked up the three stairs to the small concrete slab porch. She started going through her purse searching for her house key and I begin to walk away.

"Did he have any relatives?" she asked.

I paused shaking my head and then called back, "Just me."

Alex had been great to live with after my parents' death. He was always good about giving me space, providing me with plenty of privacy. Rarely did he have rules for me to follow while living in his house. All he asked for was respect and that was always easy to give. As he slowly filled the void left by my parents, he became more of a friend than anything else. He could never take the place of my mother or father, but he always reminded me that I wasn't alone.

When I came back from Korea, however, I decided to live on my own. While I liked living with Alex, I thought that after three years of living in a crowded barrack I could use a more space and time to myself. Living alone could be lonely, even depressing at times but I felt that I needed to try it. You learn a lot about who you are when you have no one else to turn to. Sometimes you have to be by yourself before you can fully understand the inner you or relate well to others. It's like "Know thy self" or some Freudian shit like that.

Looking back on it all, the army seemed right for me when I signed up to go. I had seen the slogans and thought the army could make me a man. I thought the experience would help me mature and teach me who I really was. I believed the ads and propaganda hook, line and sinker.

A problem emerged early on at boot camp, however. The army didn't want to help with my form or discover my own identity. To the army, we didn't have our own identities. The army wanted to tell me who I was, or rather who they wanted me to be. The leaders tried to cut me down, fill me up with their own philosophies and rhetoric. They wanted machines. I left basic training a half-empty shell, with the knowledge of how to fight and how to kill. I went off to war filled with the false understanding of what life really meant. Death would open my eyes and then contradict what my superiors had taught me. I knew life was not about the kill, but I didn't know anything else. Killing came easy. It was living with it every night that was hard.

Alex had been passionate about politics of the present and the past. He loved researching ancient politics like Caesar's battle with Pompeii, the uniting of the upper and lower kingdoms of Egypt by the Pharaoh Meni, and the emergence of Confucianism led by China's Emperor Wu. The politics of Mark Anthony partnering with Cleopatra to destroy Caesar could really get Alex's blood pumping. It wasn't until after the war that I realized how useful history could be. I preferred modern history over ancient history because of the direct effects on the present day society. Reading about the industrial revolution could keep me occupied for days on end. The growth of the British Empire, the end of slavery, and the shooting of the Archduke Ferdinand would keep me engaged in my studies more than any myth from Mesopotamia.

I had been a sucker for good and bad movies. Sometimes seeing a bad movie was better than seeing a good one. I could never pass up a chance to see one just because of a bad review. I took Alex to see Mankiewicz's version of Shakespeare's *Julius Caesar* last year. Brando's Anthony was great and very believable, but I couldn't get into Mason as Brutus, too stiff I suppose. Alex didn't care about the acting. He was too busy watching Greer Garson play Calpernia. Other than for the women, Alex hated the whole show. He thought the death of Caesar was too dramatic. I thought it was supposed to be dramatic, not like in real life, where death was the most undramatic event of your life.

The scene Alex disliked the most was the stabbing part when the Senate kills Caesar. Caesar was able to get off one of the greatest last lines according to Shakespeare, "Et tu Brute?" Real life didn't give you last lines like that. Historically, when the members of the Senate stabbed Caesar to death, Caesar probably couldn't identify anyone from Adam, much less single out Brutus from the others. He likely died having no idea who was attacking him or even why.

One moment you were alive, the next you were dead, shot in the head, stabbed in the back, falling in a muddy ditch, or to a marble floor, adding to the number of fallen slaves or soldiers, only to become a statistic in the papers or in history.

I waited for the Fifth Avenue trolley that would take me toward Alex's house. The house was a large Victorian, east of Oakland, in a neighborhood called Shadyside. Alex didn't like the idea of living near the students' dorms and rented apartments, preferring a quiet suburb instead. Alex liked the quiet streets of Shadyside, which were covered by canopies created by wide red oaks and paperback maples. Mostly rich families and single, wealthy men lived there, but Alex didn't have a family, nor was he considered wealthy. I would have called Alex comfortable, upper middle class perhaps, but not rich. He didn't own much besides the house. His possessions were few, but were elegant in always in good taste. He didn't have a car or any fancy toys.

Alex had more acquaintances and only a few close friends. My father had been one of those close friends before he died.

Thinking about Alex and how he lived, it didn't make any sense to me that he would have committed suicide. Was it possible that it was an accident? Could he have slipped and fallen out of the window? What were the odds of that?

What were the other possibilities? Was murder realistic? What motivation would someone have for killing a history professor? Was Alex having an affair with someone's wife? Maybe the husband found out and killed Alex as revenge. Possibly a disgruntled student who didn't like his or her own grade killed him. Or was it a colleague who didn't like living in the shadow of another historian? They were all viable theories, but none seemed to fit.

I couldn't remember if he had any academic or real-life enemies. He was blunt and direct, but wouldn't go out of his way to cause trouble or upset the apple cart if it could be avoided. Hell, most arguments were centered around department politics in the first place. You didn't get killed over school politics. Academics didn't kill other academics when it was much more fun to respond with a published paper. Disproving another professor's research was a prime goal and required more talent than brute force. It was pure bliss if you could publish in the same journal proving another theologian's theory wrong, especially if you despised the other researcher. Not since the Webster case has there been such a hideous act of murder for academic gain. It just didn't happen like that anymore.

It wasn't like Alex was working on anything that would redefine the field of history. History was not a physical science or a groundbreaking field of study, but a watered down *social* science. It didn't have the glamour of other disciplines like physiology or philosophy. Historians researched past societies, theorizing motives, reasons for war, and discussed the future ramifications of repeated events. Historians would be lucky if an archeologist made a discovery in an Egyptian tome or uncovered a battle ground that could catapult a historical topic to the mainstream, making it easier for them to get their research published.

A trolley car finally rolled to a slow stop in front of the sidewalk where I was waiting to head toward Alex's house. The car was full, every seat taken by the morning commuters and housewives out shopping but I didn't care to sit in the first place. I paid the fare, and found a suitable location to stand. I was thrown forward, not able to gain my balance as the driver put the trolley car in drive. I stumbled, almost missing the black leather strap extended from the ceiling. I managed to catch it just in time and pushed my cane down, jamming it between two sets of legs for support.

After the car reached a steady speed, I was able to regain my balance. I heard a scratchy groan from a man sitting in the seat directly in front of me and realizing that my cane had come down on the man's foot as I pressed it down to keep my balance. What I had mistaken for the ground was actually the man's leather shoe.

"I'm so sorry, sir," I apologized, removing the cane from his foot.

The man took off his expensive brown Gahan hat, setting it down on his lap. He wore a sleek and clearly expensive suit. The fuzzy hat was worth more than what I could make in a month. The suit and Gahan matched his shiny winged tip brown leather shoes, one of which I had managed to scuff. Looking up at me, the man gave a snarl that was part human and part mutt. He was older than I thought originally. His hair was completely white, and he had some wrinkles. His chin protruded with multiple layers, lying like a mountain over his tight red tie. I judged the man to be in his late fifties or early sixties, older than Alex had been, but less refined, and overly eccentric.

My stop was approaching. The man stared at me with a certain hatred that I hadn't seen in a human being wearing civilian clothes before. I purposely tried not to make eye contact while I limped to the exit, placing my cane close to my leg with each step. I nodded to the driver and practically jumped down from the car without another glance behind me.

The sun was out rising by the second, as I made my way down South Negley towards Walnut Street. It was beginning to get warmer and the sunshine was providing an uncomfortable brightness, burning my eyes. I was sweating more than usual, but not enough to cause any discomfort. The house wasn't far from the intersection, so I began to shuffle over the couple of blocks to Alex's house.

I crossed the street and noticed out of the corner of my eye a figure in all brown following right behind. At first I wasn't sure if it was coincidence, but I realized right away that it was the man from the trolley. Either he was extremely angry about his wing tips or it was oddly his stop too. I stopped, ready to stand my ground and saw that the angry glare hadn't left his face. He was my height, but broader, and even though he looked to be older than Alex, he seemed as if he'd be able to hold his own in a fight. The man didn't waver as he approached.

"Is there a problem, sir?" I asked ready to defend myself. Three years of army training returned in a flash. It was so ingrained in me that I didn't have to think through a plan of action. I was functioning on instinct alone.

I didn't want the encounter to turn into a violent display of male aggression, but I knew sometimes there was no way around it. My nerves were shot and I wasn't sure how much rage I might take out on him. I realized that if I allowed the floodgates to open I wouldn't necessarily be able to close them quickly.

"Jamie?" The man smiled, exposing a yellow smoked stained grin. "I thought you recognized me, but I must have been mistaken." The man set out for a hand shake. I didn't understand. My mouth fell open revealing my confusion.

"I am right in thinking you are Jamie Schmidt?"

"Ahh, yes … I am," I said and closed my mouth. The blood began to return to my opening fists as I relaxed. I couldn't figure out who the man in front of me was. A moment ago I was ready to throw fisticuffs in his direction, but now he was happy, almost giddy.

"It's been so many years. The last time I saw you, you came up to my knees. I must say, I heard you were back from the war, but Alex did not say anything about how big you had grown."

"Alex?" This man was a friend of Alex's? He just couldn't place him.

"I'm going to visit him right now." The man said.

"I'm sorry?"

"Oh my, I completely forgot. You were just a boy when you met me. My name is Longmont, Dr. Mark Longmont"

"Dr. Longmont, I'm so sorry to have to tell you this, but Alex

. . . he's. . . dead." It felt uneasy explaining his death to a virtual stranger. "The police found the body early this morning."

Longmont grabbed his chest staggering backward. "But that's not possible," he said surprised. "I was just on the phone with him yesterday. We were supposed to meet for lunch at his house today. That was where I was going when I ran into you."

"When did you talk to him?" I had tightened the grip on my cane. My knuckles were bright white, and I tried to keep from grabbing Longmont by his lapel to shake the answer out of him.

"I really don't recall the exact time . . . "

"Please, try to remember doctor, it's very important." I was pleading. An hour ago I had learned that Alex had taken a swan dive from his twelfth-story office window and now I was looking for any clue to explain what happened and why.

Longmont rubbed at his chin trying to remember. He seemed fairly calm, but the shock probably hadn't settled in yet. Sometimes it takes hours for people to fully comprehend terrible news.

"About six in the afternoon, I think. It had to be around that time, now that I think about it. I usually have dinner around five and called him right after that." He paused. I wasn't sure if he was done or trying to remember something to tell me.

"I called from home, in Ann Arbor." He began again, "I'm a professor at the University of Michigan. I had to confirm our meeting for today, but it was a brief call really. Alex seemed to be in a hurry." The professor pulled out a silver cigarette case tapping one on the hard surface to pack it.

"What was the meeting supposed to be about, Dr. Longmont,

if you don't mind my asking?" What was Alex doing in his office so late?

Longmont opened a book of matches and struck one. A bright orange flame took shape as he lit his cigarette. He took a deep breath, inhaling the nicotine and tar before letting it out in a cloud of white smoke.

"We were working on a project together. Alex had just informed me he had a breakthrough in our research. He said he could not wait to tell me."

"Why not just tell you over the phone?"

"I'm not sure. He sounded very excited and wanted to tell me in person, I suppose."

"And the research, what were you working on together?"

"A boring subject I'm afraid, but not due to your professor's doings. I had designed the theory myself and was working it into a paper for a small journal in the Midwest. It was a standard research design, really. Alex had been researching the historical content of the paper. As I said, it was a very dry subject, but Dr. Gerlach had found something that even he became excited about."

"Dr. Longmont, are you sure you didn't have any idea what Alex found?"

"I'm afraid not. We had only been working on it for a short time, maybe six months."

Six months? Alex had kept six months worth of research from me. I guess I could believe it, with as much time as he spent at the office working without me. He could have also as easily done the majority of the work in his own home office. He had far more books and papers at his house.

"I'm in a bit of a spot here, Jamie. I was planning on staying with Alex while I was in town, but now I'm not sure what to do."

I gave Longmont the names of several hotels in the area.

"Maybe I should give a statement to the police. I might be able to remember more later, after I've rested."

I agreed. If they obtained more evidence, the police might think about reopening the case. Dr. Longmont decided on The William Penn Hotel. He would stay in town for several days and I could reach him there.

The house was only a block away and I hurried over without stopping again. I took out my spare key and opened the front door, entering the house. I was dumbfounded by the shear scene of chaos before me. Every piece of furniture in the living room was knocked over. The end tables were broken on their sides. The couch and love seat were flipped over. The fabric was ripped open, exposing the white stuffing.

Books and papers were thrown everywhere. The high fidelity stereo was thrown across the room, revealing shattered glass tubes. I had never seen a house in this condition before. Alex was religious when it came to cleaning. He paid more attention to the cleanliness of his house than to what was in it. A maid came to his house once a week to clean what little of a mess he made. Alex lived by himself, but he liked everything square and tidy. But this was beyond a mess that someone would make on his own. This was vandalism. I hoped the maid wasn't here when whoever did this was around.

I walked over to the opposite side of the room where the turntable had sat. It was split open down the center, never to work again. Surrounding it were all of Alex's records. Some were still in their sleeves, but many were shattered into hundreds of pieces all over the floor. I picked up Nat King Cole's "Unforgettable", which was cracked down the middle. Alex liked all types of music, but was a huge fan of Jazz. I put the two pieces back down and remembered when Alex bought the album a year before.

The television awkwardly lay against the coffee table, the screen shattered. I was pretty sure there was no chance it could be repaired. It didn't matter anymore though. Alex would never watch it again even if I had it fixed. He purchased that set after my parent's funeral when I had just come to live with him. Alex thought buying it would make me perk up. I wasn't in the clearest state of mind and wouldn't come out of my room except to use the bathroom. Alex had to bring all my meals to me, forcing food down my throat on a daily basis. I had locked myself away hoping the pain would stop.

Amazing how much the damned television impacted my life. I wasn't proud of the positive affect it had on me. I had never seen a TV show in my life before, and I wasn't sure if I was going to be able to live without television ever again after that. I liked watching Sullivan on *Toast of the Town*, but you couldn't pay me to sit through that *Hallmark Hall of Fame* crap. They would butcher Shakespeare, not to mention great stage plays.

Their version of *The Tempest* made me want to throw a brick at the television.

In the kitchen, cabinet drawers rested on the laminate floor. Alex's silverware was spread out along the counter as if someone was ready to melt it down to make a quick buck. The refrigerator was wide open and even the food had been thrown out around the room. I tried to put some of the food back into the cooler, but it was useless. It would take an hour to put it all back and I was pressed for time. Besides it was a drop in the bucket when you considered enormity of the mess throughout the house. The smell would start to grow pungent, but the mess would have to wait until later.

When I closed the refrigerator, a postcard dropped down, sliding under the kitchen appliance. The postcard had been kept in place by a small magnet in the shape of a pineapple. No other items were on the front of the cooler. I reached under the grate hoping not to find any slime or dirt. I couldn't reach far enough and had to lie on my stomach. Once I was eye level with the floor I saw the card right behind the black panel and pulled it out.

Looking at the postcard, I didn't know if it was sent as a joke or if it was meant as a serious postcard from a friend. It featured a picture of the Eiffel Tower against the Paris skyline. It was because Alex despised the monument celebrating the French Revolution, with a revulsion that would make the Prime Minister blush, that I didn't understand why he would display it. I turned it over, but it hadn't been sent by anyone. It was blank.

Alex went to France several years ago for a conference on irrigation and agriculture in Eastern Europe in the 1300s. When he returned, he didn't have a single nice thing to say about France. He claimed that he could barely focus on the conference due to his displeasure with not only Paris, but the French people as a whole. I thought the conference might have been a tad bit dry even for Alex, but he blamed his French hosts for his mood. He had so much hostility towards the French as a whole after his trip that I was amazed he didn't make it his goal in life to wipe out the whole country. I had never heard the word frog used in such a bigoted manner before he returned. To say Alex had a dislike for the French was a gross understatement and the irony of the situation was almost too much to accept.

I took the postcard, slipping it into my pocket. It would at least remind me of Alex's sense of humor, possibly making me laugh when I needed to most.

The rest of the house was much more of the same mess. Alex's office looked like ground zero after an atomic explosion. Books were spread in disarray along his bookshelves, desk, and floor. He had gone to the painstaking effort of organizing every book based on topic, author, and the year it was published. Whole shelves were devoted to genres of ancient civilizations, Greek, Mayan and Egyptian, just to name a few. European history was divided by the country of origin. The largest collection was modern American history, which took up a whole bookcase by itself. Now everything was strewn everywhere.

Several of the desk drawers were open. Alex wasn't what you'd call a pack rat, but he did keep a lot of crap around. He was a collector by nature. Never knowing for sure what was worth keeping and what wasn't, he just kept it all. In the corner of the room was a stack of newspapers going back about two months. Current events were vital to a historian's research, because the next day they became part of history. When the stack got too big, he would store the newspapers in the basement. There must literally be two tons of newspapers going back decades that he had stored downstairs next to a random and lonely toilet. Oddly enough, the toilet worked, and was used only on special occasions to check if it still worked.

Deep within the unfinished basements all over the city, there stood working toilets such as this one, installed to add resale value to the houses. Theoretically, that is. Anyways, it was such a widespread practice to install these toilets, that nearly every house built in the 1930s had one. The toilet would be isolated, but without any sort of enclosure, thus making it an undesirable place to do *one's business*. Alex, however, had stacked up enough newspapers around this toilet to create a private space.

The cops could not have done type of damage that existed throughout the house. They might have flipped a few items over. Hell, they've been known to be a little disrespectful at times, but if they thought it was a suicide why would they go to all this trouble searching the house in the first place? That fact started to gnaw at my brain. If it wasn't the police, then maybe the murderer broke in before or after Alex's death. I decided it was time to call the police and report a break in. I gave the emergency operator details and then hung up the phone. I sat patiently on the front steps of Alex's house, waiting for the cops to show up.

After my parents died, I couldn't stay in their house for extended periods of time. It was troubling for me to be in the empty house alone. I had fresh memories of my mother and father eating breakfast in the kitchen as I came downstairs to join them. I jumped at the chance to move in with Alex when he offered. He helped me sell the house, but it felt wrong to keep the money. He had convinced me to keep it and I put it away in a bank to collect interest.

It wasn't long before a police cruiser pulled up and two uniforms stepped out. I gave my statement to how I found the house. I also informed the cops that the owner of the house was Alex Gerlach, the man they found at the base of the Cathedral.

"Anything stolen?" one of the officers asked. He was older than his partner, but it could have been the mustache that gave the impression. He began to fill out a form as he asked me questions.

"I don't think so, but I'm not sure for certain," I replied. Whoever went through the house it didn't seem like they found what they were looking for.

The uniform I was speaking to turned to his partner and asked, "Isn't Gerlach the guy that committed suicide?" When his partner nodded he finished filling out the paper work and had be sign my name at the bottom.

The other copper went back to the car to radio in. When he returned he took his partner to the side. I couldn't hear what they were saying, but I didn't think it was going to be helpful. The older cop's partner walked away, leaving us alone.

"Listen, we're sorry kid, but if there's nothing stolen there's little we can do. Homicide doesn't think there's foul play, and they aren't too concerned about this break in." The cop looked sincerely apologetic. I saw sympathy in his eyes as he added, "How about my partner and I look around, see if we can find anything you might have missed?"

The cops looked around for close to five minutes, and then left without saying anything else. In a city like Pittsburgh, the police had more to worry about than a break-in where nothing seemed to be stolen I guessed. I wondered who would have thought the two incidents weren't connected. Could Detective Bloom wanted to have the case closed after tagging it as a suicide?

I sat on the stoop trying to piece together the day's events. After making my head hurt with a hundred different possibilities, I stopped and tried to relax. It was finally beginning to really hit me; Alex was dead. I would never see him smile again. I would never hear him tell his bad jokes or listen as he spoke to an undergraduate class about the Declaration of Independence.

Alex could make the most boring subject come alive, acknowledging the dryness and humor of any given situation. It was hard for students to remain attentive during lectures, but Alex had a quality that demanded attention. Also, if you fell asleep in his class, he would take a black felt marker and write the next day's assignment on your forehead. He would even write it backwards so you could look in the mirror to read it.

I slipped the postcard out of my pocket and smiled at its absurdity. I flipped it over in my hands looking at the Eiffel Tower, following the metal beams crisscrossing into odd little shapes. As I studied the view from the Champ-de-Mars, I realized something was added to the picture close to the tower's side. It wasn't part of the original picture. The handwriting had pushed the paper in, causing a small indentation.

There was tightly packed, tiny cursive handwriting along the side of the tower, blending into the picture's structure. I had almost missed it a. Written in black ink were the letters *GR*, followed by the number *119*.

I could identify his penmanship from the smallest written word, and knew right away that this was Alex's handwriting. It was fluid, not hurried, and the curve of the lettering rolled in just his style. Alex didn't use a typewriter. He wrote everything in long hand. I couldn't understand what the letters and number meant, but knew they had to be important. Was there something special about the Eiffel Tower, an attraction he despised? Did I have to go to Paris and find *GR 119*? There had to be more to it, something else to explain what this meant.

I sat still, examining the postcard intently. I scanned it over and over again making sure I didn't miss any of its minute details. I held it up to the light for a better look. Nothing else was written anywhere on the card. Could it be a measurement, maybe a location? *GR 119*? What did it mean? I gazed at the picture of the famous French landmark, but nothing else came to me. I was a blank slate. Was I missing something? Alex always said to follow the most obvious line of reasoning; the answer with the simplest explanation was almost always right.

Was this a clue? Could it be something else? Maybe it was just a picture to humor Alex. Or was it something more, something important? Could it be a number for a safety deposit box? I wanted to call Sara, but I didn't want to seem crazy. GR 119.

What was *GR 119*? The postcard on his fridge didn't make sense in the slightest and GR 119 meant something only because it didn't have a direct reason for being there. Only Alex would have used it as a clue in some way, I was sure of.

I got up from the stoop and walked the neighborhood streets to clear my head. Several blocks away across the street there was a light blue Victorian home with newly painted white trim and auburn highlights. A young woman was sitting with a small girl, no more than two years old on her lap. The girl was laughing as the woman read the girl a book. The woman would point to the pictures and the girl would let out loud innocent giggles.

Something about woman and her daughter reading the book intrigued me, but I wasn't sure what it was. I hobbled over to the blue house, taking slower steps. The woman stopped reading to her daughter as I approached. I didn't want to scare her, but something about the book seemed familiar to me. On the cover of the book were several fairies, knights, and different goblins, all characters in the fairytales from my youth.

"Sorry, to bother you ma'am, but I couldn't help noticing the book you were reading to this young lady. Could you please tell me its name?"

The woman paused not comfortable with the complete stranger before her. The neighborhood had always been friendly, but my appearance must have flustered the woman. A moment later, the little girl held up the book toward her mother. The woman must have seen something in her daughter's eyes, because she relaxed and read the title of the book out loud so I didn't have to get any closer.

"*Anderson's Fairy Tales*," she said.

"Thank you. Sorry to have bothered you. Have a nice day," I apologized and waved goodbye to the girl. She waved back, but the woman pulled her arm down still unsure of her unwelcomed stranger.

I tried to settle the woman's fears, but didn't know how. I didn't know if was the woman's motherly instinct, but I felt I could tell this woman anything. I wanted to reach out for the woman's motherly touch.

"Did you know Alex Gerlach?" I asked turning back. I needed to talk about him. Find out if anyone else would miss the man that had become like a father to me.

The woman nodded, "Has something happened to him?"

"Yes ma'am. I'm afraid he passed away early this morning." I didn't want to give any gruesome details. It would only frighten the woman, making everything worse.

She flung her hand over her mouth, surprised by the news. "Oh my, I'm terribly sorry."

"Thank you, ma'am."

"I take it you were close to Alex?" She asked. "I didn't catch your name," the woman added.

"I'm Jamie. Alex took me in after my parents past away when I was younger."

The woman nodded understanding my life as only a mother could. "I'm Sylvia Snow," the woman said, "and this young lady is my daughter, Linda." It was the woman's eyes that comforted me.

"Were you or your husband close to Alex?" I asked.

"Sometimes," the woman explained. As in sometimes we would see him, sometimes we would talk, sometimes we would wave. "My Martin passed away last year." She added.

"Sorry for your loss," I gently replied.

"Thank you," she said. "Sorry for yours, too."

I nodded my thanks and slowly walked away from Sylvia and Linda.

As I walked the streets my mind raced back to the book, *Anderson's Fairy Tales*. I didn't know the title, and had never seen the book before, but there was something that was very memorable about it. What was it? Anderson didn't bring up anything, but what was it about the book that had interested me?

I stopped, beating my cane against the ground, making quiet thumping noises against the concrete. I knew why the book was so familiar. The fairytales Alex had read to me as a boy. His fascination with myth and legend only added to the overwhelming joy those stories would bring. Of course, I thought, the Grimm's, the authors of the most common fairytales, two brothers who wrote the stories together. *GR* could stand for Grimm. It was a long shot, but seemed right in my desperation.

Chapter 3

The Brothers Grimm, the authors of the fairytales! Was that what Alex was referring to on the postcard? I only knew a few of the tales, but I didn't need to know all of them to remember the Brothers Grimm. The stories were never written to entertain children. Instead, they were lessons, meant to scare the little ones into following rules and listening to their parents. Watching Disney's *Snow White* made me wonder if the stories were ever meant for kids to hear or see at all.

The clue, if in fact it was one, could be referring to the actual stories or to the authors. Besides several of the main stories, I didn't know much about the authors or their work. Assuming the GR stood for Grimm, what was it about Grimm?

I went back to Alex's house, entered his office and pulled down from a shelf a book with a map of the University of

Pittsburgh. Could there be something locally called Grimm? I didn't remember any buildings named Grimm on campus, but the numbers could be a room number or an address. There were hundreds of buildings. I couldn't possibly search out every *119* in every one of them. Maybe it was a page number of a book in Alex's library, but I didn't remember seeing a fairytale or even a mythology book anywhere around the house. Possibly, there was such a book in his office at the Cathedral, but I doubted it. Alex was a grounded type of person focused on realities not fantasies. I couldn't recall a time when he read or spoke about a work of fiction.

I threw down the map book and grabbed my bag. I rifled around inside, looking for some change and found a dime hiding at the bottom. I had to get a call to Sara. I needed her help with this. I couldn't tell her what was really going on, not yet, but I still needed her support. I threw my bag over my shoulder and headed out the door.

I didn't own a phone so I had to use the one across the street. I dialed Sara. One of her housemates picked up, and went to get her. Sara picked up the phone as she mumbled thanks to the other girl whose name I didn't catch.

"Jamie?" Sara's voice questioned.

"I thought you might want to help me with a little game, sort of a puzzle. It could help take our minds off of everything for a bit."

Not the best lie, but it would have to work until I was sure about this. I didn't want to upset Sara anymore than I had to. If I was right and there was something important about the postcard

I would tell her soon, but if I was wrong, I could really make things worse for her if I went into detail with her now.

"What type of game?" She perked up, almost excited at the thought of doing anything else.

"It's a scavenger hunt. The clues seem really hard. Well at least this one."

"A scavenger hunt? Okay Whatever. I'll bite." Good, she was already into it. I knew Sara couldn't pass up a puzzle. "What's the first item?" She asked.

I cleared my throat. "Grimm 119," I spoke, reciting each syllable slowly and accurately.

"Where did you get this scavenger list from, Jamie?" Had she heard through my lie already?

"It was from . . . orientation." Why did I say that? Sara had been there, too.

"Our graduate orientation at Pitt?" She asked.

"Umm, that's the one," I responded.

"I don't remember any scavenger hunts during orientation. Weird." There was silence on the other end of the phone, but I could hear Sara's breathing every few seconds.

"Hello? Sara, are you still there?"

She broke the silence. "I'm thinking, Jamie."

"Oh, sorry," I said. I waited a few more moments as I listened to her breathing at a constant speed.

I was going to give up and forget the whole thing, but Sara called out, "Okay, I'll meet you on campus."

"Why on campus?" I asked.

"We'll start in the most likely place," she responded. I didn't know what she was talking about. "The Cathedral," she said with a slight satisfaction to her voice.

"I'm not following." What did the Grimm Brothers or their fairytales have to do with the Cathedral of Learning?

"In the German nationality classroom, there's a series of stained glass windows depicting some of Grimm's fairytales," She said. "I thought you would have known that."

She was right. How did I miss something so obvious? I told her that I'd meet her there and broke the connection, hanging up the phone. I got on the rail car and headed down Fifth. I needed to think back. What did I know about the German classroom? It was the first of four nationality rooms built in 1938, after the Cathedral was finished. The other three were the Scottish, Russian and Swedish rooms. Each room represented the national heritage of a particular country. The rooms were an attempt to bring together different cultures and nationalities for a unified university. The concept was part of a big public relations campaign for the city and school.

There were tens of thousands of Germans in Pittsburgh by '38, and many of them donated money to have the German room built. I must have been in that room a hundred different times for class. Alex loved that room. His parents were born in Germany and came to America for the same reasons everyone else did at that time. They searched for better jobs and a new prosperous life. Alex was extremely proud of his German heritage, and even donated a large sum of money for the room's construction.

The German classroom's structure was based on an old German schoolhouse from the mid 1800s. A wooden plaque in the front of the room, written in a Gothic German script, had a quote from one of Alex's favorite German poets, Friedrich Von Schiller. Six of the letters were highlighted with blue and red blocks, making the words stand out on the dark brown wood of the rest of the room. This particular quote from one of Schiller's poems had something to do with the search for truth through hard work.

Unfortunately, it also sounded like *Arbeit macht frei*, the quote the Nazis placed at the entrance gate to the Auschwitz death camp. *Arbeit macht frei*, roughly translated, means *work will set you free*. I had seen the pictures and read stories about the death camps. I had even spoken to survivors of the war. They marched in through the gate to their death, their extermination.

Alex had been ashamed of his people, outraged at the atrocities committed during the war. The Germany Alex remembered was from his youth. His was during a happier time, when there were no such things as Nazis, Hitler, or any mention of exterminating a whole group of people.

When I arrived at the Cathedral of Learning, Sara was waiting for me in the main sanctuary. She sat at one of the many oak worktables reading a small paperback book. Her long blond hair was pulled back into a ponytail. I could tell she had been crying because of the blotchy red puffiness around her eyes. No matter how puffy her eyes were, she would always look like Grace Kelly in *Rear Window*.

Jimmy Stewart had a quote in the film referring to Kelly. Every time I saw Sara I thought of it. Stewart says, "She's too perfect . . . too talented . . . too beautiful . . . too sophisticated...

too everything than what I want." Unlike Jimmy's character, I loved this girl, Sara, for being all those things. I respected her because of them.

"What do you have there, kiddo?" I asked, walking around the table.

Sara wiped her eyes again. "I found it after you called." In her hands was a small copy of *Grimm's Fairy Tales*, which could come in handy. She pushed the book into my hands and I flipped through to the 119th story.

"I tried that all ready," she said. "In that copy the 119th story is *The Stolen Farthings*." She raised another copy of the *Grimm's Fairy Tales* from her bag. It was a larger hardback version from the English department's library on the sixth floor.

"In this one, it's *The Seven Swabians*. The order is set by the editor."

"Could it be a room number instead?" I asked. But Sara didn't respond. She slipped out of her chair and began to walk away. I followed, not sure if I should ask the question again. Maybe she didn't hear me.

I didn't like seeing her upset, so I was happy that this was taking her mind off the morning's climatic event. I would do almost anything to stop a girl from crying, especially Sara, but right now the best thing to do was to follow this trail and see where it led. I felt like Bogart in *The Maltese Falcon*, but without any little black statue of a bird. Keeping Sara occupied for as long as possible was the only thing I could do to help her.

I followed her down the main hallway toward a series of classrooms. We walked over to a dark walnut door with wrought iron hinges. In the middle of the door, there was a small square window covered by black wrought iron bars. On the wall next to the door, in brass, the number *119* was nailed in place. Sara already knew it was the room number to the German classroom. *GR 119* stood for the German classroom in the Cathedral of Learning. It would have taken me forever to figure out that clue, but Sara did it without a moment's hesitation. She was born to be an investigator.

Sara went in first and I followed right behind. The room was set in a light brown mahogany, which covered the walls, and then a darker brown wood covered the floor. Even the ceiling was made to match the darker wood of the floor. To the right and left of the entrance, two blackboards hung along the walls. In the center of the room were twenty brown glossy oak desks, which were right out of a real German village schoolhouse.

Sara walked over to the glass windows on the opposite side of the room. Having been in the room so many times, I would see the glass panels without ever really looking at them.

In multi-colored glass, the Grimm Brothers' most famous tales were depicted in glorious shades of blue, red and orange. Today they were backlit by an afternoon sun. The stained glass was added several years ago, after the room was already finished. You wouldn't know there was any lapse in time between the room's construction and the addition of the stained glass because everything matched rooms perfectly.

Sara's face took on an overpowering blue and yellow glow as she stepped in front of the transparent colored glass. During class, the glass would let in bright colored light that would dance along the faces of the students. If a lecturer wasn't keeping the students' attention, the brilliant shades of colored light were sure to hold their thoughts.

I knew all of the stories depicted in the windows of glass. They were the most popular stories, which had been taken and made into softer child-friendly versions. The *Sleeping Beauty* story was the fifth series of windows. Two columns of stain glass windows displayed the story of the King and Queen and their baby daughter Beauty, the curse given to the baby by the old witch, the spinning wheel, and the Handsome Prince waking his love up with a kiss.

The other windows depicted *Snow White, Red Rose, Little Red Riding Hood,* The *Frog Prince,* and Alex's favorite, *Rumpelstiltskin.* What did it say about Alex that he favored a story about a dwarf who ate babies? I'm amazed to think that not every child who heard the real story of Rumpelstiltskin had night terrors. I looked around the panels for some sort of clue. Nothing I could see was much help. I told Sara the story, as she gently placed her hands on the window pane, searching for something not readily seen. She touched each square of the story, looking for a glimmer of truth.

Alex wouldn't have led us here without a reason. There had to be something here. *GR 119.* He must have written it expecting someone would latch on to the clue. He was about the details. He was the type to put everything into context, explore and re-explore until he exhausted every possibility imaginable. He must have known I'd find the postcard. No one else would look that closely. He foresaw everything. He learned from history, understood the ramifications of the chain of events. It could be the actions of the Chinese government, or just a model like Marilyn Monroe making a bad movie. He understood how everything could play out. He understood the present and future because he analyzed the past.

What were we supposed to find? I slid down onto the floor leaning my back against the wall. I felt cheated. I was sure this was the answer to Alex's clue. The stained glass, it had to be the stained glass.

I hung my head in shame. I wasn't able to figure it out. I looked up, gazing into space. I didn't want to think anymore, but the blackboard in the front of the room reminded me of Alex even more. Each donor of the room was either from Germany or could trace his or her heritage back. Alex cherished his German heritage, even during the war he held strong, believing the Nazis would be defeated — that they were not representative of the entire German people. After the war, he celebrated with the rest of us.

Pittsburgh had a large German population since its early days. There had been thousands of German immigrants in the city who had donated money to the school in support of the Cathedral of Learning. The city even has a neighborhood nicknamed Duetchtown over in the north side of town.

Oddly enough, the first committee secretary, Fritz Ueberle, would take notes in English, translate them to German, and then send them to the German press with progress reports on the room's construction. Considering the room wasn't finished until '38, it was odd to think of Ueberle communicating with the

German press when they were going to be censored by the Nazi party anyway. I could just imagine the racist twist the German people read in those reports.

Even weirder, after the war the Holy Roman Empire's eagle remained above the doorway, which I began to look at. Hitler adopted it for his Third Reich, but even with the negative connotations of the war, it remained in the room.

"What's wrong?" Sara asked. She still thought it was a game. She was looking for a clue in a scavenger hunt. I was searching for an answer to something with far more significance.

"Maybe, we're wrong about the whole thing," she whispered.

"Huh?" I tried to play dumb, which I could do extremely well at times.

"I know there's no puzzle Jamie. You never could lie to me. You must have found something of his. Something that led us here."

I pushed my head back against the wall looking up at her blond hair. The blue light from the windows made her look like an angel. A halo seemed to glow by her face. I didn't want to upset her, but I didn't know what else to do.

"He didn't jump," I said as a matter of fact.

"I'm not sure what happened, but I don't know what we're doing here. Please let me see what you found."

I reached into my pocket and handed her the postcard. I told her where to look, but she found Alex's handwriting without my help. She giggled at the Eiffel Tower, just as I had.

I was searching too hard, maybe looking at things that didn't have any meaning. Was I connecting unrelated ideas? *GR 119* was too much of a coincidence not to be something important, but was it related to Alex's death?

Sara smiled while she looked at the postcard. "He hated Paris," Sara said as tears started falling from her eyes. "I was wrong," She added.

"What do you mean?" I responded in a low quiet tone. I was tired and didn't want to play any longer.

"GR didn't stand for Grimm." I searched her expression. She began to smile. "German Room." She gave the *G* and *R* emphasis.

I looked up in shock. It was too easy, but she was right. He was directing us to the classroom itself, not the stained glass depictions. We had been right and wrong at the same time. I got my second wind and was now ready to continue the search.

Sara leaned over and held out her hand. I took it and she tried to pull me up. My new enthusiasm ended quicker than it began as a pain shot down my hip causing my leg to buckle. She couldn't support my weight. I slipped through her grasp, tumbling back, and hit my head against a window ledge. The pain was instant, sending a razor sharp explosion directly into my skull. The pain traveled down my neck and into my back, as tiny pinpricks tickled my spine.

My tail bone landed on the hard wood floor, breaking the floorboard below me. I grabbed my head with one hand and the other I attached to my ass. The pain in my head began to subside as quickly as it manifested, but the pain in my backside was beginning to grow as the initial shock took hold.

"Jamie, are you all right? I thought I had you. I'm so sorry." She was worried and felt guilty, so I waved my hand to reassure her.

"It's okay. I'm okay, just a little thump on the head." Not to mention a pain in my ass.

I looked under my bruised butt to see a small panel of wood that I jarred loose by my impact. I picked it up examining it with admiration. I had broken only one board in the floor. At least there was a positive side to everything. That was me, Mr. Positive.

Sara smiled through the pity on her face, "I think you broke it," she said, trying to hide her laughter. It was rude to laugh at a friend's pain and suffering, but sometimes that couldn't be helped. Even painful experiences could be funny.

I started to laugh at my own predicament following Sara's lead. I tried to stand once more, this time grabbing onto the window ledge for support. When I was able to stand, I was directly facing the opposite wall where the Golden Book was kept. The Golden Book was the nickname given to the registry of all the room's donors, which happened to be a book with gold-edged pages. Alex's name must have been written in the book since he was a donor years before. I wanted to see his name in the book, but realized a moment later that I *needed* to see it. Something inside me wouldn't let me leave the room without seeing my dead friend's written name. I was being pulled along by the strange urge.

Sara followed behind as I walked towards the book's case across the room. I was in a trance, unable to turn away. The book was lying on a red velvet cloth bed inside a glass cabinet. The cover of the book was hand-carved ivory and had copper hinges running down its spine. Just as its namesake suggested, gold leaf covered the edges of the pages. Without realizing that the cabinet would be locked, I pulled the door open, popping the lock with ease.

"There you go, breaking more stuff Jamie," Sara snickered.

"I'll make a donation later," I smiled back.

I flipped open the book and traced my finger down the old parchment. Hundreds of names were written in long lists. Alex was on the second page and was actually one of the first donors in the list. I took the book out of its display cabinet and held it in my arms staring at the written name of Alex Gerlach. It was what I wanted to see, what I needed to see. My friend was gone, but I needed to know his legacy lived on. Knowing he made a donation to a cause made me feel happy to have known him.

"What is that?" Sara asked as she shoved me out of the way.

I held the book out thinking she might want to see it, but she bent down in front of the cabinet's velvet liner. Sara felt around tracing the outline. She moved her hand to the side and pulled away the cloth to reveal a yellow envelope underneath. She pulled the envelope out into the open. Without hesitation, she began to open it by sliding her delicate index finger along the fold.

She pulled out a single folded piece of paper, which she read silently. After she read the note, she handed it to me.

"You aren't going to tell me what it says?"

"Just read it, smart guy," she responded.

Could this be what Alex had led us here for? At the top of the note were the words *Salk vaccine*. Below were written five names: Park Davis, Eli Lilly, Wyeth, Pitman Moore and Cutter. The last one, Cutter, was circled with a black felt-tipped marker.

I didn't have to tell Sara what the Salk vaccine was. Everyone knew about the vaccine here in Pittsburgh. It was the polio vaccine developed over the past couple of years by Dr. Jonas Salk at the University of Pittsburgh. I would have been surprised if the whole USSR didn't know the name, Jonas Salk. These days the name *Salk* was almost as famous as Joe McCarthy or Eisenhower.

Since developing the vaccine, Dr. Salk has been in every paper and tabloid in America. If that wasn't enough, just a couple of weeks ago hundreds of thousands of kids from across the country were vaccinated with Salk's polio vaccine in a huge field test. Moms and Dads everywhere were cheering Jonas Salk for protecting their children against the evils of polio.

There might have been some debate over how effective the vaccine was in the medical community, but to everyone not holding an M.D., Salk was a saint.

I read the list again, going over each name slowly, but none rang a bell.

"Do you recognize any of the names?" Sara asked.

"Not a single one. How about you?"

She shook her head no. I was wondering if the five names were people who might have helped Salk in making the vaccine. Could Cutter be a disgruntled laboratory technician?

Frustrated, Sara paced the room. I watched, wanting to do the same, but my leg made it hard to pace without looking like Quasimodo, and besides my ass still hurt. The near impaling I received from the broken board didn't make me want to make any sudden movements so soon.

I shuffled over to the blackboard and was amazed that I remembered what was written above the board, a quote by the German poet Friedrich Von Schiller: "Nur dem Ernst, den keine Muhe blichet, Rauscht der Wahrheit tiefversteckter Born." Alex would recite that saying over and over again when he was researching something with a hard answer. He said it out loud so many times, I even memorized it. "A Stern endeavor, which no arduous task can shake, to the hidden font of Truth attains!"

Alex would look for the answer to any question until he found it. He never gave up, no matter how hard the obstacle seemed. He wouldn't move on until he figured out history's riddles, always straining over different manuscripts and books of long dead authors, making connections and solving the mysteries of historical importance.

Sara came over to the blackboard to look at the Schiller quote with me. On both sides of the blackboard were the names of four German scientists. Humboldt, Koch, Siemens and Roentgen, each etched into the soft walnut paneling on either side of the blackboard. Four names all together, two on each side. She raised her hand over the etching and followed the outline of Koch's name. I saw her eyes move along the letters following her finger's movement. She was contemplating the connections and possible meanings of potential clues.

"Koch, Robert Koch!" Sara yelled without warning.

"What about him?" I asked while I leaned against the wall.

Sara turned to me and started to explain, her voice was booming and the energy in the room grew monumentally.

"Koch discovered what caused Tuberculosis and then developed something much like a vaccine, in this case Tuberculin. But Koch exaggerated the positive effects of his cure. It only worked some of the time." Sara paused, waiting for her explanation to sink in. I waited with her, unaware of when my own epiphany would present itself. After a long pause, I bit my lip and shook my head. I still didn't understand what she was driving at.

"Don't you see, Alex must be telling us there is something wrong with the Polio vaccine," She said with a giddy appeal.

Maybe she was reaching, maybe the shock finally set in. Either way I was exhausted. I wanted to sleep, take a shower, and when I'd wake up, eat, and then go back to bed. I wanted nothing to do with this wild goose chase anymore, Alex was dead, and nothing I did could change that.

"Sara, I miss him too, but I think we should . . ."

Sara started to jump up and down excited by her own conclusions. I thought about what she had said for a moment, a split second really.

"Sara, I think I should walk you home."

"Don't Jamie!" she said, while her demeanor changed without a beat and her smile dropped away for good. "You brought me here. Don't start cutting me off now."

"But, the polio vaccine? Sara, we know it works, the doctors know it works."

The polio vaccine did work and actually quite well. Early in the month, Thomas Francis, a protégé of Salk's, did a double

71

blind study and expressed the success of the vaccine in front of the whole country. On behalf of the United States Health Department and The University of Pittsburgh, Francis had conducted his own third-party testing of the vaccine at the University of Michigan concluding that the vaccine a success. He proved the vaccine worked, just as Salk had said it would. During the past three weeks, a story about the Salk vaccine has been in the paper almost every day.

"It's the connection to the room. Why would Alex leave the letter in this room, unless it had some meaning?" I could feel the Sarah's need for a connection.

"Maybe the room means nothing," I went on, "Maybe the letter was only put here because the room was easy for him to get into." I paused and then continued. "We don't even know if it was Alex who placed the letter here."

"Who else would it be?" Sarah yelled. "Jamie, you know as well as I do, that Alex did not do things randomly. If he placed the letter here it would have to mean something. The room must mean something."

She was right on several points. Alex was exact and never random in his approach. She was using the same reasoning I used to get us here. I pressed my hand against the stained walnut doors, feeling the wood grain against my palms. Wood inlays, called intarsia, depicted the fountain of Rothenburg. The central square of Nierenberg caught my attention as I ran my fingers along the wood. Colorful bits of wood were fitted together to make wonderful pictures of the German cities.

Sara could be right, hell she was almost never wrong, but the vaccine did work. If Sara was correct, Alex uncovered something that got him killed. Worse, if she was right, we were walking right into the same dangerous situation.

I didn't know what to do. This was something much bigger than anything I thought I could handle. Alex was dead, and he left us information knowing we'd find it. Had he known he was being watched? Had he known all this would happen? Why the secrets? Maybe, Alex wasn't sure of what he knew.

I limped over to a bench across the hall to stretch out my bad leg. Sara sat next to me. I extended my leg and then bent it to get the blood pumping as I tried to massage some feeling into my thigh. It wasn't completely numb, but I did have a growing loss of sensation further down toward my foot. I looked down at Sara's legs and wondered if a girl like her could ever love a man like me. Would she be embarrassed of me in public? Would she introduce me to her parents? Thoughts of growing old with her flashed through my mind as the feeling came back, first in my thigh, then my knee, and then finally my foot. I wiggled my toes and set my leg back down. I was ready to go.

"Hungry?" I asked Sara.

She nodded yes, smiled, and stood up without a word. She bent down and set a small kiss on my cheek, which made me blush. I smiled and she helped me to my feet. We walked down the Cathedral hallway together, both pondering the riddle before us in silence.

We got a quick bite at Hayden's Diner on Fifth Avenue. It was a dive, but they had really good burgers. I traded two sips of Sara's malt, for some fries off my plate. The French fries were

25% potato, and 75% grease, but hit the spot like no other food could.

Over the noise from the undergraduates, the jukebox was playing Joe Turner's "Shake Rattle and Roll." Several greasers were near the box looking for another song. The kids wore leather jackets right out of *The Wild One*. Those fellows probably thought they were real hip, really cool, without really understanding their own rebellion. Didn't think they went to Pitt, but you never knew. Thanks to the G.I. Bill, everyone had a chance at a new life. There were all different types in school these days. Unfortunately, they thought they were all as cool as Marlon Brando.

After lunch we decided to split up. Sara thought we could get more done that way. I agreed, but was worried about how safe it was.

"Don't worry so much Jamie. No one knows about the postcard or the letter Alex left for us. What about Dr. Longmont, do you think he could help?"

"I'm not sure about that guy," I replied.

"You don't trust him?" Sara asked.

"It's not that I don't trust him, but the guy came out of nowhere claiming to have been working with Alex, and the only person who would whether in fact they were working together happens to be dead."

"He could be telling the truth," Sara shot back.

"Why wouldn't Alex tell me about the research or mention this guy, Longmont? We were a team." I didn't think there were any secrets between the two of us. "Why didn't he trust me with this?"

Sara didn't have an answer for me. There were too many questions running through her head to add another one about trust issues. Sara shrugged her shoulders and decided to try finding some information at the library.

The university didn't have any one central library. All of the departments had their own separate smaller collections that generally had useful selections. Unfortunately, each library was too far spread out over campus, that it made it impossible to do a general information search. Fortunately, when you needed to do general research, going to the Carnegie Library on Forbes, was a viable option.

There was a rumor that the university was going to build a central library somewhere in Oakland, but I couldn't even begin to speculate where they would find the space. They'd have to demolish something as big as Forbes Field for something like that. The Pirates were one of the worse teams in baseball, but even if we were in last place, the team was a part of the city. I was sure no one would demolish the field.

Maybe I'd get lucky and get a talkative technician from his hospital lab on campus. Sara said goodbye and we parted ways. I began my trek up the hill to the hospital, forgetting how steep my journey was before it was too late. My leg was already throbbing, but I was able to limp my way up to Lothrop Hall, working through the pain. Half way up, I had to stop. I watched doctors, nurses and patients hurrying to different appointments and procedures as I took a break under a small oak offering shade.

Salk had been honored at the White House by Ike this past weekend and was probably still in D.C. Maybe he got to stay in the Lincoln bedroom. Famous celebrities always carried on about the Lincoln bedroom being the place to stay at the White House. The president called Salk "a Benefactor of Mankind," which wasn't a bad title to carry around the rest of your life. I sure wouldn't have minded something on that scale. If that didn't make someone a celebrity, I'm not sure what would.

I left the pleasant shade of the oak behind and continued. Pitt's football stadium came into view up on the right soon after. It was a massive structure plopped down in the center of a residential community. I didn't even want to think how many family homes were uprooted to set a path for the *pride* of the university. Pretty soon the whole school would be taking over the area.

I looked around once more and realized the school had already done so. The University of Pittsburgh owned the neighborhood and its logo was virtually everywhere. If it wasn't there yet, it would just be a matter of time. Families were uprooted, sent packing on their merry way, as new and better classrooms were built where their homes once stood. There was a trade off – education for everyone in exchange for a few lives to be uprooted. Alex had helped me sell my parent's place a couple of years ago to the university. I wasn't sure what they were planning on doing with the land, but I could think of at least twenty different ideas.

On my way to the hospital I had realized I had only been to a hospital at home once when I was seven. I tried jumping a curb on my bike, but missed the landing completely, breaking my arm in two places, at my wrist and further up my arm. My dad brought me to Children's Hospital to have it set. It was a short drive as we lived in South Oakland and the hospital was right up the street in Central Oakland. We were there for two hours before we were seen. A broken arm can't compete with traumatic accidents. The doctor finally saw me, took an x-ray, and slapped a cast on my arm without a second thought. I was sent home with a bottle of children's aspirin and a new toy to play with. The cast was hell to keep dry. Six weeks later when it was supposed to come off, it was so loose and spongy that I could have pulled it right off myself. It reminded me of a papier-mâché science project. I had to wrap my cast in a trash bag when I took a shower, but it didn't make a bit of difference. By the end, all the signatures and "get better" notes had blended together into black and blue swirls.

My wrist had healed in its own funky way, and I was lucky not to have a long-term problem with it afterwards. The memory was still so fresh in my mind. It was more than eighteen years ago, but I remember it as if it happened yesterday. I remember my pops carrying me into the emergency room, never leaving my side even for a second. I knew my father was not a perfect man. I know now that he had his share of problems, but at the time, to as a seven year old, my father was like Superman.

The Municipal Hospital was owned by the University, one of the first in a long list of hospitals in Pittsburgh they planned on acquiring. I was close. The hospital sat on the left, a few hundred feet away. The hospital had just been built in 1939. I was guessing someone would want to name it after Jonas Salk, considering that he had discovered the vaccine in the same building. That was how things went. The university would obtain money from donors to build something. They named it after whoever donated the most money or gave it a nice generic name, and then they changed the name eventually when someone made a meaningful discovery like the cure for the common cold. I would bet after Chancellor Fitzgerald retires at the end of the year, he'd get his name somewhere on campus too.

On Terrence Street, across from the hospital, a steel skeleton stood as a testament to the growth of the university. Its next expansion project was underway at this very moment. Maybe if I got rich and famous I could donate money and call the building Schmidt Hall. I liked the ring of that. What about Schmidt Library? No, I couldn't have my own library; they reserved those for the presidents of schools and the country. At the end of the day, I'd settle for a hall. I'd rather have a whole school, but I wouldn't be picky.

I took the final part of my stroll over to the hospital to see if I could strike up a chat with someone from Jonas Salk's research team. I was surprised by how extremely quiet the lobby was. Where were the doctors, the nurses, and where were all the patients? Where were the researchers? I knew Salk's lab was on the first two floors of the hospital. I walked over to a set of double doors, which I assumed led to his laboratory. I looked through the glass panel, and realized that there were no lights on. I tried to open the door, but it was locked. The whole hospital seemed to be vacant, everyone taking a day off. I was beginning to wonder if I was the only person in the whole building.

A voice rang out. "Can I help you?"

I pivoted my body in surprise, not expecting anyone was here. I would say it was my military training to put me on edge, but the fact was I was scared, like a little girl. I could be fairly calm when I was firing a mortar at the enemy, but when it came to people sneaking up on me, I sometimes thought I would wet myself.

"You always try to give someone a heart attack like that?" I said while struggling to catch my breath.

I was thankful to see a middle-aged man in a white lab coat. He wasn't wearing a stethoscope or any other medical equipment. He was probably just a low-level technician.

"Sorry, I didn't mean to surprise you like that," the man said.

"No problem, really," I lied. I checked to see if my heart was in its right place and felt relieved when I found it on the left side of my chest.

"Didn't think anyone else was in the building. We haven't been very busy around here with the vaccine going into production." The man paused and continued, "Is there anything I could do for you?"

"I know this sounds strange, but a friend of mine was found dead early this morning, Dr. Alex Gerlach." The man didn't acknowledge knowing Alex, so I added, "He was a history professor at the school."

"I'm so sorry to hear that," he said with surprise. "I've been taking care of some loose ends up here all day. Haven't even taken breakfast yet."

I looked down at the name tag on the lapel of his coat. It read Keith Ontario. I pulled out the list of names Alex left in the Golden Book for me to find.

"Mr. Ontario, my name is Jamie Schmidt."

"Please, call me Keith." He smiled, shaking my hand.

I looked back down at the list and asked, "I'm sorry to call bother you Keith, but does the name *Cutter* mean anything to you?"

The man took a peek down at the piece of paper I was holding, pondering the question for a moment. He started to shake his head, but stopped. He did recognize the name after all. He looked up and smiled.

"Yeah, if you mean Cutter Laboratories."

Cutter was a laboratory? "Would you know what they do there?"

"They make animal vaccines. I order some of the supplies for the lab and I remember seeing some medicines for our animals."

"Animals?" I was surprised he had animals in the lab at all.

"Oh yes, we keep a group of Capuchin monkeys on hand for experiments and the like." Keith smiled. "You're not one of those activists are you?" he jokingly asked.

"No of course not, just surprised is all. I guess you would need animals to test instead of humans, right?"

"Exactly right you are. We don't want our monkeys getting sick around here. Even if we get them sick, we still want them to get better. We treat our animals very well, after all. Those little creatures come in handy all the time around here."

"Do you get animal activists up here a lot?"

"You actually wouldn't believe it. Just the other day we had a whole group of twenty of them camped outside. I tell you, I don't know what this world is coming too."

"Well, sorry to take up your time Keith."

"Sorry I wasn't more of a help. If there is anything else I could do for you, please don't hesitate to stop by."

I approached the front doors, and remembered I should have asked about the other names on the list. I turned around holding the paper up once more, but Keith was already gone. I must have been keeping him from something more important. At least he had known about Cutter. I should have known Salk would use primates to test the vaccine before humans, but what was so special about a company that manufactured products for monkeys?

I wanted to kick myself for not asking more questions when I had the chance. Sometimes you only got one shot and then the opportunity is gone. I would have to remember that for next time.

Since the war, I was never much for walking, so I jumped on the first rail car I found. The fans were on and the windows were open on the rail. The cool breeze dried the moisture from my skin. At least I didn't have to sweat.

The driver had the radio tuned to KDKA, the first commercial radio station in the states. At first it was a novelty to hear the music and sound from the speakers, not just mindless chatter. Occasionally they played something worth listening too. Right now, Jazz was playing, but I couldn't identify the musician. Sounded like Davis or Coltrane, but without vocals I never could tell for sure. As the song was ending, the car slowed down to a stop. I took a look outside. This was not a scheduled stop and there wasn't red light.

The driver called back, "There's a car in the way." He jumped out of his seat leaving the trolley with the engine running. I watched as he walked up to the closest house and began knocking on the front door. A sense of déjà vu overcame me as I realized I had seen the same seen several times before. An older man wearing red suspenders, white t-shirt, and black pants opened the door. The driver pointed to the car in the street blocking the trolley. The man shook his head, angry that he had to waste his time with another person's problem, and went back inside. The driver walked over to the next house in the row and proceeded to repeat the process.

I could have walked the rest of the way to the Library, but I was already too tired. The music playing on the speakers stopped, transitioning to the news. I listened as a voice gave a sports report about how bad the Pirates had become in recent years. The team had come in last place for the past several seasons and this year they had even been worse than previously. I could understand why the city did not have any faith left in its baseball club. Another voice chirped in about a new rookie, Roberto Clemente, a guy the Pirates recruited from the Montreal Royals, the minor league club of the Brooklyn Dodgers. The opinion was that Clemente would be able to give the team the added boost it needed to help win some games, and hopefully one day a pendant. I was skeptical about one man being able to change the outcome of a baseball game, but then again, there was Babe Ruth.

I checked out the other passengers waiting patiently, looking to see who else was stuck waiting for the driver to get back. A couple of business men happy that they were getting to leave work early and an elderly couple, oblivious to the pause in their slower paced day were among the other passengers. The sports report ended and the station was now covering the day's headlines.

After waiting ten more minutes, the driver climbed back onto the trolley. A moment later a man rushed out of a nearby house across the street. His black slacks unbuckled, and his tie hung loosely around his neck. He carried his ruffled jacket under his arm as he franticly dug around for his keys. A moment later, he was pulling forward and out of the rail car's way. The rest of the trip was more or less uneventful, and I was let off at Forbes and Bigelow.

Waiting for the crosswalk sign to change, a man in a grey raincoat and a Stetson fedora appeared on my right reading *The New York Times*.

I took my time crossing the street, putting more weight than usual on my cane. I was tired and didn't know how much more walking I could take. I was approaching the library when I heard footsteps behind me, heels steadily clicked against the pavement. All of a sudden I realized that I was physically drained, and didn't have any more energy to keep up my guard.

I felt like I was being paranoid, but decided to take a few more steps before crouching down, pretending to tie my shoe. I listened for the footsteps, but heard nothing, only silence. I tried to look behind me. The man in the grey coat was there, stopped only several feet behind me. He lowered his paper in confusion as we acknowledged each other's presence.

I stood up, trying hard not to seem worried. I continued walking to the library, keeping my steps controlled. Still following,

I could hear the man's footsteps fall in place right behind, keeping close.

I walked into the Carnegie Library and, just as I feared, the man in the grey coat followed me in. The foyer was vacant, except for a lone security guard sitting by himself in the corner. That got me worried. I needed a crowd if I wanted to make this spook go away. The guard could have been sleeping, it didn't matter. There would be little he could do anyway.

I entered the atrium and was relieved when I saw at least two dozen college students sitting around various tables. Most were working on homework, but some were there just to flirt with the co-eds. The undergraduates used the library as a makeshift hot spot, when they were tired of the usual overlooks, car hops, drive-ins, and malt shops. It was well known around the campus that studying was secondary to what really went on in the library.

I spotted Sara sitting at a table near the stacks. Books were piled high along the table, some open, as she tried to cross-reference several at once. I decided to walk behind her and kept going. She was too engrossed in the research to notice me or the man following behind.

I was glad Sara hadn't seen me. The guy following me could use her against me in a number of different ways. He followed me into the stacks with no subtle pretenses. He was blatantly following me. I pretended to look for a particular book on the shelf, grabbing something at random and then I pretended to read it. Scanning the pages, I was able to peer off, but the man was nowhere to be seen. Had I lost him that easily? How was that possible? I wasn't even trying to lose him yet. I put the book back on the shelf to find him.

Peaking around the bookcase, I didn't see the man in grey, only several students staring oddly in my direction. I hurried back to the man sitting area where I found the man in grey doing exactly what I was trying to avoid before. He had begun a conversation with Sara. She was smiling as he examined the books she was reading. She had no idea the man had followed me in. I made my way toward them and cleared my throat when I was an arm's length away. Once she saw me, Sara gave a sigh of relief.

As I closed in on Sara and the man in grey, the man slipped his right hand into his jacket. I was ready to charge him if he pulled a gun, but saw a white business card materialize out of his inside jacket pocket. I relaxed not realizing how tense I had become.

"Mr. Schmidt?"

"Yes," I said with a yelp

I nodded as the man handed me his card. "I was told to find you if anything happened to Dr. Alex Gerlach. My name is Victor Wheeling."

I looked down at the man's card. On it was a logo of one of the names from the list, Parke-Davis. Dr. Victor Wheeling, Vaccine Production was written under the logo. "How did you know who I was?" I asked hitting his card against my hand.

"Alex described you fairly well, down to your military injury. I came to you because I need your help."

For the first time, I looked into Victor's eyes. They were sincere like his dark oval face. He seemed to be the same age as Alex had been, maybe a little younger. The hair along his temples was already graying, and there were lines forming around his eyes.

"He told you about her, too?" I asked pointing over at Sara with a thumb.

"Of course, he said wonderful things about Ms. Thompson, too. I'm sorry I gave you a fright." Dr. Wheeling began to laugh. "As I was returning to my hotel, I found you on the trolley outside. At first I wasn't sure it was really you, but I followed you off just the same, hoping in my gut that I had found you." Dr. Wheeling became much more serious and quietly, almost under his breath he said, "You see, I believe I was being followed and I wanted to make sure I didn't lead them to you."

"Who would be following you, Dr. Wheeling?" Sara slid in.

"Let me start at the beginning. You see, I was feeding Alex a certain amount of information concerning a product my company had been in the process of manufacturing for the Health Department."

"The polio vaccine." I guessed.

"Correct. Parke-Davis had been assigned to manufacture the vaccine on a small trial basis. Then recently, we were awarded a contract to produce the vaccine in large quantities. But I had stumbled onto several problems we were having."

"Maybe we should sit down for this," I suggested as I pulled out a chair and slumped down on it. The doctor pulled off his coat, then his hat and took a seat across from the two of us.

Dr. Wheeling took a deep breath and looked into Sara's eyes, then mine. "I met Dr. Alex Gerlach four years ago here at the

University of Pittsburgh. On the orders of my superiors, I came to see for myself the progress Dr. Salk was making with the polio vaccine. I was told to do anything in my power to persuade the good doctor to push the trial start date for the vaccine up and let Parke-Davis have exclusive rights to produce the vaccine.

"You see, as soon as Salk declared the vaccine finished, a competitive public bidding process would be used to determine the manufacturers, and then of course the larger contract for mass market production would be up for grabs. Of course I knew Jonas would never consider a shady dealing of this sort, but it was my job nonetheless to try to convince him. The proposition would have made the doctor a very rich man, but would have been unethical, if not illegal. Either way, I was sent to accomplish my job for good or bad, but was unable to fulfill my task because Salk would not budge on his morals.

"During one of my visits I met Dr. Gerlach at a press conference. He had spent much of his time around the Salk laboratories, documenting the series of events for its historical significance. I got on quite well with Alex and enjoyed our time together a great deal. As a man of science myself, I could only imagine how important the creation of the polio vaccine would be for mankind.

"Months later, while discussing the vaccine with Alex, I let him know how much trouble we were having in creating the necessary amount of vaccine for the trials. Using Salk's protocol for the vaccine, we were trying to produce eleven consecutive batches. We hit roadblock after roadblock using Salk's protocol, designed by Salk himself, but for a different purpose. He had created this particular protocol when he was making only a small amount of the vaccine. When we tried to apply his instructions when producing larger amounts, we were failing miserably."

I broke in, "Why was it so important to have eleven consecutive batches?"

"The government put in place a set of procedures it thought would help ensure the safety for vaccine recipients. Each vial of the polio vaccine contains a small amount of inactivated polio virus. This is how most vaccines are made. To get the actual virus that causes Poliomyelitis inactivated we needed to follow Salk's protocol of adding formaldehyde. Unfortunately, Salk didn't foresee the problems we would have with such large quantities. Adding formaldehyde would only work if we soaked the virus for twelve to fourteen days in this liquid solution. At first, we couldn't produce a single batch without it being infected. We realized the problem before it was too late and began to use ultraviolet light instead of formaldehyde in the deactivation phase."

"At the time, did you know whether or not the others trying to produce the vaccine were having the same problems?" Sara interrupted.

"We were all competing for the same contract, so just like us, no one would speak out if they were having difficulties with the production. I assumed they were. The National Foundation on Polio was supervising the trials, but as soon as the trials were completed we only had to answer to the Laboratory of Biologics Control, a branch of the Health Department. The Laboratory of Biological Control gave us just five-pages of protocol to follow, instead of the 55-page protocol that Dr. Salk recommended, omitting most of the safety procedures that Salk had planned for. This included omission of the formaldehyde deactivation process we had already stopped using. We had switched over to ultraviolet light to kill the virus because it was cheaper, but hardly as safe. I made my concerns known to my superiors."

Dr. Wheeling paused, lost in his thoughts. He cleared his throat and then continued.

"Shortly after I spoke out, I was taken off all vaccine production responsibilities, given a raise, and put behind a desk. They thought I'd keep quiet if they gave me more money, but I had been supplying Alex with whatever information I could obtain, and had no intentions of stopping."

"Alex died because of this?" I asked Victor once he was finished.

"I don't know. I received a call several months ago from Ralph Houlihan, the associate director of Cutter Laboratories."

"Cutter!" I nearly shouted. Students at the other tables all looked our way. I lowered my voice and pulled out the list. "Alex left this for us," I said giving Victor the list of names. He read the list, sighed, and handed it back.

Dr. Wheeling nodded his head as he slowly explained, "This is the list of the five companies that were given a contract to produce the vaccine for commercial use. Cutter was the smallest and newest producer of vaccines intended for people. It started out as merely an animal vaccine firm, but began expanding with the polio vaccine. Its intention was for the polio vaccine to bridge the gap from animals to humans.

"Houlihan asked if we were having problems inactivating the

virus. I didn't want to tell him we were, so I asked him why. It was then that he informed me of something that was so surprising I didn't even consider the ramifications until it was too late. He said that they could not produce one single unit of the vaccine that didn't have the live polio virus in it. Every batch they made was infected with the virus."

"Several days later, I called Ralph about the ultraviolet light we were using, but it was obvious Cutter couldn't afford anything on that level. At this point, Cutter should have dropped out of the contract. A week later, Cutter declared to the public that it had a working vaccine ready to ship across the United States. When I told Alex, he actually went all the way to Berkley to see the Cutter facility and doctors for himself. He returned dumbfounded, amazed that they were even legally licensed to manufacture vaccines for animals, let alone people."

Sara cut in, "Could Cutter really have perfected the vaccine in less than a week?"

Victor raised his eyebrows, looking at Sara. "That is exactly what Alex and I were trying to figure out. Unfortunately, we didn't have any conclusive evidence at the time. Then Alex called me several days ago. He found something that he thought could expose the truth once and for all. He wanted me to come as soon as possible. I'm sorry to say that I was too late."

"Who else knew about the companies making the vaccine?" Sara asked.

"Do either of you listen to the radio? There have been reports from the start. This is the problem with young people today.

There is no interest in current affairs. All you care about is your rock and roll, and your hula hoops."

I didn't want to correct the doctor on any of his cultural "insights". Alex had singled out Cutter on the list for a reason. He must have found something that was important enough, but enough to get him killed?

I told Sara and Dr. Wheeling about the man I met at the hospital. There was a chance Keith didn't know who was making the vaccine, but if he was involved with the testing, he would certainly have some knowledge, some information that might prove helpful to us.

Victor was tired from his train ride and I was somewhat exhausted myself. The doctor was staying at the Schenley Park Hotel, which was right around the block on Bigelow and Fifth. Sara and I walked Dr. Wheeling to his hotel and agreed to meet in the morning and try to find any files Alex might have left behind. I had so many questions to ask, but they would have to wait until the next morning.

"Dr. Wheeling?" The doctor turned around. "Was there anyone else helping the two of you? I mean would anyone else know what you and Alex were trying to do?"

Wheeling shook his head. "No. We both promised each other that we wouldn't involve anyone else. Alex said he had a feeling he was being watched, but wasn't entirely sure by whom. I thought he was just being a bit paranoid. Now, I'm afraid that he was probably right."

A sense of dread came over me as I thanked Dr. Wheeling. It was a little after four, and I had this feeling that I had forgotten something. The feeling stayed with me as Sara and I strolled around the hotel trying to decide our next course of action.

The day was getting cooler, but the air was comfortable. Other students were already walking around enjoying their time outside after the end of day's classes. The sun wouldn't set for another three hours, so we still had time before night fell around us. It was during the dark hours that the sadness would become the hardest. I wasn't looking forward to the first night without Alex being around.

Chapter 4

Leaving the hotel, Sara and I walked without a destination in mind. I was following her, but I had the strange feeling she was actually following me. Neither one of us was leading, but only mindlessly walking the other around in the general direction of the university.

We ended up by a small concrete fountain, at the base of the Cathedral, in front of a large stone staircase. Water flowed from a small panther's head embedded in the soot-covered fountain wall, streaming into a stone basin overflowing into a larger pool below. Heavy black soot had built up on the beige limestone over the past thirty years. The building was so black, new students thought it was built from black stone. The color was like the butt of a smoked cigarette, disguising the natural color of the stone beneath.

Sitting on a bench across from us, a young beatnik in a black sweater and the week's growth of facial hair was busy writing franticly into a notepad. When I returned from the war, I realized that the country had gone through a cultural revolution. I wasn't sure if it happened while I was away or grew slowly around me before I left, but had gone unnoticed by me until after I returned from Korea.

Alex would send me books and comics every other week. I'd digest them on a regular basis and trade them for all sorts of reading materials with other men in my unit. We never wanted to be bored. Reading was a great way, and sometimes the only way, to pass the time. One book I couldn't put down was *The Catcher in the Rye*. Even in the cold wet mountains of Korea, I could relate to Holden Caulfield, the main character. He was lost in a world he didn't understand, a world stuck in the past as he tried to move on. As I looked around, I knew the world was moving on whether I was with it or not.

"Hey!" Sara's soft voice boomed, drawing me back to the present, "You could at least throw your garbage away!" She was giving the beatnik a verbal lashing for tossing his finished cigarette on the ground. He rolled his eyes, but decided he was better off cleaning up than to further anger the blond girl. I was surprised at the anger pouring from Sara's small mouth. She was upset, and needed to burn off some steam before she popped.

"The nerve of that guy," Sara said shaking her head in disbelief. "They blow smoke in our faces all day long and don't even have the common decency to find an ashtray."

My attention was drawn to Sara's words as the wheels in my

head began to turn. We needed to find the smoker. There was another person smoking in Alex's office. *Find an ashtray ...* she said. We had seen the ashtray in Alex's office, filled with cigarette butts. Now we needed to find their source.

"I have an idea," I quickly said.

I grabbed Sara and pulled her up the blackened stone steps. I was too worked up to explain my epiphany to her. I felt an urge to see Alex's office right way. I needed to see it as soon as possible. I almost pulled Sara through the revolving door as I went through, but realized at the last second we couldn't fit together.

I released her hand, but the momentum had already done its job and I plowed into the glass doors. The glass held and didn't even vibrate as my entire body was bounced backwards onto the rough stone. Sara didn't know if she should start laughing or help me up, but tried both at the same time. It must have been hysterical to watch, but I was on a mission and didn't have time to joke around. I recovered my cane applied pressure, slowly entering the revolving door slowly to the Cathedral. I picked up momentum as Sara added her weight.

It was harder for me to run, so I ended up practically skipping through the sixty foot commons room. While I extended my good leg, I tried to brace myself with my cane, and then swung my bad leg in front of me. Rose marble pillars began at the floor, rising up and forming wide arches toward the ceiling. Cylinder bucket-sized lights hung from each arch's keystone. Several dozen students were scattered around studying at the large brown mahogany tables. They turned away from their studies long enough to see a limping madman trotting past. I knew they were staring, but I just didn't have the time to care. I was on a mission. No . . . a quest . . . a quest to find a piece of evidence that could tell us what happened to Alex.

I ran under the twenty-foot brass gate dividing the atrium from the elevators. I waited for the lift doors to open, pausing to catch my breath. Sara caught up to me just as the doors began to open. I jumped into the elevator, realizing too late that other people were still on it. I quickly jumped backwards as several students and faculty members got off the elevator trying to avoid being trampled to death by the gimp with the cane.

Once again I tried to catch my breath as they filed out avoiding me as best they could. This time they were avoiding me more because of my actions than because of my appearance. When the lift was empty, I slid in with Sara following right behind. As the doors began to close, a large wrinkled hand slipped in between them causing the steel doors to bounce back open.

I was going to apologize as the doors slid fully open, but stopped as I stared in disbelief at Dr. Longmont smiling wildly outside of the car. His yellow teeth made his skin appear pasty and cartoonish. His Gahan hat rested comfortably on the top of his head, while his dark brown suit appeared worn, with wrinkles.

"Jamie, what a surprise once again to see you. Room for one more?" he asking walking in before we could even respond.

I was speechless, but nodded as Longmont entered the lift. Sara tried to press the twelfth floor button, but the large hairy man beat her to it.

"Dr. Longmont," I said in greeting the man. The smell of cigarette smoke was overwhelming as it filled the elevator, causing a light cough to escape from my lungs. "What are the odds of us meeting like this twice in one day?" I figured that the odds were good if he was following us.

Longmont laughed and didn't bother to answer a question he took as rhetorical. "You must be Jamie's girlfriend. I didn't catch your name dear."

Longmont's paw-like hand encompassed Sara's small fingers as they shook hands. Was it possible Alex had several projects he hadn't told either Sara or me about? He obviously didn't tell us about the vaccine.

"Oh, we're just friends, Dr. Longmont. I'm Sara," she said as she fought back a blush. I shot back a look at Sara as she said we were *just friends.* For some reason there was a small pain deep in my stomach. Although I knew our relationship was just a friendship, I had wanted it to be more. Hearing her confirm that our relationship was only a friendship was almost devastating.

"My apologies dear," Longmont said to Sara as he tried to bow slightly in the small confined space. "Jamie, I'm glad I caught you. I was wondering if Dr. Gerlach left any files for me in his office."

I scratched my chin, pretending to wonder. "I don't recall the actual topic of research you and Alex were working on," I said while I tried to bait him, intending to get him reveal something. I didn't trust the man. He reminded me of a man in advertising. I didn't trust ad men.

Without skipping a beat, Longmont answered, "The Roman senate." If it was a lie, it was very quick and well designed. Alex did much of his research on the Roman senate. "As I said before, I designed the research methods. Alex was providing the historical relevance of the political system at the time, mainly Cicero's point of view on the public sphere."

Was that the truth? How could I be sure of anything now? I stared at Longmont for what felt like a long time, but must have only been seconds. If he had been telling a lie, would my pause indicate my distrust? He knew Alex's favorite topic was ancient Rome, but that wasn't hard to find out. If he was telling a lie, what was it that Longmont was really looking for? What was he trying to hide? Alex had written paper after paper about Rome, but Longmont missed an important detail. Alex had always focused on the political analysis of war, not the senate. Was this important, or was Alex simply helping a colleague with his work?

I gave Longmont a friendly smile, trying not to gag from the cigarette fumes radiating from his person.

"If you like, you can take a look for yourself," I said. I felt a small pinch along my elbow. I looked over at Sara seeing her worried expression. She understood the discrepancy too. It was a subtle point, but Longmont's mention of the senate as a focus of Alex's research was off. Was that enough to cause worry? Sara thought so. The elevator stopped, and a moment later the doors opened onto the twelfth floor.

"I have to grab a drink," I said, "I'll meet you there." I didn't want to leave Sara alone with Longmont for any period of time without knowing what his motives were. If he was really here to pick up research Alex had been helping him with, I didn't want to get in his way. A little voice inside of my head told me to call the cops just in case, but I wasn't sure that was a smart idea. I still didn't have any real evidence to disprove Alex's suicide or to substantiate a murder theory. Murder? Could it really have been murder?

I was still coughing as I made a beeline for the water fountain down the hall. I turned the little metal knob causing water to shoot out and up in the air. I tried to clean the foul taste out of my mouth, spitting the nicotine and tar away. I tried to swallow more water, focusing on the excess liquid swirling down into the drain. I took a final sip. Then headed to Alex's office.

Once again, I found Alex's office with the door open, the yellow police tape hanging down from one side. Sara must have used the keypad to open the door for Longmont.

Sara was reading book titles along the wall, when I entered the room. Longmont was rapidly searching through the filing cabinets. I didn't know how I felt about a total stranger going through Alex's things. First someone ransacked his home. Now I was actually watching as this strange man sifted through the memories of my mentor. Something wasn't right about the whole experience. I had given approval to his search with doubt in my mind, and now I was having second thoughts. I didn't want to be rude. If Longmont was Alex's friend, than I didn't want to interfere.

I looked around the room. At least maintenance covered the broken window with plywood.

"Do you need any help doctor? Maybe Sara or I could help you with your search."

"No worries lad. I think I can handle it," he said without bothering to look up.

I pattered around, taking in my dead friend's office, probably for the last time. I wanted to grab some of Alex's things before the school decided to clean the office out. I searched for the silver elephant lighter on the desk. He had never used the lighter for its intended purpose. Alex preferred using matches over a fuel lighter to light his smokes. He was a man of habit and even a present from a faraway land, given to him by a close friend couldn't change that. I couldn't find the lighter. The elephant wasn't anywhere on the desk. I looked in the drawers, but didn't have any luck there either. I remembered moving it when I was in the office earlier that morning.

Sara turned to me. She looked worried, almost scared. I started to move toward her, but all of a sudden she moved her hand up for me to stop. She looked back over at Dr. Longmont as he continued with his search. She brought her hand to her mouth and mimicked smoking a cigarette. The man was too engrossed in his investigation to notice our silent conversation. I didn't understand what Sara was trying to tell me until I realized Longmont was smoking a cigarette. He flicked ash down into the ceramic ashtray. Without finishing it completely, he put the cigarette out walking away from the cabinets, frustrated with his search.

"I only wanted to help the professor get published one last time," Longmont said with disappointment. "Well, no point crying over spilled milk right? Jamie, thank you. Sara it was a pleasure to meet you." He shook Sara's hand, then mine, and walked out without another moment's hesitation.

We waited in silence until he caught the elevator. Then Sara picked up his half smoked cigarette. We compared it to the butts from the night before. They were all the same, Lucky Strike. Alex wasn't a heavy smoker, but when he did smoke, his brand was Kool.

"Could Dr. Longmont have been here last night?" Sara asked.

I looked at the butts in my hand. I didn't know if I wanted to believe it, but I had to think it through rationally. If we were looking for a killer, I couldn't jump to conclusions that I might regret later. We needed to be careful, thorough in our investigation. We'd need very strong evidence before we could go to the police or accuse anyone of murder.

Sara and I thought the situation though. It could be a coincidence that Longmont and the person in the office last night smoked the same brand of cigarettes. After all, Lucky Strike is a popular brand. I tried to convince myself that Longmont could not be the same person who killed Alex. While there was an inconsistency in Longmont's story, and he happened to smoke the same cigarettes as the person in this office the night before, that wasn't enough to start crying murder.

I couldn't think clearly in this office. There were too many emotions swirling around in my head. I went out to the hall, not realizing my legs were moving. Sara followed, turning the lights off, and closing the door.

I wandered over to a bench at the other end of the hall in

between the elevators. We sat in silence as hundreds of thoughts raced around in my head while I tried to grasp a logical explanation for everything. For some reason, I knew we had thrown logic out and were relying on pure speculation.

"He's got something to do with this. I just know it, Jamie," Sara said with a tremble.

My attention turned to the brass keypad above the handle to the office door. Alex used to change the combination once a month, each time making us solve a riddle to guess the code that would unlock it. Sometimes, it would only take moments, but the professor occasionally made the puzzle harder so that it could take days to solve. One month, the riddle was so difficult that it took me an entire week to figure it out. Alex thought it was hilarious that it took so long to decipher the code. It occurred to me that all this was just another game for Alex. Even in death, he could overwhelm us with a disturbing mystery.

The puzzle would always take different forms and require different skill sets to figure it out. One month it would be an easy, mathematical logic problem. Other times it would be a riddle referencing popular culture or mysterious foreign words. Alex's favorite was to give us a historical riddle referencing a moment in time. He would make these as hard as possible, never giving a hint to the answer. He would savor the days he could stump us with an obscure detail only he knew. Sara was good at decoding the obscure, while I was a crack ace with popular culture clues. The last one had been a tough one. I didn't know if Sara had even figured it out.

"When did you figure out the combination?" I asked Sara pointing to the door.

She repeated the riddle out loud. "The birth of the first comrade to Klauder's prize?"

"Yeah, that's the one."

Sara dropped her head down with a hint of remorse. "I never solved it," she responded.

"Really? I thought it was pretty easy. Klauder referred to Charles Klauder, the lead architect on the Cathedral of Learning. His prize was the building itself. Just the prestige alone carried him through his career. The Cathedral's first comrade was the Cathedral's Russian brother, the central tower at the University of Moscow, was the only educational building taller than the Cathedral itself. It was built in 1755."

Sara looked up into my eyes. "Neat," she murmured. She hadn't thought about the clue and didn't care about the answer at this point. What was the point if Alex was gone?

I looked back at the door and keypad. A question crossed my mind. "If you didn't know the combination than how did you unlock the door?" I asked.

"I didn't. Dr. Longmont did," Sara said, the words hitting a raw nerve.

"1755, that bastard knew the answer!" I yelled, jumping up from the bench and jammed my thumb against the elevator down button. I continuously pushed the button waiting for the doors to finally open. Longmont must have known the combination because he saw Alex open the door the night before. He was there with Alex the night of his death. Time went by slowly for the next few moments as we waited for the elevator. Once it arrived, it took its time descending, stopping at every other floor.

When we finally hit bottom, Sara was the first out, rushing into the commons room searching for that manipulating bastard. I went the other way, first looking inside, then moving outside and searching around the Cathedral. Sara and I met outside on the Cathedral's lawn. We had lost him. He knew the combination. He had to be the one smoking last night in Alex's office. We lost the one man who was with Alex the night he died. Longmont knew what transpired and we had let him get away. It was possible that Dr. Longmont killed our friend.

We ran back to get word to Victor at the Schenley Park Hotel. He said he'd meet us in the lobby and hung up. Sara went to the front desk and called the William Penn Hotel. The clerk at the front desk said that they didn't have anyone registered under that name. According to the clerk, the hotel was full so it was possible that he went somewhere else. Sara proceeded to call every hotel in the downtown area. She called everywhere from the Hilton, to a little bed and breakfast called The Sunnyledge Inn at Fifth and Wilkins. Longmont wasn't at any of them. I realized we had a big problem on our hands. Not only had we let a complete stranger comb through Alex's personal possessions, we had even welcomed it. We waited for Victor in the hotel lobby contemplating what to do next. Victor must have been taking a nap because he came down with his hair messy, tucking in his shirt. After we explained what had gone wrong, he began calling around to his colleagues. No one had ever heard of Dr. Longmont before. It was clear that we had been lied to by the good doctor, whoever he was.

We decided to part ways from Dr. Wheeling. We'd see each other in the morning, after a good night sleep. It was still too soon to go to the police. We hadn't come up with anything worth reporting, only minor facts that could be interpreted in many different ways. It was vital to produce some sort of evidence that the cops could use to reopen the case.

Sara was tired and I was beyond beat. I needed a cup of Joe to keep going. I knew we had a major problem at the moment, but I couldn't stay awake to save my life.

We stopped at a nearby diner and took a booth in the back. The waitress came over to take our order. She had long black hair pulled back with a pink ribbon. Around her eyes were dark circles and the hint of crow's feet. Aside from the crow's feet, her skin was flawless and pale like it hasn't seen the rays of the sun in years. She wore a short pearl necklace and carried a warm smile. I ordered two cups of coffee and piece of apple pie to share. The waitress brought mugs, filling them to the top. She returned with our pastry and two forks, which she set down on the table.

"What's the grin for Jamie?"

I hadn't realized that I was smiling until Sara pointed it out. It was the waitress. She reminded me of my mother, a few years older, and maybe the age she would have been if she were still alive today. I didn't want to share the memory, so I just shrugged my shoulders and kept the thought to myself.

"I can't remember the last time I had pie," I said with a smile. "I hear they have great apple pie here." It was a lie, but a small one since places like this always had good apple pie.

I had wanted to say, *Thanks mom*, when she brought the

pie, but I restrained myself. No reason to make Sara think I was a complete weirdo anymore than she probably already did. I had too much on my mind already and didn't want to make myself any more depressed than I already was. I tried to force my mother's memory from my mind, hiding it once again with the rest of my childhood.

"Spill it," Sara said, not letting the subject rest.

"It's nothing really, just a sentimental moment. There, it passed."

Sara sat back frowning because I wouldn't share my innermost thoughts with her. What was it about women and their feelings? Couldn't they understand we didn't like sharing, especially when it came to our mothers? Call it Freudian, it didn't matter to me. I missed my parents, but I wasn't going to talk about them.

"I think we should go to the police," I said, changing the subject.

"With what? We don't know if Longmont is his real name or where he even is." She paused to take a breath and a sip of coffee before she continued. "We broke into a crime scene and invited a complete stranger in with us. What do you think that is going to look like? They closed the case because they thought it was suicide, so we need proof. All we have are guesses and vague leads."

"Guesses and pie," I corrected her. She shoveled a fork full of apple pie into her mouth shaking her head.

"You are just not right in the head, are you Jamie?"

A full mouth of food made the words come out in jumbles, but I got the gist of the question. I ignored Sara and kept thinking. She was right, of course. We knew Longmont smoked the same brand of cigarettes that we found at the scene. Was that a big coincidence after all? How many people smoked the same brand? He also knew the combination to the keypad on the office door, which could have meant that Alex had given it to him at an earlier date. But why would he do that? I sat back angry, not knowing what to do.

"Listen to me," Sara pleaded. We don't know anything more than we did before, really. Yeah, we have some leads to go on, but that's it. We should go to the police when we have something more concrete, a bit more substantial. The last thing we need right now is for the cops to think we're two crazy kids, because then when we do really have something, they won't even want to listen."

I nodded in agreement, knowing she was right.

"I'm frustrated, Sara. There's a good possibility Longmont either killed Alex or knows the person responsible and we let him get away." My nerves were shot.

"I understand how you feel, Jamie, I do." She grabbed my hand, calming me in the process. "But we still need to stay calm."

It was funny how Sara was telling me to stay calm. I had a feeling she was saying it out loud for herself too. This couldn't be easy on her either.

We sat in silence until the piece of pie was completely gone. I wanted another serving, but thought if the waitress came back to our table I would lose it. Sara's house was only a couple of blocks away so I asked her if I could walk her home. She shook her head from side to side reminding me of a small child who didn't know she was sleepy until she hit her pillow.

"Jamie, I don't know if I could sleep now even if I wanted too."

"We need to get some sleep," I said with a smile. "It's been a long day for both of us, and if we don't get some rest we won't be able to think straight tomorrow." This time I was being the rational one.

I knew men coming back from Korea who hadn't been able to cope with what they saw or what they had to do during the war. They ended up in hospitals, wearing straitjackets, and sleeping in padded cells. Doctors would give them shock therapy and medicate them to lethargic states.

I was a firm believer in sleep. We needed to take our time and have a chance to wrap our heads around what was happening. Getting overemotional wouldn't help either of us. Sleep would provide the calm we needed.

"Even the bad guys need to get some rest," I added. Sara turned back toward me with her forehead scrunched up like a bulldog, and began to giggle, which then turned into a laugh. It was a nervous laugh, but a laugh all the same. I took it as my queue to drop some quarters on the table for the waitress. On my way out, I wanted to give the woman a hug, but decided against it.

We strolled down Atwood Street on the way to Sara's house. She pulled me close linking her arms around mine. I didn't want to get too excited because I knew she was still jumpy from the long day, but I couldn't help myself. We only found out about

Alex's death this morning after all. She had been saddened by the event and the last thing I wanted to do was take advantage of the girl. In the past ten hours, Sara and I had been through the wringer. I was more worried about her, however. I didn't know how she would handle the situation in the long run, but so far she was doing well under the circumstances.

Sara was from a small town in Ohio called Troy. It was smack in the middle of the state and had a town square, with a Main Street for only 20,000 people. Pittsburgh was no New York City, but it could feel overwhelming at times coming from a small place like Troy.

I needed the trolley lines, the automobiles, and the thousands of pedestrians running around. I liked the bustle. I thrived on the chaos of it all. Sara, on the other hand, felt otherwise. She came from such a quiet place, where the town sheriff was also the town barber. Her idea of a fun night before she came to Pittsburgh was hanging out at the one malt shop in town.

Sara's parents did fairly well for themselves during the depression. Her father made a decent living running a pub in the town square, while her mother did all the cooking for the business. Sara was the first of her family to finish high school, and one of only a handful who had gone on to college.

She received a free ride to Chatham College, an all-girls school in a small suburb of Pittsburgh called Squirrel Hill. She had started out with biology, but switched to history after suffering through a grueling semester taking organic chemistry.

We met during our first semester of graduate school, in one of Alex's classes, and hadn't parted ways since. Even though I felt more for Sara on a daily basis, it wasn't as if she felt the same way. I would love to take our relationship to the next level, but it seemed that she was more interested in a simple friendship. I didn't want to ruin our relationship by making a fool out of myself. If Sara didn't feel the same way as I did about us, there was a chance pushing her would destroy what we already had. I wasn't ready to take that kind of a chance yet.

I had been around death and could handle it better than most people. Even Alex's death was something I could deal with in my own way. I already knew the nothingness, which could occur after the last breath left a friend. Watching someone die closely could take away all faith in the existence of a human soul. Sara and I were different in that way. I knew Sara couldn't find purpose in life if she thought the way I did. I've become numb, but she hadn't and possibly never would. She would probably never see the real thing, the violent kind of death that a normal person could only find in the black and white pictures of *Life* magazine. Sara needed to know that there was something out there watching over her. She needed God to help her through life's challenges. She needed meaning, a direction. I, on the other hand, did not.

When we got to the door of her house, Sara stood there clutching my arm. She was hesitant to go inside, too scared to even step foot into her own home. I looked down into her glistening eyes. For a moment I wondered what it would be like to hold her close.

"You want me to come in with you?" I asked, wondering why I had just said that. The words had slipped out and I desperately wanted to take them back. Sara wasn't the type of girl to let anyone in her bedroom. What was I thinking? Did I really think she would take me up on it? I was just trying to help her gain some courage to face her worst fears . . . . Yeah, that was it.

Sara pulled herself together as she dug into her purse searching for her keys. After a frustrating moment and an awkward amount of searching, she found them.

"If you wouldn't mind," she said. Did I miss something? "I would like the company," Sara added.

"What did you say? It sounded like you wanted me to come in with you."

Sara blushed, "Please, it would mean a lot. But if you don't want too I'll understand completely."

"I'll come in if you think you'd feel better." Had I died and gone to heaven? I needed to pinch myself to make sure I wasn't dreaming all of this. I grabbed a chunk of skin on my arm, pinching it to make sure. It hurt, but I wasn't sure if that was enough.

"You wouldn't mind? I don't want to be alone tonight, Jamie." She said as she stepped inside the house.

She kept the door open waiting for me to walk through. I couldn't say no. Even if I wanted to, I wouldn't be able to. It's been a lifetime since a girl asked me inside her home. Actually, I'm pretty sure I've never been asked in a girl's home before. Not that I was a virgin, of course. I had my share of flings in the past. I was just not the type of guy who got asked back to a lady's place.

I followed Sara into the dark foyer. I couldn't see much and didn't know my way around. She didn't want to turn the lights on and draw any attention from her housemates. I bumped into what I thought was a chair and Sara reached back, grabbed my hand, and led me the rest of the way, all the way up the stairs to her room. I tried my best not to trip, but the butterflies in my stomach wouldn't settle. My legs felt like rubber as I climbed the stairs. I felt like a little boy waking up on Christmas morning to a room full of presents. When we got to the top of the stairs, Sara pushed me aside and unlocked the first door on the right. She stepped inside and I followed keeping my cane close so I wouldn't bang it against the doorway.

Sara closed the door behind us and turned the lights on. My eyes took a moment to adjust. Her room was a dull white, nothing like I pictured it. I thought it would be pink or something more colorful, full of spirit and energy. There weren't any posters of Hollywood stars or pictures of her family. Nothing besides a small mirror hung near the doorway. A small white desk with a green typewriter on top stood in the corner. Books were scattered around the room, most resting in stacks by the desk. A small cross hung over her bed. All of a sudden I felt like I was invading a sacred place. I was out of my element, with little if anything in common with the woman standing near me. We were from different worlds. We were in the same class, but that was where the similarities ended for both of us.

A green three-cushion couch was set against the opposite wall. There seemed to be more books on the couch than anywhere else. Directly across was Sara's bed against the opposite wall. It was a twin, which probably came with the room. A light green quilt neatly lay under several oversized plush matching pillows. I would have assumed that the size of the bed would have dissuaded her from having nighttime visitors. Sara took off her coat and placed her purse down near the desk.

"I know what you're thinking. It's plain. The landlady won't let us redecorate." She looked at me and giggled. "And don't worry," she winked, "the cross isn't mine."

"What? I mean I didn't . . . " I paused, feeling a rush of relief take over. The differences disappeared, and I suddenly was aware of my own irrational thoughts. I wanted this woman so badly that my emotions caught me off guard. I began to walk towards Sara, seeing if I could kiss her. She blushed and walked over to her desk, avoiding my reach.

Sara spun toward her bed as a sense of dread came over her. "I hadn't thought this through," she said. "I guess you should sleep on the couch."

"Oh," I sighed, "right, the couch . . . ." My fantasy fizzled away.

Sara laughed again. "Jamie, did you think that . . . I was asking you to . . . "

I cut her off before the situation became any more awkward than it already was. "No, of course not. I'm just joshing you. Of course I knew." I wanted to hide. I couldn't believe how naive I was. A woman like Sara didn't just invite you into her bed. She wasn't a hussy after all.

"I'm going to change in the bathroom," she said as she grabbed a pile of clothes. She looked back not sure of herself. "Stay here. Okay?"

I nodded as she left with her small bundle. I looked down at the couch and began to clear a space for my feeble-minded person. How could I have actually thought I'd be so lucky? Sara wasn't interested in me like that. I should have known better. I paced around the room peering at the small yellow bookcase standing next to her bed. I scanned the books on the two shelves. More books were spread out over the floor, most likely for school. I looked back to the shelves. The books on them were the typical women's books you'd expect to find in any girl's room. There were some mysteries by Agatha Christie and a few romances, but nothing out of the norm. I saw *The Catcher in the Rye* half way along the first shelf. I went to grab the book, excited to see it.

"Looking for something?" Sara's voice echoed through the room.

I didn't hear the door open as Sara had walked in. She spoke with all the seductiveness of the woman from my dreams. I turned around to see Sara who was watching me, wearing a short white gown that left little to the imagination. She could have easily been a centerfold in one of the smut rags. I've seen *Playboy* before, and I have to agree with Mr. Hefner's taste in women. They were elegant, classy, never leaving you feeling dirty for looking. Sara was the all-American girl and definitely pin up material. I thought that might be what attracted me to her in the first place.

"Jamie?" Sara called trying to distract my attention away from her body.

"Yeah?" I said not registering where the crack in my voice came from.

Sara starred at me from across the room.

"You might swallow a fly if you keep your mouth open like that."

I came out of my trance, wiping at the dribble that had started to run from the corner of my mouth, but I couldn't manage to form any words. I had to come up with something to talk about. I grabbed *The Catcher in the Rye* off the bookcase, holding it up for inspection.

"This is my favorite book," I said with a type of giddiness reserved for seven-year-old girls. Realizing how I must have sounded, I lowered the book turning away from Sara. "J.D. Salinger must have remembered every awkward experience he had when he was young." Just like the awkward experience I was sharing with Sara at this very moment.

"Me, too," Sara added in almost the same giddy voice I had shared moments before. Her excitement suited her girl next-door look. "Can you believe I almost did the same thing as Holden in high school?"

"Dropping out of prep school?" I asked.

"No, the big life question." She said as she grabbed the book from my clutches. "He doesn't know what to do with his life, but he feels the weight of the world on his shoulders." Sara took a seat on her bed and I took a seat next to her. "He wants to experience life and grow up so badly, but at the same time doesn't want to end up like every other adult he knows." She took a deep breath continuing as soon as her lungs filled. "Like at the museum what he's looking at the Eskimo exhibit. He relates to the never changing museum exhibit, like it's his own life. He wants it to change and move, but it won't. That's how I felt in high school too." She stopped speaking as she sat staring at the cover of her book in my hands. I leaned in for a kiss, not sure if it was the right time, but not even noticing, she stood up and put the book away.

"Do you want a blanket, maybe a pillow?" Sara asked as I quickly moved back into the same position she last saw, before I leaned forward.

I shook my head and stood up. "All I need is the couch." I moved toward the opposite end of the room. "I'll sleep like a baby as soon as I lay down."

Sara followed me to the other side of the room, standing next to me. She put her hands on mine and gave me a kiss on the cheek. "Thank you for staying Jamie. It really means a lot to me."

"It's not a problem, really."

"You're a good friend," Sara added as she continued to stare into my eyes without turning away. Her face grew into a frown and she stepped away without another word.

"What's wrong?" I asked.

"How did your parents die Jamie?" Sara replied.

"What brought that up?" I wanted to know.

"Alex's death can't be easy on you," she explained. "I knew how close the two of you were. To me he was a mentor and friend, but he replaced your parents after they died." She shook her head, indicating that she wasn't sure what else to say, but then she found the words. "It would mean a lot to me if you told me," she finally said.

"They were on their way back from Jersey in my father's

'43 Plymouth coup. It was an auburn color, with shiny chrome highlights. The curves of the sides and the long hood made the car the slickest thing on the road, but its glamour certainly didn't protect my parents," I explained. "They were driving on a curvy patch of Interstate 80S, and my parents' car was hit from behind. My father lost control of the vehicle and nothing he could do as the car went over a cliff, falling thirty feet down into a gully. The police were never able to find the driver of the other car. He got away, never realizing the damage he caused." I finished and silence swept over us for the next several moments.

Sara finally broke in, "I'm sorry Jamie."

She turned off the light and darkness filled the room. Sara climbed into bed pulling the covers up. I lay down on the couch setting my cane on the floor next to me. The couch was comfortable enough, but I tossed around anyway waiting for sleep to take hold. I could sleep anywhere. Since Korea I could even sleep standing up. I once slept through the worst snowstorm Mother Nature could throw at me during the war, only waking up to take a leak. I wondered how I'd sleep with Sara so close. I would be lucky if I could drift off to sleep without going crazy first.

"Good night, Jamie," Sara said cutting through the silent darkness. "I really do appreciate your keeping me company tonight."

"My pleasure, Sara," I responded. "Good night." I felt my chest tighten. I wanted to be cool, but wasn't sure if I could pull it off. I wanted to be like Brando or James Dean, cool as ice. They always knew what to say and how to act. Sometimes I had to remind myself that they were actors and in real life they were probably completely different people. Unfortunately, even in real life those actors still could get the girl on a daily basis. I kept my eyes open in the dark for as long as I could, but slowly my eyelids closed and my exhaustion took over.

I fell asleep thinking about Sara.

In my dream, I was on a motorcycle with Sara riding behind me, clutching my waist. We were on a Triumph 149cc OHV Terrier with a full tank of gas ready to ride as long and far as we could. The bike was humming between my legs. Sara's arms encircled me and her face pressed against my neck. We were riding off into the sunset together, out to the country, away from the city and its dark shadows. The air was clean and we were having the time of our lives.

I saw cows in the distance watching as we zipped by on the open road. We were alone out there, not another car in sight. Brando would have been proud and Dean would have been envious of the terrain before us. The pavement was completely flat, no potholes to worry about. The sky was light blue, clear of all clouds, and not a chance of rain ever.

The bike hummed as we took the turns, watching the full green trees pass us by. The air screamed around our heads, but I could still hear Sara's cries of excitement in the rush of the speeding wind.

I wasn't sure how it would end and I didn't care in the least. I was happy and with the girl of my dreams. I set the bike in gear speeding along the highway. There was no friction, no dampening of my senses. It was pure. It was good. But, of course, I knew deep down, it was only a dream.

Chapter 5

I woke up to darkness with the taste of road kill in my mouth and a weird desire to buy a leather jacket. Although it was dark, I didn't want to go back to sleep. I was still tired, but I remembered all of the events of the previous day with a vengeance. Alex's death invaded my thoughts. My back was slick with sweat and the air was damp with cool humidity. The grass outside would still be cold and wet, until the sun rose, drying the moisture. I couldn't see the clock, but it had to be before six. Sara was still in bed, fast asleep, and I didn't want to wake her. She lay wrapped peacefully in heavy blankets, hopefully dreaming of fluffy bunnies, and nothing to do with the horrors of yesterday.

Her arms were hidden beneath the two pillows under her head, and her dirty blond hair hung loosely around her face. I've had dreams of waking up next to her oval face on more nights than I cared to remember. In most of my dreams, I was laying in the same bed, holding her in my arms, never intending to let go.

All of a sudden, the weight of the world was on my shoulders. I wanted to get to the Victor's hotel as early as possible, but I didn't want to wake Sara in the process. She deserved the rest after everything that happened yesterday. I wrote a note and placed it on the pillow next to her. She would hate the fact that I went without her, but I couldn't wait around knowing there was work to be done, and the thought of waking her at this hour made me ill.

The sun began to rise as I made my way out of the house and began my trek to the hotel. It was already the beginning of a pleasant day, and the spring chill had already started to recede. There was still the morning dew on neighboring lawns, but that would soon disappear as the sun reached hirer into the sky.

I had to run through the past twenty-four hours in my head. Alex was dead and the idea that he committed suicide seemed unlikely. It seemed more likely that he was murdered. It was possible that Alex's death and the Salk vaccine were connected in some way. Did Alex discover some secret conspiracy that got him killed? And who was involved if he was in fact murdered? My biggest problem right now would be who to trust.

Then there was Dr. Victor Wheeling. He had been working for Parke-Davis, the biggest of the five pharmaceutical manufacturers. Victor had said that there was a problem with the way some of the companies were making the vaccine. Were those problems corrected before the vaccine hit the market?

If a problem was uncovered after the vaccine was released, those big firms would be in big trouble. They'd face lawsuits and the possibility of a shut down resulting in the loss of tens of thousands of jobs. If Alex found some evidence that threatened the pharmaceuticals would those companies resort to murder to hide that evidence? There were too many questions I couldn't answer. I felt my day get tougher with each nagging question I asked myself. The biggest question on my mind though was if I did find out what happened to Alex, was there anything I could do about it.

I was going to be interfering with some powerful people if I was right and Alex had discovered evidence against them. If someone was willing to kill Alex to keep these secrets hidden, how far would he go to protect those secrets now? Would he come after me? More importantly, would he go after Sara if she were implicated with me?

I made my way into the Hotel Schenley, which was nationally known and famous in the region for its clientele. The whole national baseball league had stayed at this hotel at one time or another since Forbes Field was built in 1909. Almost every president had stayed in the hotel since it opened in 1898. The most famous Hollywood stars, major league athletes, and powerful politicians have walked into the hotel at one time or another in the past sixty years.

Most likely they didn't pay much attention to the hotel's elegant design. They probably never marveled at the modern white marble pillars surrounding the building's sandstone steps and handmade brass railings. Did they take the time to appreciate the architect's grand vision at all? I had to stop myself before I continued down that slippery slope. I couldn't make any judgments about people I didn't know. These people that came to the hotel long before me had been geniuses in their fields, most of them were well educated, and knew good taste when they saw it. Who was I to think that I could understand the inner workings of an expert's mind?

A bellhop in a red suit and matching round cap nodded as I walked through the lobby. I felt completely out of place. I became self-conscious, not because of my limp, but because my clothes were in a terrible state. They were shabby looking and filthy from the previous day's activities. I looked down at my slacks, which were wrinkled from sleeping on Sara's couch. My shirt was almost yellow from dried sweat. I could have been a madman running around town the way I looked standing in the lobby of this fine establishment.

I glanced around the room realizing that no one seemed to notice my attire, or if they did, they didn't care in the slightest. I strolled up to a white and grey marble desk, but it was deserted. No one was around. I rang the silver bell on the desk and waited.

I waited for what seemed like long enough before deciding to go up to Victor's room without being announced first. I was anxious and didn't feel like waiting for assistance. If Dr. Wheeling was anything like Alex, he was already awake and reading the morning paper, having started his day at dawn. I wondered if the older you were the less sleep you needed. I think Joe McCarthy said that if a person sleeps long than eight hours a night he must be a communist. I could be mistaken, but it sounded like something the Wisconsin senator would say. I was in favor of sleep myself, but would never admit it in the halls of Congress for fear of being called a Red. At least we could sleep well, knowing the Russians were doing the same, seven hours ahead of us. That was probably one of the reasons McCarthy hated the Russian communists: they would start their days a full seven hours earlier than the American capitalists.

I took the elevator up to Victor's floor, stepping off into a slightly dimmed hallway. Green carpet covered the floor and yellow wallpaper made the hall seem larger than it really was. There were brass candelabras on tables at twenty feet intervals along the hallway. A painting of flowers appeared near every candelabra illuminating the pictures' details. I passed several white doors before I found room 3125. I raised and lowered the knocker gently, letting each thump resonate.

I waited for an answer, but no one came to the door. I knocked a little harder and the door slowly swung open exposing the interior of the hotel room.

"Victor?" I called out. "The door was open. Hello?" I checked the room number outside on the wall and confirmed it was Dr. Wheeling's room.

He could have already gone to get breakfast, forgetting to lock the door. I didn't want to go in without Victor's permission, but my curiosity got the better of me.

"Victor, it's Jamie Schmidt, I'm coming in okay?" I made sure I gave a moment for any dissent from within the room.

The elegance of the Hotel Schenley lured me in without any more hesitation. I had to see inside the room for myself. It was an odd materialist yearning that drew me in. I looked back down the hallway to make sure no one was coming. Then I quickly slipped into the room unnoticed.

I pictured an exotic hideaway, filled with lush colors, and cloud-like pillows. Reality sadly slapped me across the face as I peered into the room. The blinds were wide open, letting the early morning sun pour through the clear glass. When my eyes adjusted, I was able to make out the room's amenities. It looked just like any other generic hotel room I had been in before. There were double beds covered in floral patterned bedspreads. A small brass lamp sat on a light oak nightstand in between the beds. A large matching wooden dresser, with a tabletop radio, rested directly across from the nightstand.

I looked out the window. The room was only on the third floor and not high enough to have a decent view of the city. Still, I was high enough to see the Oakland skyline and the taller buildings in the area. The Cathedral of Learning created a heavy shadow in the rising sun, which loomed over the hotel like an orange drape.

A knock at the door turned my attention toward the colored maid entering the room. I felt my face blush. I had just been caught, like a child stealing a cookie in his mother's kitchen. I was frozen with fear of being kicked out for trespassing.

Oddly, the maid seemed to apologize. She must have thought I was a guest of the hotel and left as quickly as she arrived. Victor must have called housekeeping before going out. I took another look at the beds. Neither looked as if it had been slept in the previous night. Both beds were made, the corners still tucked in, and the pillows were neatly lying up against the headboards. Why call housekeeping if you had already cleaned the room yourself?

The taste of sleep still stung my mouth from the previous night. The taste was foul, causing me to gag. Maybe, the hotel had a complimentary toothbrush I could use to solve my urgent hygienic need. This time I was not let down. The bathroom was more than elegant, with a light blue marble sink, matching giant mirror, and a big bathtub partly hidden by a white linen curtain. It looked as if more money was spent in the restroom than in the actual bedroom.

The only issue seemed to be a lack of space in the design. Everything was cramped into a five by four foot area, elegant yet tiny. At least there was a brand new toothbrush, and a cup next to the sink. Victor's toiletries rested neatly on the opposite side. Finding no complementary toothpaste, I decided to use Victor's Colgate. I didn't think he would miss it. I made sure to start from the end and work my way up the tube. It's one thing to make a mess of your own tube of toothpaste, but quite another when it came to someone else's. I spread a small dap across the bristled brush, ran the water and began to brush the foul taste out of my mouth with an extra force reserved for hangovers. I turned the faucet off when I was finished and wiped my face with a clean towel.

I could hear the water continue to drip from the faucet. Without looking down, I tried to tighten the hot and cold handles, but the dripping continued. I looked down, but the faucet was off, no water was coming out, much less dripping. I realized the sound was coming from behind me. Victor must have run a bath earlier and not turned the faucet off all the way. The sound of a dripping faucet was enough to make me go crazy.

When I was in Korea, we heard about an interrogation technique called *Chinese water torture*. It was simple, but effective. Water would repeatedly drip onto your captive's forehead, while their head, hands and feet were tied down. It would last no longer than a few hours or it might go on for day until the victim finally broke down, revealing secret information. No horrible pain was involved. There was no cleaning up a messy pool of blood. Yet it was one of the most effective techniques used. The only problem was validating the information, of course. A human being tortured will admit almost anything to end the torture, no matter his innocence.

I reached behind the curtain, searching for the handle. I found the faucet and turned it toward the left to make the water stop dripping. The tub was filled and I was surprised to see the tip of a black shoe in the water. I pulled the curtain back a little more, exposing a leg wearing dark grey slacks. Without another thought, I jerked the curtain open, exposing the rest of the tub. The shoe was on the foot of the lifeless body of Dr. Victor Wheeling.

Victor's face was a frozen in terror, especially his eyes, which remained open. His hands were raised to his neck as if he were trying to stop his attacker from strangling the life out of him.

Victor's face was bloated. I wasn't trained in homicide forensics, but during the war I had to step over my fair share of dead bodies. It looked to be hours since he died. I knew the basic stages of post mortem activity pretty well for an amateur.

I heard the door open once again, a light voice called out. "Do you need housekeeping?" the maid asked reentering the room, this time without knocking.

I walked out of the bathroom to cut the maid off.

"No thank you, I can manage without it," I said, while I tried to block her view, but in the end it was futile.

The maid began to scream at the top of her lungs, dropping the towels meant for Victor. She made the sign of the cross and stepped back toward the hall. I moved toward her, but she started to scream louder. She ran out of the room knocking into her own cart in the hall. Linens and toiletries flew everywhere, scattering on the floor. When the maid regained her balance, she sprinted as fast as she could away from her own private nightmare. For an overweight woman who looked to be in her fifties, she was moving very quickly.

I watched the maid run down the hotel hallway, while a thought suddenly occurred to me. My life was about to become all that much harder. I had to get out of the hotel as quickly as possible. I didn't know if I was set up, but the maid's timing was too coincidental to believe otherwise. I would have bet a million to one that someone knew I was coming to see Dr. Wheeling. No wonder they didn't bother to hide the body. They wanted me to find it. They pretty much left it out in the open for the world to see. Now the maid would think that I was the murderer and she could identify me. Just what I needed to have to worry about, being booked for a murder I didn't commit. They would probably pin Alex's death on me too, an added bonus for sticking my nose in where it didn't belong.

I wasn't surprised when I heard the sirens. I didn't bother to wait around. My time would be limited. If they caught up with me now, I'd strangle in red tape, trying to prove my innocence while the evidence I was trying to gather about Alex's murder would go cold or get covered up. I had at least a three or four minutes before the cops would storm in to find me. If I didn't move fast and leave as soon as possible, I might find myself sitting in the electric chair this time next year.

I glanced around the room one last time to see if I'd missed anything. Victor's clothes were all neatly laid out on the dresser, and his briefcase was sitting on the floor by the bed closer to the door. I opened it, but it was completely empty. I searched under the bed, around the nightstand, but didn't find anything. Someone had combed though the room already and taken everything of importance.

With every wasted second the sirens grew louder. I had to get out of there. I bolted out the door and half ran, half limped back to the elevator. Victor's room was only on the third floor, so I figured the cops would come up the stairs. I just had to hope they wouldn't send another team up in the lift. Pushing the down button, I waited anxiously for the lift to arrive, scared shitless the cops would pour out as the doors slid open. I clenched my jaw waiting, not sure what I would do if they appeared.

Luckily, the lift was only a floor above and arrived quickly. I walked into the empty compartment and pushed the first and second floor buttons in a continuous motion until the doors began to slide together. I heard the stairwell door burst open as the elevator doors touched back together, allowing me to make my escape by just a fraction of a second.

I didn't think I'd be lucky enough to stroll out the hotel's front door. The cops were probably waiting for me down in the main lobby. I assumed that the dispatcher had called multiple units to the hotel. In any case, I had a plan. I slipped out of the elevator when the doors opened on the second floor and continued to limp my way down the hall to the stairwell.

The cops would be in Victor's room already, searching for clues while I made my get away. Of course they wouldn't find anything except the eyewitness who could place me at the scene of the crime. I didn't have an alibi. Even Sara never saw me leave this morning. For all she knew, I'd slipped out after she fell asleep and killed Victor last night. The cops wouldn't find any evidence that I was involved in the murder, but they would be able to place me at the scene of the crime. I couldn't take the chance that they would take me into custody for that alone.

Hurrying down the steps, I passed the lobby continuing to the basement. I came to a dark room filled with black and copper pipes running along the ceiling and the two sidewalls. Steam poured from the hot metal, accumulating in puddles of water on the floor. I had to be careful not to slip and crack my head open.

The hotel's furnace was next to the laundry facilities. I passed the housekeeping and maintenance staff, all of whom were too preoccupied with their own tasks to notice me. I wasn't worried about running into Victor's maid down here. I was sure she was giving her statement to the police and most likely would be for some time.

I followed the signs to the exit and opened a grey steel door to an overcast sky. I decided to walk calmly and slowly away from the hotel. No reason to run and draw suspicion. I was a student taking a stroll around near campus, nothing more. No one seemed to see me slip out the back of the hotel. As soon as I could, I crossed to the opposite side of the street continuing to look down at the placement. I didn't want to make eye contact with anyone passing by. I was concerned I'd draw attention if I looked in anyone's direction.

Avoiding eye contact would buy me some time. I tried not to draw any attention. It was harder than I thought it would be. I needed to disappear, but I felt I stuck out like a sore thumb.

I crossed the street and stepped up on the curb in front of the school. I was hoping that I would blend in with the other students on and around campus. The hotel was in the middle of campus, which worked in my favor. Without warning, a light grip came down on my shoulder. They had caught up too me after all. I was ready to swing my cane behind me and take off running. As I looked back, instead of seeing the boys in blue, I saw my blonde-haired friend holding the note I left for her. Sara was furious. I could tell that she was ready to bite my head off. I began to think about taking off anyway. I could let the cops catch up to me and take my chances with a murder rap. That might be easier than facing Sara's wrath. In the end, however, I took the tougher option and decided to stick around an angry Sara.

"Jamie, I can't believe the nerve of you!" Sara growled. I

thought I saw fire shooting from her mouth and steam shooting out her ears, but it could have been my imagination.

Instead of stopping, I grabbed her arm and pulled her along in the opposite direction.

"Keep moving, don't turn around. Just keep walking." I knew she'd be angry, but we couldn't be seen anywhere near the hotel. I didn't want to become a suspect in a murder I didn't commit. This had to be a set up. I didn't want to end up taking the fall if I couldn't set things straight. Everything was about to get worse before we even had time for breakfast.

"Jamie, what are we doing?" She blurted out. "Did you meet with Dr. Wheeling without me? Why didn't you wait for me?"

"He's dead," I said as a matter of fact, not holding anything back. She began to shake her head in child-like denial. I had to be blunt. If we were going to get out of this alive, I had to be direct. Someone was knocking off everyone who got too close to whatever this was. There was a possibility we would be safer in a jail cell than running around on the streets searching for answers. But we already knew too much to turn back now.

"We have to go to the police," she hissed, "We can't do this alone anymore." She was frantic and I thought she might scream.

"Going to the police won't work. It's already too late for that."

I tried to stay calm. I had to take control of the situation. If Sara freaked out there was no telling the trouble we would be in. "If we go to the police now, they'll lock my butt in jail for murder. I'm the one who found Victor's body in his hotel room.

A maid walked in and saw me standing over him. She's a witness to what she thinks was me murdering Victor. Sara, please. It's my word against hers."

"The police are smarter than that Jamie. They won't simply lock you up like that," she said, obviously trying to convince herself.

I pulled Sara along as I finished telling her about my morning. She started to tremble with fear. I moved my hand to hers, grabbing it tightly. She held on without the hint of letting go. She was frightened, and all of a sudden that I terrified me. I needed to control my emotions before I lost my nerves. Sara's fear was becoming contagious.

I was going to give it ten minutes before the cops put out a call and started their search for someone fitting my description. We couldn't go back to my apartment. That would be the first place they'd check. Sara's place was out of the question, too. The cops would be all over the campus soon. We had to get out of Oakland, but I didn't know where to go. We needed to get out of town and avoid the police.

As I thought about the problem, Sara motioned to the trolley car pulling up next to us. She was way ahead of me. The trolley would take us down Fifth, into a neighborhood called the Hill District, centered on the intersection of Crawford Avenue and Willie Street. I let Sara decide where we should go, trusting her decisions. I had to trust her judgment if I wanted her to trust mine. She jumped up onto the trolley and I followed right behind.

The police never spend much time in the Hill District. I wish

I could say it was because it was such a safe, quiet neighborhood, but the truth was that the residents of the Hill were mostly Negros, and a large portion of the police were bigots. Overall, the Pittsburgh police were good at their jobs, but minority sensitivity was not one of their strong points. They would take longer to respond to calls in the Hill area because of their prejudice. I couldn't say that the rest of the city agreed with the racist nature of the police, but I rarely saw whites take their side against them.

The nightclubs on the Hill played mainly jazz, while blues was beginning to become popular. Sara liked listening to singers like Ella Fitzgerald and Nina Simone. I liked jazz too, but what really knocked my socks off was rock and roll. Guys like Jerry Lee Lewis and Big Joe Turner could hold my attention for hours. I would always have a soft spot for Frank, Dean, and my boy Sammy, but you couldn't move to them like you could to Lewis's "Great Balls of Fire." That cat could sing.

I wasn't interested in country music, but Johnny Cash could make the worst country yokel sound cool. For the most part, the only musicians who would set foot in the Hill District were the colored ones, but every once in a while, white musicians would make an appearance, the hipper guys who didn't care about color of skin. The bars and clubs weren't open this early, but we could still hide out in a neighborhood diner.

I was glad Sara hadn't come with me this morning. Having her see Victor's corpse would not have been a good thing. Knowing that Victor was dead was enough. She didn't need to see the body. A lifeless body is guaranteed to remind you of your own mortality and the picture stays with you. It's something you never forget.

We rode the trolley all the way up Centre Avenue into the Hill, getting off at the first open diner we saw. I didn't know about Sara, but I was starving. My stomach was growling loudly and thoughts were becoming fuzzy. I felt a cold sweat start. Just the thought of going without food any longer was causing a wave of nausea. I needed to eat badly or I was going to collapse.

For me, the hardest part of the military had been the long stretches between meals. Of course, hungry as I was now, those times in the military came back to mind in full force. Try fighting for your life on an empty stomach was tougher than you could ever imagine. Oh, you'd do it, but the hunger alone was enough to make you want to surrender simply for a bowl of cooked rice.

When the Chinese joined the war, it was hell on our appetites. Even when we knew we had to eat, it was hard to do so after what we had gone through. The loss of a soldier's appetite was common. Add the long winter on top of everything and you practically had to be forced fed by your commanding officer.

As a boy fasting on Yom Kippur, I would struggle to get through the whole day without food or water. I could make it at least until lunch every year, but the rest of the day would require help from my parents to distract me from wanting to eat. I didn't have my father or mother to help me through it any longer. I think the last time I cared to fast was when they were still alive. I didn't have the motivation to celebrate the holidays since their deaths.

We walked into a diner named the Crawford Street Café, which had tables and chairs already setup along the sidewalk. We chose to eat inside just in case a cruiser would past. Sitting out in the open would defeat the whole goal of hiding. We had to be careful, and didn't want to draw too much attention to ourselves.

Sara and I both ordered a cup of coffee and the day's special. The special consisted of eggs any way we wanted them, toast with jam, two links of sausage, and a heaping portion of grits. I rarely ordered grits in Pittsburgh, but in a place like the Crawford Street Cafe, they were fair game.

Our plates came and I began to shovel food into my mouth. I was too hungry to talk, and Sara seemed to be deep in thought. I wondered how she was handling everything. My thoughts turned to her well being. Was she tormenting herself? Would she have nightmares the rest of her life? Then a selfish question popped into my head. Could I do anything to help?

It was only after I cleared my plate that I realized Sara had only been pushing her food around, playing with it, unable to eat. I was too preoccupied with my own needs to even notice that she wasn't actually eating. Sara was gripping her fork tightly. Her hands were shaking, while she moved her scrambled eggs around her plate.

I gently set my hands over hers, steadying them a bit. I only hoped her mind would follow. Sara looked up, her eyes revealing the pain she felt. She wasn't doing well. I wanted to tell her that everything was going to be all right, but I couldn't manage to say the words and I wasn't so sure that would be the case anyway. I didn't know how of all this would turn out, not any more than she did. I didn't know what scared me more, the thought of being killed or the possibility of going to jail for the rest of my life.

Sara pulled her hands away and began to cry. She held her hands over her face, trying to hide herself from the world.

The waitress came over and poured more coffee into our cups. She looked down at Sara with her dark sympathetic eyes. The waitress appeared to be in her late sixties and had a caring, dark face. Her expression showed only exhaustion, which probably had been the expression she'd worn on a regular basis for the past ten years. Her shoulders and back muscles showed through her thin white blouse and it was obvious that she was not a stranger to hard work.

The waitress smiled. "Child, nothing is that bad that this food here can't heal."

Sara made an attempt at a smile. "Thank you," she said. "I'll try the food. It really does look good."

"Is this fellow giving you a hard time baby?" the waitress inquired. "You tell me the truth and if he's givin' you a hard time, I'll make sure he never talks to you again."

Sara's face suddenly brightened and her smile was genuine. "No, it's nothing like that. He's great." Her eyes were still wet, but her smile grew by the second. "Thank you though."

The waitress nodded her approval at Sara's transformation. "You want me to heat those eggs for you?" she asked.

Sara took a big fork full of eggs and shoved them in her mouth. "They're still good like this," she said with a mouth full of food.

The waitress showed her approval once again. "You call over if you need anything else sugar." The waitress walked away happy carrying the pot of coffee.

Sara started to let out a small giggle in between bites. That got me laughing and just like that the tension lifted. A cloud of unease still remained, but we were able to push it back for the moment.

Sara continued eating the cold food on her plate, getting bigger bites into her mouth. The body required a high amount of energy to produce the emotion of sadness, but sadness would cause a loss of appetite in most people. Watching Sara eat, I understood that her sadness had lifted, maybe only a moment, but at least long enough to allow her to eat. Sara's hunger had actually returned with a vengeance and she cleared her plate.

"I didn't realize how hungry I was," she said in between each mouth full. The toast was the first to disappear off her plate, followed by the eggs.

When she was finished eating, Sara put her fork down and pushed her plate to the middle of the table. "Let's go through everything from this morning again," Sara said to my surprise.

"Are you sure you are up to that." I didn't want her to shut down again from fear.

"I think I'm good now," Sara said smiling for my benefit.

I thought it over and decided that it would be good for the both of us if I went through the details of the morning once more in case I missed something. Sara had wanted to know everything, even the goriest details surrounding what I found. I tried not to leave anything out, but held back when I recounted his facial expression. Some things I didn't even want to recall.

Sara drank her coffee as she replayed the details in her head.

"Are you sure Victor didn't hide anything in the room?" she asked, making sure I told her everything.

I thought about it. "I didn't have much time, but I think I got a good look around."

Sara wasn't satisfied with my answer. "There is still a chance that Victor left something for us. You said it yourself that his briefcase was empty. Maybe he was able to hide something before whoever it was killed him."

That seemed plausible. "What do you suggest we do? Go back to the hotel and search through the room with the police waiting for us?"

"Waiting for you, maybe," Sara corrected me. "They didn't see me anywhere near there. I could walk right up to the hotel room and no one would be the wiser."

"It's too dangerous," I expressed my concern. "What if they catch you?"

"They are probably only looking for you anyway!" She almost screamed. The waitress looked over, but lost interest when Sara began to smile. She continued and lowered her voice, "Jamie, we don't have any other option. We are going to have to split up. While I'm at the hotel, you go back to Alex's house and try to find his notes. Alex and Victor were going to exchange information, so Alex must have had something substantial prepared. He wouldn't leave anything like that on campus for just anyone to find." She paused, and then added, "You know I'm right."

Even if I thought she was right, I didn't have to like the idea of her going to the hotel, especially alone. I didn't like the idea of putting Sara at risk, at the center of this crazy scheme. There was a chance the killer would be waiting for one of us to do something stupid. Unfortunately, we still needed to know what got Alex and Victor killed. Sara was going back to the Hotel Schenley, while I was supposed to go back to Alex's house. There would be cops in both places and I bet they would be looking for me.

I found a Post-Gazette on the table next to us and started to flip through it. I needed a distraction, something to get us off the subject for a bit. At first I pretended to read the paper, but then I noticed a review of a movie I had wanted to see before this whole mess started. It was playing at the New Ganada theater.

"Fine, you want to split up? Then I'll meet you at the New Ganada at 3:15."

Sara's face eyebrows arched as she shot back, "How can you even think about watching a movie right now?"

I knew the timing was wrong to catch a flick, but I also knew the movie would calm my nerves. At the same time, it occurred to me that if we ran into any problems, the dark theater could provide us with a safe house. What better place to hide than in a dark movie room where no one spoke?

"We can blend in at the movies. It would make a great hiding place."

"Unless someone sees us go in," Sara snapped. "What if we're followed?"

"If you have a better idea, let's hear it," I demanded. I didn't want to sound mean, but I was feeling a bit defensive.

Sara paused, opened her mouth to provide another suggestion, but closed her mouth instead. Her squinted eyes, declaring defeat by whispering "Fine."

We caught the first rail car heading back to Oakland along Forbes Avenue. After Sara got off at Bigelow, I sat back and wondered how I was going to get into Alex's house if it was being watched. There was a chance the cops closed Alex's case because of the mess they found at his house, which indicated there was probably more to Alex's death than a suicide. Maybe they made a connection between Victor and Alex. They may have found out that they were knew each other and were planning to meet. I had no way of knowing. Would I be able to sneak in? Maybe I could creep in like the comic book character Dark Night or even appear out of thin air like the Spectre. That would really be something.

Batman didn't have anything on the Spirit of Vengeance. The Spectre was a dead cop brought back to life to seek revenge on the evil of the world. He wore a green cloak, covering his bare grey skin. I read *The Spectre* religiously before I left for Korea. While my childhood friends went for the lighter books, I was content with the more serious and darker ones.

During the war, all the fellows carried their rifle, rations, and a couple of comic books in their packs. They read them in '42 when we ran into Germany, and again in '51 on the way to the Orient. The cape comics pulled a lot of us up by our bootstraps and gave us the strength to march on. The cover of *Superman* #24 alone almost single handedly provided us with the fortitude to win the war back in '43.

By the time I got to Korea, horror comics were already dominating the comic book racks, but we would still get shipped comics like *Blackhawk* and *Action Comics* on a regular basis. War and western comics were sent to us by the thousands, but the government was limiting the number of horror books coming though. I couldn't blame them for the censorship. It was all about morale. We were out there fighting for our lives every day. I guess they thought only books with positive messages were needed at a time like that.

The brass shipped us the cornier and silly, *World's Finest*, where Superman and Batman teamed up to fight crime. They were two of the oldest superheroes, but they still managed to entertain grown men overseas.

I cautiously looked around when I arrived at Alex's house, but didn't see the police anywhere. Clearly the cops hadn't made the connection between Alex's death and Victor's, which was lucky for me. I'd have some time before they got around to connecting me to both of them and their murders. Just to be on the safe side, however, I went around back to enter the house through the basement, where I was less likely to be seen.

In the back of the house I found the double red storm doors on a slight incline from the ground. Alex had always kept them unlocked and I opened them with little effort. I went down a small flight of concrete stairs where a white metal door to the basement stood. I unlocked the door easily enough with my spare key.

I knew the house well, having moved in with Alex after my parents passed away. Everything I owned was moved over quickly after they died. Most of those things were now sitting down in the basement collecting dust. The basement was darker than any other room in the house. A single light bulb hung from the center of the room, providing just enough light to the narrow pathway in between boxes and piles of papers.

The floor was a red brick instead of the cement that was used these days in laying foundations. Over the years, some bricks had sunk or pushed up sometimes making the journey hazardous. It was an unfinished basement, covered in old newspapers, and had an open ceiling showing the floorboards above. Copper pipes and electrical wiring were visible throughout the whole room, making it much easier for repairs. A toilet in the middle of the stacks seemed out of place.

I went over to the brown cluster of stacked boxes in the corner. There was a cool dampness throughout the room, which gave my hands a clammy feel. A light mildew fragrance hung in the air, filling my nostrils. The cardboard boxes contained mostly clothes that I had grown out of years ago. I wasn't surprised that Alex hadn't thrown anything out. I swiftly checked the boxes. He had even kept the college papers I'd written, saving each one no matter the grade. Old comic books were left untouched in another box. I always had the feeling that Alex was sentimental, but until now I hadn't known to what extent. Sitting here was my entire life. Nothing had been thrown out.

I moved on to the opposite end of the long room. In the shadows, where the light bulb could not completely reach, I could make out the maze of newspapers Alex had saved to create his vast archive.

I could have stayed down in the basement for days, reminiscing about the forgotten past, but I had more important things to do. Looking through my own particular past was not one of them. I walked up the wooden staircase to the kitchen, and then down the hall in the direction of the den. The house was still in total disarray, littered with battered furniture and broken possessions. Did I think a cleaning crew would have gone though the house, fixing lamps, and setting records on the shelves? I hadn't known what to expect as I walked down the hall passing the main bathroom, pushing open the door to Alex's private study.

Alex could have hidden a message in one of the books around the room, hiding it from curious eyes. I began to read the titles of the book along the wall. Full sections of books on ancient civilizations like Rome, Mayan, and Mesopotamia filled the shelves. Others were strewn around the room, thrown around by the person or people who ransacked the place.

I picked up a few books and placed them back on the bookshelves. Using my cane, I limped over to the grand desk in the middle of the room. The desk was a heavy walnut, stained a light brown. Alex had bought the piece at an auction in Boston, twenty-five years ago, a month before I was born. Before Alex gave the winning bid, the desk had been owned by Andrew Carnegie and kept in his New York penthouse. Before Carnegie had owned it, the desk was said to have been owned by Robert Morris, a founding father who had signed the Declaration of Independence. It was never proven that Morris had owned the desk, so there were only three competing bid that day. I sat behind the desk and opened several drawers, but the majority of their contents were already scattered around the floor.

I left the desk for later and went back to the books. United States history had its own section with subjects ranging from the War of Independence through the constitution, and even included several books on World War II. I ran my finger across the book spines, while I skimmed the titles.

Going to the next bookcase, I stopped in my tracks. An odd French book caught my eye. It was on a shelf where only American ones should be. Alex was meticulous about categorizing his books. On the second shelf from the floor I found, *Last Time I Saw Paris* by Elliot Paul. It was a small blue hardback, and I would have missed it if it were not for the color and the fact that it was out of place. Then I made the strange connection with the Eiffel Tower postcard I had found earlier.

I bent over and tried to slide the book out, but it wouldn't move. I pulled harder, gripping the entire spine, but it still wouldn't budge. I bent closer to a better look, bracing myself close to the floor. Deep in the back of the case, a small metal anchor was secured and hinged to the back of Paul's "benign" novel about France. I pulled the surrounding books off the shelf to gain access.

Instead of pulling it, I pushed the book to the right, flipping it up on a hinge. I heard a click when the bottom of the book touched to top of the shelf. A panel shifted at the back of the case, exposing a small rectangular hole built into the wall. Alex had installed a secret hiding compartment behind his bookcase.

This was it. The search was over. I must have found whatever it is Alex wanted me to discover. I reached in, grabbed a small rectangular object and pulled it out. I held it up to examine it. The object was a brown leather-bound book wrapped with a band to keep it closed. I removed the band, opened to book to discover that it was Alex's journal. A creak in the floorboards made me look up as the butt of a gun came crashing down toward my head. I was able to throw my cane up just in time, stopping a direct impact. The block knocked the gun out of my attacker's hand, throwing it into a pile of books. I pushed my attacker's arm back and got a glimpse of him, a man in a dark suit with a look of surprise on his face.

He took a running start and collided into me with enough force to project my body into the corner of the room. The book slipped out of my hand and fell in front of the man's feet. The intruder picked it and turned to leave.

Before he could take another step, I swung my cane, and held on tight. I caught the base of his knee with the cane's solid brass handle. The impact was hard enough to send the stick splintering one way and the handle in the opposite direction. The man staggered backwards, giving a loud yell, while he clutched his leg in pain.

I regained my balance and was finally able to clearly see the man's face. It was the lab technician from Salk's laboratory, Keith. He was wearing a dark blue suit instead of the white coat I saw him in before.

He scanned the room searching for his gun, but didn't see where it landed. That gave me the time I needed to sweep my good leg behind him, knocking his footing out from under him. I didn't even give Keith the chance to regain his senses. I grabbed Keith's gun from among the books and swung the butt around, smashing it against the man's head.

I grabbed the book from Keith's limp grasp and took off,

flying down the hall. I fumbled down the stairs, almost falling twice, and out made it to the front door. I checked behind me, but he wasn't following, and after hitting him as hard as I did, I doubted he would be after me for some time. That would give me the time I needed to get away before he could find me.

Chapter 6

My chest was clenching and it began to burn after running only several blocks. The pain was enough to slow me down. My breathing was heavy and my heart was racing. If that wasn't enough my stomach began to cramp, making me grab my side in frustration and pain. I had to catch my breath or I would end up throwing up again. I knew I wasn't in good shape, but this was ridiculous. Two years ago, I was able to run miles on end with a fifty-pound pack strapped to my back.

As I caught my breath, my heart rate started to slow, but my stomach continued to spasm as a result of my exertion. I took a moment to look around, realizing I was in the middle of Walnut Street, the neighborhood's shopping district. Middle class consumers were walked the streets around me looking in the windows of clothing stores and markets, searching for products to buy and consume.

No matter what it was you were looking for, you could find it on Walnut. There were grocery stores, hardware stores, bakeries, and where I stood, an electronic store. New televisions were positioned in the window allowing passersby to sample the afternoon's entertainment. Every day, "Love Story" and "The Jack Paar Show" would entertain hundreds of thousands of stay-at-home wives between twelve and one. Even after close to fifteen years, midday television programming was something that captured people's attention.

I had to hurry to the New Granada Theater to meet Sara. I was only four miles away, but without my own car, it might as well been a hundred. The sky began to get overcast. The air was still, no wind at all. If it rained, it wouldn't be for hours.

I walked down to Negley Avenue and hopped on the first trolley car heading toward the Hill District. I made my way to the back of the car and threw myself onto one of the cushioned benches. Shifting my weight around, I was finally able to make myself comfortable. I made sure to hide my face as we rode through the campus, before the car turned north away from Oakland. All it would take was for one cop to think he saw me on the trolley. Our trolley system had two central stops on the majority of its lines, Oakland and Downtown. It would cause a problem if I were spotted too close to an open investigation.

I looked down at the brown leather cover of the small 6 x 8 brown book. What was so special about the book? It had white lines forming along its spine from extensive use. The leather was creased and wrinkled from the abuse Alex must have inflicted during its use. I flipped through the book and found clippings of daily newspaper articles and Alex's handwriting next to each one. I scanned the titles of some of the clippings. A report on the total yearly chemical sales from 1954 was towards the middle. Another claimed *Vaccine for Polio successful*, and others painted Jonas Salk as a national hero. Alex's script filled the pages around the news clippings, under and above pictures, and carried on for pages at a time.

I flipped through pages until I reached a series of articles that caught my eye. The name Cutter appeared in each headline. I quickly read the first couple of sentences of each. They were all part of the same theme, all from different papers. Cutter was using its own manufactured polio vaccine to inoculate their employees. Four different papers had told the same story with only minor difference in details. One even was accompanied by a small black and grey photo of a happy line worker receiving the shot.

I continued to shuffle through the pages until a folded piece of paper fell from the back of the journal to the floor of the rail car. I reached to pick it up, realizing that it was actually several 8 x 10 pieces of paper, folded over three times, like a mailed letter. It was a business letter from a Sylvia Moore addressed to Alex at his home, not at his work address. I skimmed the letter quickly at first, but then slowed down when I saw Cutter's name once more. Moore appeared to have worked at Cutter Laboratories under Walter Ward, the chief laboratory director, who was solely in charge of the polio vaccine's production.

In the letter, Moore suggested that the vaccine Cutter had

used to vaccinate its own employees and family members was not made at Cutter Laboratories as the newspapers had reported. In fact, according to Moore, the vaccine that was used was actually made by another pharmaceutical company, Parke-Davis, the same company Victor had worked at until his untimely demise.

Alex documented in detail and the facts set forth in her letter. The next page was a second letter from Moore. Judging from her opening statement, it was a response to skepticism Alex had expressed concerning Moore's first letter. Proof of the validity of her claim that Parke-Davis was the maker of the vaccine used at Cutter was provided in the form of an invoice for the purchase of ten cases of the Poliomyelitis vaccine. I checked the invoice's date and then looked back at the four articles I had just read. The date on the invoice was one day before all four news articles ran in their respected papers.

The Parke-David invoice showed a total price for the vaccines of $120,000 and was signed for by Ted Cutter, the brother of CEO Robert Cutter, and the head of Cutter Laboratories' research department. I read Alex's own written entry after the Parke-Davis invoice. It said:

There can only be one reason why the Cutter brothers would buy a competitor's vaccine -- to replicate it for their production line. I imagine that it wouldn't be so difficult to reverse engineer, thus recreating the vaccine and producing it in their own factory. The question is why would they do that? They were supposed to be producing it on their own. I believe the Cutter brothers must have been uncertain about their own product. Rather than infect their workers, they switched the vaccine with another company's, this avoiding the risk.

I slipped the letters back into the book, wrapping the bands around securely so the letters and clippings wouldn't fall out. I suspected Ward, Cutter's chief laboratory director, would have understood all of this too. He would have been aware that Cutter's version of the vaccine was infected with live polio virus, but did not bother to share that information with the Health Department.

If Cutter sold an infected vaccine with live virus in it, certainly the people in power over there would have known it. Instead they kept quiet to avoid losing the three million dollar contract it had with the government from production of the vaccine. This contract guaranteed Cutter a hefty sum. It was too valuable to simply drop out. Even the large drug companies would have been tempted. At was all about profits. I had a feeling that the other companies would have been tempted as well, especially if they were having problems with creating the vaccine. Alex was planning to expose them all and had enough evidence in his journal to do it.

Who else was involved? I wondered. Parke-Davis knew it was selling its own vaccine to Cutter, and I had the feeling the other three companies would have shared some communication. But would they have gone to such extremes to cover their own mess? If so, the entire vaccine production line was keeping hush. Each of the five companies likely feared an investigation and responsible.

So how did Keith, the lab tech attacker fit in to all of this?

Was it possible that he was trying to protect Cutter or one of the other companies? He would want the journal and any other evidence we had. Alex and Victor were dead. Who else would he kill if he or she got in his way?

Hopefully, Sara was able to find something at the hotel. There had to be clues left behind by the murderer or by Victor, things I may have overlooked in my haste. Regular people would leave a number of clues behind. The majority of people were sloppy when they were involved in anything they wanted to keep secret. If there weren't any clues at the crime scene that would mean that we were dealing with a trained professional who might kill anyone who got close. I didn't even want to think about a professional hit man at the moment. It was scary enough knowing we had two murders to contend with, but throwing a professional into the mix would raise the body count exponentially.

I got off the trolley in front of the Sparkle Super Market on Centre Avenue. I went inside, bought myself a pop and slapped a nickel on the counter. Using the bottle opener bolted to the side of the cooler, I opened the pop and took a long swig. The cold liquid felt refreshing going down my throat. The bubbles had just enough kick to get me going once again. After draining the whole bottle, I placed it in the rack for the empties. I wanted another, but decided to head straight for the theater.

A dark-skinned colored man, in his early thirties, was straightening bottles behind the sales counter. His hair was cropped low to his scalp and a black mustache hung neatly over his upper lip. He wore a white apron over a pressed blue shirt and beige slacks.

"Excuse me, buddy, you got any canes?"

The man didn't turn away from the work he was doing. "I'm sorry?" the clerk asked unsure what I meant.

"A cane, a stick you walk with?" I mimicked an old man, hunching my back forward, pretending I had a cane in my hand helping me walk. "You know, it keeps you from falling down." How ironic was it that I was pretending to be an old crippled man when the old man before me was perfectly fit? The man stopped stocking his bottles and took a glance in my direction.

"We don't carry anything like that here." He made a move to turn back to his chore, but stopped and continued, "Try the drug store across the street." Satisfied with his answer, he turned away and continued with his stocking responsibilities. I was already running late, so I decided to wait until later to pick up a cane.

The theater's marquee was positioned so anyone walking on either side of the street would be able to see it. In big red block letters, "Rebel Without a Cause" was spelled out along a white background. It was the only picture showing today and no one was rushing to get in.

I staggered in and a cool gust of chilled air engulfed my whole body. I hadn't realized how hot it was outside until I experienced this fifteen degree drop in temperature. The sweat I accumulated throughout my morning began to dry. I felt cold and wet, an uncomfortable sticky clamminess.

I bought a ticket from a young fresh-faced colored girl at the ticket booth. She ripped it down the middle and handed me the stub. I thanked her and walked toward the concession stand. Even though I wasn't very hungry, I bought a small bag of popcorn and another pop. This time I'd wait until I was seated before consuming the food and drink. I always felt obligated to buy popcorn at the concessions before a film. There were certain foods that had to be eaten with certain activities. The first is apple pie at a diner. The second is cotton candy at a carnival. And the third, of course, is popcorn at the movies. I blamed the dancing box of popcorn and soft drink before the previews. I was a sucker for clever advertising.

I continued into the theater where *Rebel without a Cause* would be playing. I glanced around but didn't see Sara or anyone else for that matter. She was even later than I was. What if something had happened to her? There wasn't a way for her to contact me if she needed my help. I checked my watch. I still had five minutes before the movie would begin.

I took a seat near the back, letting my mind wonder without wanting it to. I was beginning to get nervous. I started to grab handfuls of popcorn, stuffing my face. I had to slow down, calm myself before I choked on a lone unpopped kernel of buttery goodness. I tried to focus on the red velvet drapes covering the screen, the golden electric lamps set throughout the giant room, anything to distract myself. In the middle of the ceiling, a crystal chandelier hung over the audience seating.

When the New Granada was built in 1927, the second floor was used as a music hall for the nation's most famous jazz musicians. Performers like Ella Fitzgerald, Count Basie, Cab Calloway, and Duke Ellington stopped at the New Granada on their way to bigger venues in cities like Chicago or New York. The first floor of the building had been built as a movie theater designed with large, red-velvet, plush seats and matching giant drapes across the screen that could open and close with the pull of a cord.

Then in 1940, the building was burned down in an "accidental" fire. The police could never prove what happened, and some suggested a lack of investigation. When the police didn't want to do their jobs, it was hard to change their minds. The theater was sold and rebuilt soon after, but this time without the second-floor ballroom. If musicians came into town, they would set up in front of the silk screen, and constantly complain when the acoustics did nothing for their playing.

Without realizing it, I had eaten half the bag of popcorn and drank the majority of my pop. I was starting to feel ill, worrying where Sara could be. I was imagining the worst possible scenarios of what could have happen to such a pretty young woman, when Sara finally stomped in, each step indicating her fury.

She passed right by me enveloped in her anger. When she didn't see me at anywhere near the front of the theater she became nervous. She took a moment to study her surroundings and finally turned caught sight of me. She hadn't expected me to be behind her. She came over, plopping herself down in the seat next to me. She grabbed the bag of popcorn from my hands and gobbled down the rest with the speed of a near-death, starved alley cat. She also finished off the rest of the pop with one long slurp, even pulling the ice through the straw.

"You want more?" I joked. "I can see if the soda jerk can fill a garbage bag for you next time."

Sara gave me a glare that would frighten just about anyone,

but then she smiled. "Sure, if you wouldn't mind," she said handing me the empties.

I wasn't expecting her to actually want anything else, but I went back to the concession stand and loaded up on soda and popcorn. When I came back, she grabbed the food from my clutches and proceeded to fill her entire mouth with popcorn before starting to chew. After seven handfuls and several long pulls from the straw, she sat back and let out a long sigh.

"You're not going to believe what I just had to go through," she said, pushing several pieces of popcorn off her blouse. "There was absolutely nothing there. No cops, no crime scene, no body. Whoever cleaned up did it in a hurry. Where's your cane?"

I showed her the journal and explained about my day. I handed her the brown leather book, which she took to examine, flipping through the pages and skimming randomly.

"Would they really send someone to kill for this?" she asked while turning the pages. "Do you really think this little book could destroy whole companies?"

I furrowed my forehead as I thought about the questions. If millions of dollars worth of medicine were infected with live polio virus, someone might go to that sort of trouble. There were millions of dollars at stake, the companies' reputation and the careers of thousands of people to think about. A whole industry could collapse if the media got wind of anything like this, assuming it was all true. I knew there would be a great need to protect certain interests, but would they resort to murder?

I hesitated about saying anything that would scare Sara, but finally I answered. "If this book could really stop the production of the vaccine? Then yes, I think someone would."

The lights started to dim and the projector turned on with a low hum, running 35mm film off spools in front of its ultra-powered lamp. An image of dancing candy and cups of soda filled the screen. Even after weeks without seeing the cartoon, I could still clearly remember the dancing products. As the credits began to appear, James Dean made his appearance on the screen, playing with a toy monkey clapping symbols.

Sara asked, "Are we really going to sit through this whole movie?" She was nervous.

"We're just hiding out until we can figure out our next move." It wasn't a complete lie, but the hell with it. I really wanted to see the film. "Tell me what else happened at the hotel?" I asked, trying to change the subject.

"Nothing much," She began. "I checked out Victor's room like you wanted me to, but there wasn't anything left. The cops had already shut down the crime scene, clearing out any evidence. The hotel room looked as if nothing ever happened there. Even the tub had been cleaned."

"I wonder why they cleaned the room so fast," I pondered. It wasn't like the cops were known to be slow, but even one day was fast to dismantle the scene of a crime. Especially, on a homicide, the cops would tape off the scene to preserve any evidence and return to investigate further to make sure they hadn't missed anything.

"You're tearing me apart!" Dean yelled. He couldn't deal with his parents and police going back and forth. He was confused, scared of growing up, and screaming for help.

I never had problems with my parents like Dean's character did. Mine were loving, caring, and always supportive people. It was sad, but I'd trade his character's rebellious life just to be with my parents again. I would give anything to hear my mother's voice. I would drink up every demand and overprotective motherly moment, indulging in each blessed second of it.

Sara turned her attention to the movie. She seemed to relax and actually begin to enjoy it, turning her attention away from the journal in her hands. Leaning back we watched the end of the movie, killing off the remainder of the popcorn. She drank down the rest of the pop, making the liquid bubble in the cup.

After an hour and a half, Dean held his dead friend Plato, cradling him in his arms. Their rebellion had caused his friend his life. Dean's character seemed to be absorbing the fact that he was really only a child, not ready to be an adult. He had been fighting against established rules, but now he was realizing that he could never fully win.

Sara turned to me, "What now?" she asked as a tear ran down her cheek.

Moments later the credits began to roll and the lights came back on. I stood up, raising my arms to stretch, and surveyed the room. Nobody was waiting to surprise us in the theater, which I took as a good sign. After all, we had been the only ones in the audience.

It was early evening when we walked out of the New Granada. Dusk set the mood perfectly after a movie as dramatic as that. A melodramatic movie was always well accompanied by a melodramatic night. I still hadn't responded to Sara's question because I truly didn't know what we were going to do. I was completely out of ideas. We couldn't go to the cops. That much was clear. They would be looking for me as a suspect in Victor's murder, maybe even Alex's now. I could try to plead with them, give them the journal, but would that be enough?

My leg had time to rest while we were in the theater, but now the dull pain returned as we walked. It reminded me of the cane I broke before. I looked around, finding the Home Drug Company a block down the street. Sara followed me as I limped into the local drugstore.

I paid the pharmacist three dollars for a new cane, leaning on it as we walked out of the store. I immediately redistribute my weight, leaning on the cane and relieving some of the pressure on my hip. The pain started to fade into a dull annoyance. Sara must have felt my relief. She seemed to become more relaxed herself. As the tension faded from my hip, my mind began to clear.

"We could go to Salk and ask him for help." Sara suggested.

"What if he already knows about the problems?" I didn't want to believe that Jonas Salk would secretly put that many people's lives in danger, but I was having my doubts about many of my preconceptions. I had to remind myself that Salk was a man, the same as any other, and we still needed to be cautious about talking to him.

"We have to do something, Jamie. How many kids do you think have died already?" It was horrible to think about. Children would catch the polio disease from the vaccine their parents thought would protect them from it. They went to the doctor with a trusting innocence. Their mothers told them the vaccine would protect them so that they wouldn't get sick. Their mothers trusted the vaccine, so why shouldn't they? Who else would have to suffer if we didn't do something quickly? We might be the only ones left who could do anything — the only ones with the information and willingness to make a difference.

"What would happen if Salk didn't believe us? We might come off as insane if we go at this alone. We don't have any credibility at the moment."

"Fitzgerald?" Sara then suggested.

I knew the name well. Fitzgerald was the president of the school, a highly respected leader, but one who was very approachable. He would be the one man who would have the patience and be open-minded enough to look at the evidence without bias and then try to help us. If he believed us, the police would think twice before placing me on their most wanted list. Fitzgerald would be able to help prove my innocence, while getting to the Health Department to stop the production of the vaccine before the pharmaceuticals hurt any more children. Sara started to play with her hair, twirling it around her fingers, waiting for my reply. It was a nervous habit, one she used when waiting for a test grade. I knew from experience to give her an answer before she made a total mess out of her hair.

"That's what we'll do then. We'll go right to the top. We'd go see Chancellor Fitzgerald."

Last year, Chancellor Fitzgerald announced that he was going to retire from the University of Pittsburgh. A few months later, the truth came out that he was being let go, forced into an early retirement. The school's board of trustees forced Fitzgerald out before his time had come. After ten years of hard work, he was forced to leave because the trustees didn't want him to lead the growing campus's development. The board as it turned out did not agree with the direction the school had gone in. Under his tutelage, the campus had doubled in size. The Chancellor excelled at fundraising for the now thriving college. Word spread. People began to gossip and word spread. Students gathered to protest the Chancellor's dismissal, but decent from it was too little too late. Fitzgerald had no other option but to leave. At the end of this year, Chancellor Fitzgerald would step down and be replaced by another able body -- another man who would do the bidding of the board for perhaps another ten years. Four years ago, the Chancellor's name was placed on the school's field house on the upper campus. Now the board members decided he was past his prime, wanting nothing to do with him. I assumed having your name live on in history was enough, but I heard he was parting with a large severance package that would make the wealthiest of men jealous.

I knew he would help us on principle, upset or not about the board's decision. He wouldn't turn away a student in need. We had respected the man for a reason and now we needed his help. He would understand our situation and the need for intervention.

Alex had trusted Fitzgerald throughout his tenure and thought the man was being treated unfairly. In class, like he did with history, he had rooted for the underdog. Alex showed his support for Fitzgerald by using him as an example in lectures of someone succeeding in life without the support of those around him. Alex would pair Fitzgerald's name with the great leaders of our world, leaders who were denied their rewards in life, suppressed when their name became too great.

Sara and I rode a trolley up Fifth Avenue toward the Chancellor's office. Sara had been quiet since we boarded the rail car near the pharmacy. She stared out the window, watching nothing, deep in thought.

"What's on your mind?" I asked. "You seem preoccupied." Sara continued to watch the scenery outside the car, but began to move her lips, thinking out loud. Her words came out as a whisper, intended only for herself.

"If a hospital orders the vaccine, who would the hospital get it from, the producer or a separate distributor?" Sara asked, turning her attention back to me.

I didn't know what Sara was talking about. Why did she care how a hospital would get the vaccine? Didn't we have hundreds of thousands of products being shipped around the country on a daily basis? Why would it matter who shipped it where? I threw out the answer that I thought would be right.

"I guess a distributor. The drug company would send the finished product to maybe a hundred central locations and then ship the drug out regionally." Other products were sent like that, why would pharmaceuticals be any different?

Sara turned back to the view outside. We were stopped at an intersection's red light. My eyes wondered to the view around us. A bridge leading to the South Side of town was directly in front of us. Outside the window I saw the Monongahela River, which intersected with the Allegheny and Ohio Rivers at the Point downtown. I didn't get what Sara was driving at. Then she pointed to a building on the right side of the street.

It was finally apparent what it was Sara had been looking at and why she had asked the question about distribution. I saw the giant billboard sign for Burrell Scientific. I had completely forgotten about the laboratory supply company only a mile away from the campus. I hurried to grab the yellow wire across the top of the windows, but realized that someone else had already pulled it. Sara must have already pulled it. Before I knew it, we were jumping off the car across the street from Burrell's front door. Burrell Scientific supplied the University of Pittsburgh with medical and laboratory supplies. Most of the supplies were beakers and test tubes, but they also carried the majority of the chemicals and medicines the school used. Burrell was the regional distribution center, a centralized location from which companies across the world shipped their products.

Looking through the windows of the white brick building, we realized right away that Burrell Scientific was already closed for the night. The lights were off and we couldn't see much beyond the front ten feet. I banged on the front door hoping the night security guard would hear us, maybe opening the door to see what we wanted. After several minutes, however, no one answered our pleas. I stepped back looking for another entrance, maybe where the trucks were loaded.

Without warning, a rock the size of my fist flew past within a foot of my much softer head. It broke through a window, shattering the glass. The rock's velocity kept it sailing through the large warehouse where it finally hit something somewhere deep inside. Sara took a look around hoping no one had been watching her illegal act. I was probably wanted for murder, so the breaking and entering we were about to commit didn't seem like such a big deal. Sara pushed the rest of the glass out of her way as she reached her arm in through the window frame and unlocked the door from inside.

"Where did you learn to do that?" I asked her in amazement.

"An episode of 'Dragnet'," Sara grinned in triumph. "It was the episode…"

She opened the door and walked in as her voice trailed off. I didn't bother to ask her to repeat herself. Whoever said that television had no social benefit? I glanced around, waiting to be caught in the act of breaking in. The place appeared to be deserted and it seemed as if no one was paying any attention to us in the slightest. No security guard came running upon hearing the shattering window or the loud echoes from the rock landing in the warehouse. But still, I was hesitant when I followed Sara in against my better judgment.

The inside of Burrell Scientific's warehouse was huge. Wooden crates of every size were stacked throughout the entire building's empty shell. Tall metal racks stored smaller crates above their bigger cousins.

Sara wandered off into the dark, reading the labels stapled to their crate. I found a stack of catalogs lose to the door. On the cover were three scientists conducting a lab experiment. They had multiple beakers and tubes with different shades of liquid. It looked like they were playing with a large glass chemistry set instead of conducting actual research. It occurred to me that I hadn't been aware of any real chemical research outside of the discussed in my undergrad Introduction to Chemistry class.

I could never resist thumbing through any type of sales catalogs, even if I would never have a use for the products in it. I put a copy in my back pocket, slipping it out of sight. If nothing else, it would give me something to read when I was in the john.

"Found something!" Sara's voice echoed out from deep within the warehouse.

I walked further in, my eyes adjusting to the growing darkness. I found Sara squatting in front of a medium-sized crate reading its packing label in the dark. She silently read off a number, which she started to repeat to herself so she wouldn't forget it.

"What did you find?" I asked, knowing she wouldn't answer until she was done.

She rose quickly and jogged past me. I went over to the crate she had just come from and bent down to read the packing slip. It was dark, but I was able to make out the numbers on the crate. But it didn't matter anyway because I couldn't make heads or tails out of what the sequence of numbers on the box could mean. Why did Sara think the number was important? I grabbed the crate and pulled myself up, while I pushed my cane down. I popped up easy enough, without straining my hip. I followed Sara, retracing my steps.

When I caught up, Sara was searching through a clipboard,

flipping the pages, while she traced her index finger down one side of the paper. She repeated the crate's number over and over again, comparing it to the numbers listed on the page. I waited patiently, realizing Sara was trying to find out what was in the crate. She had seen something on the crate that had gotten her attention.

"The suspense is killing me," I said, cutting the uncomfortable silence. "What did you find?"

"The crate I was looking at is being shipped to Children's Hospital tomorrow."

"Okay." We were in a medical supply company. Children's Hospital would need supplies like any other hospital. What was it that she had found? "And what are you doing now?"

"I'm looking at the shipping manifesto for every order for this week."

Her finger continued to glide down the page, and then suddenly stopped. She rested her finger close to the bottom of the page. Sara's face melted, as her excitement turned into dread.

"What? What is it?" I asked. I couldn't wait any longer. I needed to know what she had found. Sara slowly lifted her eyes off the page, shifting them in my direction.

"California," she whispered through her clenched lips. Sara paused as I drew in close to her. I still couldn't understand. I looked down at the shipping log and found the line her finger rested on. I read the rest of the entry. The crate was filled with polio vaccine from Cutter Laboratories.

"We have to do something before anyone else dies," she cried.

I read the entry once again. The shipment came from California and was ready to be shipped to Children's Hospital tomorrow. We didn't have much time left. Across from the shipping address was the description of contents. My mouth fell open as I finally understood Sara's dread. In the crate were ten thousand doses of the Poliomyelitis vaccine from California-based Cutter Laboratories. Ten thousand doses of the polio vaccine that could infect ten thousand children with the polio virus.

I tore the page off the clipboard and stuffed it into my pocket. We had to go find the Chancellor because time was running out.

Chapter 7

The sky was a mixture of different shades of blues and reds, as the sun set behind the city's hills. The clouds absorbed the colors, making their middles appear grey.

Sara and I hurried into the Cathedral pushing through the set of revolving doors. We didn't have to use the lift since the Chancellor's office occupied a large chunk of the first floor. The powers that be could have put the office closer to the top of the Cathedral, but decided to leave it at the base of the building. The thinking was that having the office on the first floor symbolized a connection between the students and the administration.

We jogged through the main hall. Situated beyond, in a dark dead end, was a set of heavy mahogany doors leading to the Chancellor's suite. Sara opened the doors as I trailed behind, limping as quickly as I could. A middle-aged secretary sat behind a small green desk. Her fingers were busy hitting keys of a typewriter directly in front of her. Her hands moved at a steady pace as each finger found its letter without any pause. Each key stroke created a loud clucking noise, as she rhythmically typed away.

We stood near the woman's desk waiting for her to look up from her work. She had a small round face, thick squat shoulders, and a neck like a Thanksgiving Day's turkey. She worked with determination, peering down at hand-written text though thick reading glasses suspended beyond the laws of physics from the tip of her nose.

"Ahh, hello," I finally said. It hadn't occurred to me what we were actually going to say. I brought the shipping manifest out, clutching it for moral support. I did not want to sound rude, but simply went blank. I paused to clear my throat, buying some time. Sara solved the problem for me, when she stepped in disregarding my insecurities. If she was trying to make a brilliant first impression, she was succeeding marvelously.

"We need to see the Chancellor," she demanded with the authority of the mightiest of mortals. I had full confidence in Sara's take-charge attitude was impressive. If anyone could get us in to see the Chancellor, it would be Sara.

"Do you have an appointment?" The secretary asked without looking up from her typewriter. She had ignored Sara's glare like a seasoned professional. How many years must it have taken for her to disregard emotional students during her tenure?

Sara turned toward me in frustration. I shrugged, not wanting to upset her even more. She sighed then continued, "No we don't have an appointment," Sara retorted. "What we have to see the Chancellor about is a matter of life and death."

Sara might have been a bit melodramatic, over the top, but she was accurate just the same. I would have gone for a completely different approach, one that would make the secretary actually want to help us, but to each his own.

The secretary looked up for the first time, giving the two students in front of her a once over with special attention to our disheveled appearances. She zoomed in on Sara and gave a sigh that expressed her deep irritation. Then the woman's eyes darted toward me, but she averted her eyes just as quickly when she discovered my cane.

The wheels turned as the secretary thought how to handle the situation. She could throw us out without a moment's hesitation or she could have sympathy on two worried students.

"I'm sorry, but the Chancellor is in a meeting." she said and then smiled. Her apology was only intended as a formality. It lacked the empathy it should have had. "If you leave your name, number and a message as to the nature of your visit, I will be sure to give the Chancellor the message after his meeting."

She placed a pad of paper and a pencil on the edge of her desk in front of Sara, and then resumed hitting the typewriter's metal keys, falling in a rhythm once again. The secretary chose the hard line. She was tougher minded than I had assumed she would be when we walked in. It might have been her usual attitude, but I highly doubted it.

I decided to intervene with a completely different approach. "I'm sorry, Mrs. . . . ?"

"Babcock," the woman responded at my prompt.

"Mrs. Babcock, please excuse our behavior. We barged in demanding something we had no right to demand. But please understand the significance of the situation. We really do need to speak to the Chancellor immediately. I'm sorry for the urgency, but it concerns the murder of Dr. Alex Gerlach, Dr. Victor Wheeling, and the Salk vaccine."

"Murder?" the secretary squealed, focusing the most dramatic word.

I played along, hoping she would help. "Yes. Murder!" I loudly cried back, not sure why I was shouting.

Mrs. Babcock paused, preparing to accept my plea. She rested her eyes on Sara with irritation, but returned them back to me, unable to turn them away like she did before. Her expression changed to empathy. It was subtle, but I could tell, having seen that expression on others hundreds of times before. It was different from pity. I could tell by the furrowing of her forehead and the pained expression in her eyes. I could see the wheels turning as she connected my handicap with someone she knew or had known once before. She could have lost a son, maybe a husband, but the pain was real, and she understood it.

Mrs. Babcock looked hastily back at the Chancellor's door. "Fine," she said, "Stay right here." She began to get up from her desk. "I'll see what I can do." The secretary wiped the wrinkles from her floral print blue dress, making her appearance presentable. She knocked lightly on the Chancellor's inner office, while pushing the door slightly open as she must have done on many previous occasions. Several of the voices from inside the room suddenly stopped in mid-conversation.

Another voice, this time, very deep, but calm from the years of working in high-stress environments, called from inside the office, "Come in, Nancy." Mrs. Babcock, slid into the room with a backward glance and mouthed "I'll be right back."

I could hear murmuring from the secretary and Fitzgerald, but nothing more. The others in the Chancellor's office had fallen silent. I wanted to hear what they were saying so I moved closer to the door, able to see in where the door had remained opened. I could see the large, dark brown conference table with at least ten middle-aged men in dark suits sitting around it. I thought one of the men looked familiar. He was thinner than his contemporaries and wore a pair of round spectacles. In an instant I recognized him from his picture in the paper. It was Dr. Jonas Salk.

At the far end of the conference table Nancy was whispering into Chancellor Fitzgerald's ear. He nodded every so often, and then asked a question. Mrs. Babcock would then answer, causing the Chancellor to nod once more in agreement. I could hear Fitzgerald say, "That's fine" and a moment later Mrs. Babcock walked away from the table of men out to the reception area.

I backed up from the door as she approached. Before she closed the Chancellor's door behind her, I thought I saw another man I recognized. I could still recall the man very clearly from the past two encounters with him. The first had been helpful, if not pleasant, but the second had been horrible. It was Keith, sitting at the opposite end of the table. He was wearing a dark grey suit and looked much cleaner than the last time I saw him. I would never forget the man's face.

Some people couldn't recall their attacker's face even if they got a clear picture of him. Most people unconsciously block out shocking memories and are not any help in identifying their attacker. I wasn't one of those people. I could recall my attacker's face with great precision, right down to the cleft in his chin and inch-long scar below his ear. Keith's face was clear in my mind and would never fade after what he tried to do to me.

The same man that broke into Alex's house and attacked me was meeting with Chancellor Fitzgerald and Dr. Salk. What was going on? Our last resort was washed away and now I couldn't trust either the Chancellor or Dr. Salk. As Mrs. Babcock pulled the door shut I remained quiet. I didn't want to scare Sara so I waited, staying cool. What was worse, Keith had just made eye contact with me and knew I was on to him.

"The Chancellor can meet with you after his meeting," Mrs. Babcock said, "I'm sure they won't be much longer. If you would be kind enough to take a seat, I'd be happy to bring you some water if you like."

Sara chirped up, "How much longer do you think it'll be?"

Mrs. Babcock squinted her eyes, unable to hide her annoyance with Sara. She turned back at me.

"They should be adjourning in the next fifteen or twenty minutes."

That meant we had very little time to get away. We needed to hide and we needed to hide fast. Keith would come after us.

He wanted Alex's journal and this time I was afraid he would use whatever force was necessary to get it.

"That's all right, we... made a terrible mistake." I had to get both of us away and fast. Mrs. Babcock twisted her head in confusion. "We've taken this to far already, right Sara?" I tried to pull Sara's arm, but she yanked it back. "We'll just let ourselves out." Sara backed away with eyes widened like I was a mad man.

"Sorry to bother you, Mrs. Babcock. Please let the Chancellor know it was all a misunderstanding. Thank you."

"But Jamie . . . ," Sara cut in.

I grabbed Sara's arm, this time pulling her with more force. Instead of fighting, she let me push her into the hallway. When we were out of sight, Sara pulled away from my grasp, stopping dead in her tracks.

"What the hell are you doing Jamie?" She raised her voice, loud enough for the secretary to hear us.

I spoke quietly, very carefully pronouncing each syllable as I told Sara whom I saw in the Chancellor's office. I knew she would start to panic. I covered her mouth just in time as she tried to scream. Her body shook, convulsing, as she squirmed in my arms. Sara grabbed my hand covering her mouth and tried to pull it away. I tightened my hold.

"Sara, I'm going to need you to stay calm." I told her with the same soft peaceful voice I needed her to mimic. Sara slowly stopped struggling, either running out of energy or relaxing. Either way, it worked. "If I take my hand away are you going to be okay?" I asked.

She nodded her head up and down without hesitation. I slowly moved my hand away, waiting for another meltdown. I watched her for several moments as she calmed down. When I was sure she wouldn't freak out I lowered my guard.

I took her by the hand and started to lead her away. We needed a safe place to hide. It was a last ditch effort to hide out. If nothing else, we could buy some time. We needed to be close, but far enough away when their meeting would end. If we ran, it would attract too much attention and we needed to keep a low profile. We patiently took a stroll down the sidewalk feeling the pressure of each minute as it passed by. I wanted to make sure Keith wasn't able to follow us. The more normal we acted, the less likely anyone would become a compass for our enemy.

I pulled open St Paul's large oak church doors and waited for Sara to walk in first. She led the way, passing a basin of holy water in between the long wooden pews. I followed as she walked toward the ten-foot cross at the front of the chapel. I stopped and took a seat close to the front. Sara continued up the aisle only slowing when she got close to the front of the sanctuary. She bent down in front of the giant cross and touched her head, chest and shoulders, making the sign of the cross. I didn't know Sara was religious or that she even believed in God, but I realized now was as good as any time to become a believer.

Death profoundly affected those imbued with a sense of spirituality. It always had the opposite effect on me. Having seen terrible deaths, I had a hard time believing in a higher power. There might have been a time when my faith was present or even strong, but that was a long time ago. Every time I witnessed a person's death, my faith in God lessened until one day, I just stopped believing all together. I was happy that Sara could still hold on to some form of hope in a time like this.

We sat in silence for what seemed like an hour, more for Sara's sake than mine. We were alone. Yes, we had each other, but we needed more than that. We needed the safety of the police, or our friends, but had no one to turn to. We had evidence. We had letters from inside sources and notes left by Alex, and yet all that seemed useless because we had no one turn to.

Sara rested her head on my shoulder. It was warm and comforting, and I returned the favor by wrapping my arm around her. She sighed, closing her eyes. I kissed her forehead, and was glad she was with me. She lifted her face to mine and opened her small amazing mouth to ask a question.

"Why would a man who attacked you be sitting at the same table as the Chancellor and Dr. Salk?"

I thought about the question, but could only come up with a lame theory. "Maybe, they were all in on it," I said.

Sara wasn't happy with that answer. Neither was I. "Salk wouldn't want to give anyone polio. He's a decent man. I can't imagine him throwing away his sense of humanity after inventing something like the polio vaccine. The same person who created a vaccine that could save millions of lives wouldn't just say to hell with life."

Millions of Americans praised the name Jonas Salk every day. Millions of parents could rest easy all over the United States while their children swam or enjoyed a summer's day in the woods. Sara was right, of course, but I realized I needed to play devil's advocate. We needed to examine the facts, considering all the angles and possibilities.

"What if the vaccine didn't work from the start?" I asked.

"It worked," Sara responded with certainty. "There would be no plausible way to fake that large of a field test. The majority of children in the city would have gotten polio from the vaccine if it were infected with the live virus."

I thought about it for a little bit longer and replied, "They could have administered a placebo."

"It still wouldn't explain the meeting at the Chancellor's office. What would Fitzgerald have to gain by being involved in all of this?"

I began to play with the prayer books in front of me. The man was being fired for being a success. If that didn't make him a disgruntled employee, I don't know what would.

"What if Cutter was bribing Fitzgerald to hush up about any mistakes they made?" Sara said, playing with the idea in her head. "The research was being done at the University and Fitzgerald could have found out about any number of mistakes being made."

"Let's pretend for a moment that Cutter was trying to cover up everything. The Chancellor would be an obvious resource, of course. He was being fired and would probably be an easy target to bribe. Maybe he decided he wanted more money, but that still doesn't explain about Salk and his presence at the meeting. I'm sure he wouldn't take a bribe. He wouldn't need to. His vaccine worked. The tests already proved that."

I tried to go along with Sara's train of thought.

"So Salk isn't in on it and the drug companies decide to shut up anyone else who won't go along with their plans? Kill them if necessary? Then pay off anyone who will take the money and keep quiet." The longer I thought about it the more it didn't make any sense. "But Salk was in the meeting, too."

She let it settle in as she paced in front of the pew. "The Health Department would also have to know. This would be too big for the drug companies to cover up alone. If Fitzgerald was playing both sides, he wouldn't want Salk to know anything was wrong."

That made sense. Everyone would want Salk to stay a hero, a poster child for American health care. Without Salk, there could not be a hero. The American people needed a *good guy* dressed in white.

"Maybe Keith did work in the lab," Sara added. "It would make a good cover. Not only could he learn who was asking questions, he could make sure that Salk didn't suspect anything. He would have to have been there for some time though."

Sara was about to continue, but a deep voice yelled out from the back. "Give me the book!"

I had just enough time to tackle Sara to the ground before gunshots exploded from behind us. Two bullets flew by, hitting the pew and sending wooden splinters scattering everywhere around us. Lying on top of Sara would have been a pleasant experience if not for the present circumstances.

I picked my head up over the pew to see Keith pointing a .357 Magnum in our direction. I thought it might have been overkill for the situation at hand, but effective nonetheless. I ducked my head back down just in time as Keith fired again, this time hitting the stained glass windows on the side.

Keith's shoes clicked on the chapel's marble floor as he walked closer to us. He wasn't in a hurry. He basically had us trapped. I silently motioned for Sara to follow my lead as I slipped under the pews toward the gunslinger. Keith's gunshots sounded like mini-explosions each time he fired. The noise could probably be heard for blocks away.

I waited for Sara to follow, but she shook her head violently trying to object, and I waved my hand again, indicating that she should follow. The sound of shoes scuffing the floor grew louder as Keith slowly made his way toward us. I could imagine him pointing the .357 at each open pew, hoping that one would lead him to his prey. I wanted to wait for help, but felt there wouldn't be time. If the Chancellor were involved at all, he would make sure the police wouldn't be coming any time soon.

I had to match my next move perfectly with Keith's steps, if I wanted to survive the next minute of my life. I grabbed a prayer book from the back of the pew and motioned to Sara. I raised my hand and pointed two fingers her two fingers toward my eyes, and then pointed in the direction I meant to take her. It was just like I did in Korea when we were approaching enemy lines. She didn't understand my hand signals, but I didn't have time to catch her up. We needed to move fast and I needed her to follow me to safety.

Keith was one pew away and the time was almost right. I counted to three and then flung the book away, watching it fly into the air. Time slowed down as I carefully planned my movements. I grabbed Sara toward me with all of my strength preparing for a struggle, but her body went limp and we rolled perfectly under the adjacent pew.

The book smashed into a set of metal candle sticks on the pulpit, causing everything to crash to the floor. It made enough noise to distract Keith. I saw his face before we completely rolled under the next pew. I thought he would see me, but the diversion worked in our favor just like I had hoped it would. He quickly ran in the direction of the pulpit.

I pulled Sara close and whispered into her ear, "On the count of three, we run."

I silently mouthed the words and on three we both leapt up for the front of the chapel. I pushed Sara ahead, making sure I was in the way of any bullet that might be aimed at her fragile body. Without aiming, Keith spun around firing another two shots with the ease of a cowboy at the O.K. Corral. I pulled Sara behind a marble pillar just in time. The gun had range and power. The bullets hit the pillar, which shattered into pieces of ruble, which rained down over our heads.

Keith was out of bullets and started to reload. He slowly walked closer filling each empty chamber with a new slug. Before he could finish loading, I broke away from Sara. He saw me coming and flipped the cylinder shut, only half full. Instinctively, I raised my cane bringing it behind my head. He pulled the gun's hammer back getting ready to fire.

I swung my cane, releasing it directly in his path.

Keith pulled the trigger.

The stick exploded into fiery wooden shrapnel. Keith tried to duck, covering his eyes from the shards of wood. I lost sight of Keith as Sara and I raced through the chapel's doors making our escape while we had the chance.

The moon and city lights were enough to light our way along the sidewalks. I couldn't see any stars in the sky, but that didn't mean they weren't there. The city tended to drown out the radiating balls of light on nights like this. There were only a few clouds covering bits and pieces of the sky, but we were still unable to see the millions of stars outside our solar system. Nights like this made you want to take a long drive out of the city and find a completely isolated piece of land for the rest of your life.

I led Sara away from campus, running behind Forbes Field and into Schenley Park. The area was dense enough to provide us with the cover we needed. I wasn't sure where we were going, and yet I didn't care one way or the other. I knew I couldn't go much further in the shape I was in. I was amazed that Sara was still moving at all. We needed to find a place to crash and the sooner the better. I saw the shadows of a small clearing under a canopy of trees. It could provide us shelter in case it rained. My eyelids were becoming heavy, while the rest of my body slowly became limp.

"We should stop here and rest," I said dropping to the ground. . I didn't wait for Sara to respond as I found the comfort of the cool ground below. She nodded in agreement and was quickly following my lead.

The night had turned chilly, with a small amount of moisture in the air. The grass was already damp, but neither of us seemed to care. As I began to lose consciousness, I was able to feel

Sara curling up by my side. She laid her head on my chest and closed her eyes, falling asleep soon after. I pulled her body close, catching the warmth of her skin. I shut my eyes, feeling my own drowsiness catch up with me. As I drifted asleep, I hoped that my dreams would be gentler than our reality.

Chapter 8

It was the lightening that woke me, not the thunder. My eyes were still closed, but the white light shown through every thirty seconds, causing me to see intense red bursts behind my eyelids. The affect was mesmerizing. I could have been dreaming, sleeping still, but the cold rain reminded me that I was lying outside in the middle of the woods. I sat up rubbing the sleep from my eyes. I took my hand and ran it through my hair, letting the accumulated water escape. My clothes were soaked, but a change would have to wait for now.

Sara was curled in a fetal position next to me. She was shivering as the rain continued to fall down around her. I wanted to let her sleep and carry her somewhere dry, but I knew I'd just make a fool of myself if I tried. I brushed my hand against her check and softly whispered her name. After several failed attempts, I gave her a small push at her shoulder. A slow groan lifted from her throat and her hand rubbed at her wet nose. It did the trick as she started to wake.

Her eyes flickered open and a huge smile appeared on her face. For a moment I forgot where I was. There was nothing else besides us. No trees, no rain, no storm, just Sara and me. She raised her right arm above her head.

"A little help, please," she softly whispered. I continued to stare until she started to giggle and waved her arm in my face. "Jamie, could you help me up?" she repeated, breaking me from my trance.

"Of course!" I said realizing how awkward I was acting. I rolled over to my side and pulled myself up, holding onto a branch nearby. I extended my hands and pulled Sara up to her feet. She examined her clothes, wiping away the dirt that had accumulated on her side. She adjusted her brown bag by her side, content everything was in order.

She realized I was staring and shyly smiled in my direction. My face became warm, but I didn't want to turn away. Sara walked towards me. I stood still as the distance between us shrank. When she was only inches away, she lifted her face toward mine. I bent my head down and closed my eyes. I felt her lips touch mine. The moment was cut short by a loud rumbling of thunder and lightning that appeared just milliseconds later.

"The storm is going to get worse," I said while my eyes remained shut. "It would be safer if we found shelter." I opened my eyes to Sara quietly laughing. My lips remained in puckering positions while I spoke.

"You really are cute, Jamie," she said with a sincerity that sounded like music when she spoke.

"I try," I sighed.

She grabbed my hand and pulled me with her. We began our hike out of the park. Sara and I looked like young lovers taking a stroll in a downpour. A romantic walk in the rain sounded like it would be fun, but it was too cold, and the romance ended even before it had time to begin.

We attempted to engage in small talk while we made an effort to forget about why we had slept outside in the rain. We agreed that we needed to go back to Memorial Hospital, back to Salk's lab. We needed to find out more about what the hell was going on. Who was Keith? Was he alone in all of this? The smart thing would be to get out of town, but we were already in too deep. We owed it to Alex to finish the work he had started and to find out what happened.

We trekked up the hill, past the medical school. We stood in front of the hospital, but didn't know how we were going to get in. It wasn't a twenty-four-hour deal like Presbyterian down the street. It was mostly a research facility and an outpatient testing center. I wasn't sure why they called it a hospital at all. We walked into the lobby, which at least was open, and found the security guard's desk empty.

The lobby resembled a library more than it did a hospital. The floor was white marble speckled with black and grey. Gold sconces hung on the walls at ten-foot intervals. Long ago, the candles had been replaced with electric flames, which flickered at a set pattern. At the far end of the lobby, four brass elevators were set behind the security desk. Getting anywhere from the lobby would require getting past security.

To my amazement, I saw a set of keys on the counter, at least twenty keys in all, just lying there, with no owner in sight. I reached down and was about to grab them, but before I could, Sara elbowed me in the stomach. I pulled my arm back and clutched the sight of her surprise attack.

"What was that for?"I asked sharply.

Without a word Sara motioned behind me. I shot a glance back in time to see a security guard walking toward us.

"Can I help you?" the security guard asked as he came closer. He looked at me as I clutched my stomach in pain. "Miss, you should really take your friend to the emergency room." The guard sat down on his chair behind the desk. "He's not looking so good."

I realized he was talking about me clutching my stomach. Sara quickly improvised, "Are you sure there isn't anyone who can see us here?" Her eyelashes fluttered. "My brother really needs a doctor."

She was acting like a ditz, like a freshman girl on campus for the first time. She moved over to the side of the desk furthest away from the keys and bent over the counter. She pushed her chest out until her breasts pushed against her thin sweater. Her hair was slicked back from the rain and the sweater was still somewhat damp, giving a molded appearance to her chest. I understood what she was doing, catching on pretty fast, but I wanted to stay there and watch the way she was trying to manipulate the guard. I didn't think he would buy it. He would see through her ruse.

"Sorry miss, all the doctors went home for the night and won't be back until working hours in the morning. The emergency room is right down the street. I could show you where it is if you'd like." He was smiling, giving off a goofy boyish grin. It was the same lame grin I've been using since the day Sara and I met.

She pouted and pushed out her lips giving him the full little girl show. "But officer, we really need a doctor now, my brother is in so much pain." The guard blushed, but didn't take his eyes off Sara. She had that effect on most men.

I rolled my eyes at the little production and tried not to be ill. I looked back toward the keys and saw a list of office numbers. The list had the doctors' names and office numbers in alphabetical order. It took some time reading the list upside down, but I found Dr. Salk's name near the bottom.

The guard straightened his back against his chair. He puffed out his chest, mimicking a pigeon's mating ritual. "I'm not a police officer miss, just a night security guard." His voice took a more serious deep tone creating a sense of importance where there wasn't one before. Sara didn't take her eyes off of him as he continued. "Sometimes our jobs can be more dangerous than even the police though. We walk around alone all night, making sure nothing mischievous comes our way. Just the other day, I had to . . ."

Sara leaned into the conversation even more as the security guard babbled along about a fraternity prank on campus. I reached over the desk as he fawned over the blond in front of him. Sara shot her eyes quickly in my direction, indicating that I should hurry.

"Do you get to carry a gun?" I couldn't tell if she was enjoying herself, but I could tell that her act was working in her favor. "It must be really dangerous out there all alone?"

Sara was laying it on thick. The guard responded, but I was concentrating too hard on getting the keys off the desk without listening to his narcissistic pickup lines. He started to turn away from Sara causing me to retreat, but she grabbed his upper arm feeling his bicep.

"Wow, look how strong you are. You must work out every day," she said while batting her eyelashes again. Her hand moved up and down his upper arm, making sure he didn't stray from her attention.

"Not every day," the guard said melting at her touch. "Maybe three times a week though."

This time I knew he wouldn't take his eyes away. I grabbed the keys not worrying how far I reached my body over the counter. I hooked the ring and slowly lifted it. I pulled the keys in carefully, working hard not to shake them. They remained silent as I stuffed them in my pocket. I started to back up as Sara wrapped up her vaudeville show.

"Well, thank you so much for your help."

"No trouble, miss. Just doing my part is all," the guard melted. "If you want, I could escort you over to the E.R."

"That is so sweet, but I think my brother and I can find it without the help." The guard frowned, unsure what just happened as Sara held my shoulder guiding me through the front door.

"You don't think that was a little much back there?" I asked playing my part as an invalid while we distanced ourselves from the guard. The part wasn't hard to play. My limp contributed to make me seem really injured or sick.

"We got the keys didn't we?"

"If I knew that was how you'd get them, maybe I would have thought of another way."

"Jamie, this is no time to be jealous."

"Who is being jealous?" I asked. Sara shook her head as we continued without another word. Of course I was jealous. I would admit it, but when I was put on the spot I became defensive. It was childish, I know, but no way was I going to admit to my jealousy now.

When we were completely out of the guard's sight, we doubled back around to the side of the building. There was an unlabeled door, possibly an emergency exit. I only hoped it wasn't alarmed. I fumbled with the key ring, trying each key in order. Sara was becoming impatient as she stood behind me playing lookout.

"Let me try," she demanded.

The key went in half way, but didn't fit any further. "I got it," I snarled, "Just keep watching."

After what seemed like twenty tries, I finally found the right key to the lock.

"Jamie, why would you be jealous?" Sara had crossed her arms and wouldn't move from where she stood.

I pulled the door open, but she stood her ground. "You want to talk about this now?" I was bewildered by her timing. I saw a hint of a smile under her stone glare. Was Sara having fun seeing me like this? Did she want me to be jealous? I was beginning to think all women were crazy.

"We really should get on with this." I wasn't really sure what I was referring to after I said it. Did I mean breaking in, or our relationship? Sara decided for us as she pulled me into an embrace placing a small kiss on my lips.

"I hope that settles it," she said with finality. She strutted into the dark hallway leaving me outside wondering what just happened. I shook it off and followed her inside.

The main lights were off, but the red backup lights remained on giving the hospital an eerie red glow. The light made sickly looking shadows behind our bodies as we moved toward the stairwell. The idea was to find Salk's office, but Sara and I didn't really know where we going. I knew it was on the second floor, room 203, but I wasn't sure where that would be. If Keith were working in the same place, he would have an office there too. We walked up the stairs to the second floor and realized to our astonishment the whole second floor was part of Salk's research laboratory. The lab was room 200, so did that mean 203 would be inside?

I expected something like the Batcave when we opened the door. I pictured large caverns extending into the darkness, filled with futuristic equipment, and a special hero's car like the Batmobile. What we found was very different from my vision. Salk was a hero after all, but I never imagined that in the dark a polio research laboratory would look just like any other laboratory in the world. It really was the most anti-climatic moment of my day, especially after getting shot at and finding two dead bodies in the last forty-eight hours. Beakers filled with chemicals lined the walls and filled the cabinets. Stacks of Petri dishes covered tables, leaving only a small amount of work space at each desk. Water and oxygen tanks were outfitted on all the large desks in the middle and along the sides of the room. The walls were plain white, a fact that was apparent even in the dark.

When I was an undergraduate I took a biology class in almost the same exact laboratory as the one we stood in. Except for several larger and more expensive machines around the room, it could have been the same one. We found three refrigerators, but didn't want to open them. There was no telling what we could get infected with if we randomly explored a lethal virus research facility. We needed to be careful. We hadn't discussed the ramifications of walking around in a facility outfitted to research dangerous viruses. One wrong peek and we could become infected with some unknown disease. When you were in a laboratory filled with biological dangers I felt it was a good rule of thumb not to tempt Mother Nature any more than we already were. We needed the written kind of evidence anyway, so we went straight for the offices in the back. The first office was unlocked and obviously belonged to Salk. It had pictures of the man and his family lining the walls. Notebooks were piled high on his desk, each with specific dates written in black marker. I flipped through the first on the stack. It was the most recent and was filled with experiment notes written in black ink. I didn't know what any of the symbols meant, much less what the calculations stood for. If I were a biologist I might be able to use them, but I needed something more for the layman reader. We crept around the office taking a little more time and peeking into the filing cabinets just to be certain we weren't missing something. There weren't any files on the actual companies manufacturing the vaccine or anything related to the distribution either. If Salk was hiding something he wasn't keeping it in his office.

The next door down the line turned out to be a research assistant's office. It was cluttered with paperwork, and the same type of lab journals that Salk had in his office. Several large filing cabinets sat in the back of the office. There was nothing out of the ordinary here either.

I turned to Sara. "You search this one," I said. "We can cover more ground if we split up."

Sara nodded her approval and started to snoop around. I walked out and began searching the remaining two offices down the hall. The first seemed to be a communal work area for doctoral and master's students. I took a quick glance, but the room was mainly bare except for the same experimental laboratory journals. I checked the last office in the row, but it was locked. I tried every key we had on the keying, but none of them seemed to work.

I took a step back and thought about my dilemma. Should I keep moving and search another area or should I try to break in? I would probably make more noise than I wanted to, but would it be worth it? The office must have been locked for a good reason and whoever used it didn't want anybody in there. With that in mind, I wanted to get into the office even more. I turned back searching for something around the lab that would help in my endeavor. My eyes soon fell on exactly what I needed.

I walked over to the wall where a glass cabinet was set up for just these types of emergencies. Written at the top of the box were the words *Break Glass in Case of Emergencies*. I took the small metal hammer hanging on a chain. I tapped the glass softly at first, but quickly realized I needed to use a more forceful approach. The next tap was harder and broke the glass with ease. I tapped out the extra glass from the frame, making sure not to cut myself. I grabbed the axe from its hook and marched back over to the locked office door.

I swung the fireman's axe at the lock, hitting metal against metal and causing a spark to ignite from the impact. I paused making sure nothing would catch on fire. Sara poked her head out of the assistant's door as I raised the axe once more. I paused, turning to question what she needed, but the expression on her face was of utter confusion.

"No key," I explained, and then brought the axe down hard once again. I used the remaining strength I had left in my upper body. All of my muscles felt like rubber as the axe made contact with the door directly above the lock. This time I hit dead center in between the door and its jam, breaking the lock and popping the door open. Sara shook her head in disapproval and popped back into the office.

I held onto the axe for moral support as I entered the room. A small name plate on the desk said Keith Ontario. The office screamed bureaucracy, with its minimal effects, and overwhelming feeling of a hypocritical efficiency. Keith's desk was clear of any clutter, an amazing display of anal retentiveness. There was nothing else besides a chair and a phone. I tried to open the drawers, but they were locked. I tried several of the keys expecting to magically find the right one, but I should have known better. No one besides Keith would have had a key to any of his artifacts. How he had infiltrated Salk's work was a question that needed to be answered. Salk must not have known he had a mole working in his lab.

It would take more than a blunt object to pry open the drawer. I made an attempt at picking the lock with a paperclip, but my efforts were futile. I was beginning to get frustrated at the lack of planning on my part. I had seen a lock picking kit advertised in the back of a *Vault of Horror* comic just last week. The story was about a murdered woman who comes back from the dead to seek revenge on her husband who had killed her at the beginning. It was a typical horror tale, but the lock picking set would have been useful.

I sat down on the linoleum floor and tried to come up with a plan. Leaning back, I banged my head against one of the filing cabinet's metal handles. I cradled the back of my head rubbing it in pain. I was frustrated and shut my eyes in defeat. There must have been a clue somewhere in the room, but my efforts were useless. The pain started to fade as I opened my eyes and looked directly at the black telephone resting on Keith's desk. If only I could somehow figure out who Keith had been talking too, I could begin to piece everything together.

I noticed that there was a small stack of paper propping the phone up, which I hadn't seen before. A rubber stopper was missing on the front right of the phone's base and the paper was placed there to balance it out. I didn't have anything else to show for my efforts so I pulled the stack of papers out. I quickly shuffled through the small pile. Each piece of paper was a secretary's written message. Some were from Salk, others were from random local numbers I didn't recognize. In the back of the stack were several messages from someone named Scheele with an out-of-town area code of 202. I slipped one of the pieces of paper with the 202 area code in my pocket and placed the rest of the stack back under the phone.

Hurried steps came running down the hall as Sara darted into the Keith's office in a frenzy. In her arms were a stack of manila file folders.

"What did you find?" I asked.

Before Sara could even open her mouth, the lights flickered on and the bright fluorescents caught both of us off guard. The sound of frantic marching filled the room as my eyes began to adjust. A whole squad of police rushed into the laboratory drawing their guns in our general direction, all the while building a perimeter around the two of us. Sara clutched the files to her chest, ready to break down from the shock. From behind the gun-toting flat-footed cops, Keith Ontario walked in followed by the security guard. The guard must have realized his keys were gone faster than we thought he would.

Two cops grabbed and cuffed my hands behind my back. They did the same to Sara taking away her bag, which was holding Alex's journal. I twisted from my captors, struggling to move toward Keith. They held me back bracing my shoulders and grabbing at the chain in the cuffs.

"He's the murderer!" I began to scream. "It's all there in that book." The cops pushed me back trying to secure the situation. "It's in the book, just read it!" I carried on. Keith didn't even blink. He just smirked, gazing into my eyes as he walked over to the officer who was holding me.

I tried to pull away. I wanted to strangle the life out of him, but the cops yanked me back with brute force. The one on the right gave me a quick right hook to my kidney. I hunched over when the sharp sting forced the air right out of me. My natural instinct was to grab my side in pain, but I couldn't with my hands in cuffs. I stood my ground, absorbing the intense sensations, and regained a steady breathing.

"It's okay officer. He doesn't seem to be able to hurt me now." Keith turned to the officer holding onto files and Sara's brown bag.

"I believe those belong to me," He said smugly, pointing to the files in the officer's hands.

The cop started to hand the journal and files over, but out of thin air Detective Bloom inserted himself between the uniformed cop and Keith. He intercepted the items before Keith even had a chance to retrieve them. I wasn't surprised to see that Bloom was part of this. After all, he had been assigned to Alex's case from the beginning. Now that he had new evidence in a homicide investigation he would want to play by the book.

"I'm sorry," the detective began to tell Keith, "I'm going to have to take this as evidence. You understand Mr. Ontario," he said with a *just doing my job* expression.

Keith frowned but recovered quickly, "Of course, I just wanted to get back to work as soon as possible."

"We will return everything once we've finished," Detective Bloom explained, "I promise."

Although hesitant, Keith nodded in agreement, obviously unhappy with how the situation was playing out. I turned to Sara to see if she understood what the hell was going on. She didn't seem to have any more of an understanding than I had. I realized Keith had power, not as much as the detective, but enough to be acting with the police. It seemed our new friend was far more important than he was letting on.

With the journal going into evidence, it was going to be impossible for Keith to get to it. It would be bagged and tagged and held by the police until Keith was able to retrieve it. They would read it, not sure what to make of Alex's ramblings. They would think we were all crazy after skimming through it.

The police read us our rights and then transported both of Sara and me to the closet police precinct. We were fingerprinted quickly and processed in the system. Our mug shots were taken. I wanted to smile in mine, but the officer taking it didn't seem to be thrilled with the idea. Sara and I were soon separated and put into different interrogation rooms. I started to look on the bright side. At least we were processed fairly quickly. The Pittsburgh police were not known for the timely manner in which they operated.

Sitting in an interrogation room was one of the most boring activities I had experienced since being a child. Watching paint dry could have been more exciting. Watching shows like "Dragnet" always made police work exciting. Sitting in the little box made me feel claustrophobic and the air was stale, making the heat almost unbearable. I could already see the sweat stains emerging at my armpits. My shirt was sticking to the back of my chair in wet patches. I was wondering if the police were using this time to torture me or just wanted to take a donut break.

I waited in the hot room for another half hour staring at a clear pitcher of water across the table from where I sat while my thirst grew expedientially. The room must have been a hundred degrees, and my hands were still cuffed behind my back. With each second that passed my mouth became drier causing a roughness in my throat.

After another ten minutes of doing absolutely nothing, I was not only thirsty, but I needed to take a piss like a racehorse. If the cops didn't come in soon, I was going to have a hard time explaining why I was sitting in a large puddle of urine. After another fifteen minutes of fighting the urge relieve my bladder, the door opened and Detective Bloom walked in followed by another plain-clothed detective I had never seen before.

I didn't know much about Detective Bloom except that he looked like your classic forty-year-old Dragnet police officer -- suit, tie and a fedora hat. The second cop was different in age and appearance. He was a younger officer with a well-groomed beard and was wearing a white shirt and slacks. He was probably about ten years younger than Bloom.

Detective Bloom tossed a file on the table, and began to pour a tall glass of water. He sat down across from me, taking his hat off and setting it down on his side. He set the glass down in front of me. The glass immediately began to perspire and my thirst became almost unbearable. This was the beginning of our interrogation.

Let the dance begin I thought. If I were lucky, they would

have some pity and give me the water early. Maybe I should tell them I needed to take a leak first.

"Fellas, I really would like to sit here and tell you all about how I didn't do it, but I really need to use the restroom at the moment." Bloom didn't respond to my bodily needs. With a deadpan expression, he took a pack of smokes out from his pocket and flipped a cigarette out. He lit a match from a small pack. When the flame sparked, he lit his cigarette and took a long inhale. He extended his hand offering the cigarette.

"I don't smoke," I declared.

That was what he wanted to hear apparently, because the next thing I knew there was a cloud of smoke being blown in my face. It burnt my windpipe and I felt like I was going to cough out a lung.

"I appreciate the gesture," I said, "but if you wouldn't mind . . ." cough, "I really need to use the men's room right now." Cough . . . cough.

"You can take a wiz right there," He said without emotion. "Until you confess you ain't going nowhere," Bloom said sucking in more smoke.

I couldn't resist. "You are not going anywhere," I corrected. For the first time since he walked in, the detective changed his expression to that of irritation and hatred. What was it about this guy that made me want to piss him off so much?

"I'm going to go soft on you here." He looked down at the file in front of him, reading out its contents. "You got a Purple Heart in the service, finished near the top of your class in college, and are now on your way to a PhD." I didn't know where he was getting his data from. I was closer to the bottom of my class than the top of it, but I didn't want to split hairs. He looked up from the file and continued talking. "You're a war hero for God's sake. I'm going to forget about your wiseass comments for the time being."

"You know, I heard cigarettes are bad for your health, detective."

Bloom wasn't paying any attention to my jokes anymore. "If you don't tell us what we want to hear soon, we're going to have to get rough on your lady friend in the other room." Bloom set his gun on the table. It was a small pistol, not very intimidating, maybe a .22, but still a gun. A weapon that would hurt regardless of how small it was. I didn't like being shot, once was enough for me.

"I didn't kill anyone," I said.

"Sure you didn't," he replied with sarcasm in his voice. "Can you prove that?"

Could I prove I didn't kill Alex? How about Victor? I was alone in my apartment the night Alex died. Unfortunately, I didn't talk to anyone that night. With Victor, I was actually seen in his hotel room standing above his dead body. Now that I thought about it, I was fucked for sure.

"No, but if you get Alex's journal I can show you why someone else wanted killed him," I pleaded. "It's all there in the book. Just give me a chance to . . ."

"Enough!" Bloom roared as he bobbed his head. He blew out a large cloud of smoke, which floated around his head and then disappeared. "We've got your prints all over the hotel room.

If that's not enough, we have witnesses that can place you at Gerlach's office and Wheeling's hotel room before and after the murders took place."

They could place me at Alex's office the night of his murder? How? I wasn't there. Was he making it up or did he actually have someone claiming I was there that night? I couldn't tell if it was a bluff or not.

"Why would I have wanted to kill him?" I asked. "Alex was the only family I had left." The detective in the corner hadn't moved a muscle once yet and I was beginning to wonder if he was really there. Maybe I was seeing a figment of my imagination caused by the stress I was under.

"It was Keith Ontario," I blurted out.

"Ontario?" The cop didn't skip a beat. "Never heard of the guy." He looked over at the man in the corner. "Drew, you ever hear of Ontario?"

The man in the corner shook his head no. At least he was real, but he might have been mute.

"Isn't Ontario in Canada?" Bloom laughed out loud.

"Keith Ontario. You have to know the guy, he was with you in Salk's office when you caught me. You talked to him when you brought us in for God's sake." What was he playing at? We both knew Keith had been there. What did he have to gain in denying it now?

The cop shook his head, "Nope, never heard of the man. You must be mistaken, Mr. Schmidt. We do, on the other hand, have several witnesses who will confirm that you were present in Dr. Wheeling's hotel room. You were also caught red handed in the offices of Dr. Jonas Salk, and we have every bit of proof that we need to prove you killed Dr. Alex Gerlach for your own academic and professional gain." He inhaled and then let out a big puff of smoke. "The evidence all points to you, son. Now if you know what's good for you, you'll give yourself up. Admit to the crimes and maybe we can cut you a deal."

"You are so off, it's unbelievable," I complained.

Detective Bloom sat back and took a long drag. How was I going to convince them I didn't do it?

"Alex was like a father to me. I loved the man more than anything. I only met Dr. Wheeling yesterday. He found me after Alex was murdered. You have to believe me. I didn't kill anyone. It had to be Keith Ontario. He was the one who broke into Alex's house and tried to steal the journal." I was pleading, but I didn't think anything was getting through.

"You mean the journal that you stole from Dr. Gerlach's private residence?" Bloom said while he stood up and flicked his cigarette butt at me. I flinched as I felt the heat of the butt against my cheek.

"Unless you cooperate with us Mr. Schmidt, this will be a very unpleasant experience for you." He nodded to his partner and said, "Take him to the john." Then he walked out of the room. I almost forgot about Drew, the detective with the beard. He nodded and walked behind me. I stood up and the cop pulled me along.

He took my cuffs off once we got to the men's room. After I was able to take a leak, I washed my hands and walked back over to him. He turned me around and put the cuffs back on. A small metal object was slipped into my hand before the cop turned me back around to face him.

He looked into my eyes. "Your friend is in the forth room down the hall on the left. Get her out of here. Hide out and meet me at this address in two hours." He slipped a piece of paper into my pocket.

"Why are you helping me?"

"You have at least three minutes to get your girl and then find your way out. There won't be anyone except for the desk sergeant and he's useless. You can just walk right out of here. I'll take care of the others."

He escorted me back to the hot little interrogation room and sat me down.

"Who are you?" I asked wondering why a cop would help me escape from police custody.

"Andrew Dunn. Now get the hell out of here," he answered as he left the room without another word.

I waited thirty seconds after Detective Dunn left and fumbled with the key to the cuffs. I heard the click on the fourth try and was finally able to pull my arms free. The other side was easier and the cuffs fell to the floor with a rattle that I didn't count on. I waited another five seconds, but when no one came in I carefully pushed open the door taking a peek out into the hallway. It was empty, but I could still hear officers down the hall. I listened, realizing they were talking about baseball. They were completely preoccupied with the subject. I opened the door wider, counted to five and slipped out.

I followed the hallway looking for the fourth interrogation

room. I slowly made my way down the corridor. I glanced around the corner making sure the coast was clear. I watched as Detective Bloom left his office heading in the opposite way with a cup of coffee in his hand. I continued stepping slowly toward the open office. I knew I should have gone directly to find Sara, but I wanted to know if Bloom was telling the truth about a witness on the night of Alex's murder.

I slipped into Bloom's office going directly to the case file on his desk. The file was open to my mug shot paper clipped to the case report. I flipped through the file, finding pictures of Alex's distorted body lying alone on the pavement. Other pictures of items around the body were numbered. I couldn't help but choke up seeing the photo of my dead friend. It was grotesque, but I continued to stare unable to avert my eyes until I heard Dunn's voice.

Bloom was standing in the hallway a couple of feet from his office door. Dunn had called his name from down the hall.

"Yeah, I'm coming Drew," Bloom responded and then walked off.

I took that as my queue to hurry. I glanced again at the beginning of the case report to an eyewitness report from a Tim Murphy. He had seen someone walk out of the Cathedral in a hurry following Alex's fall. I didn't have time to finish reading over the report. I scratched Murphy's address down, planning to find the man myself and ask him some questions. I was hoping he wouldn't know who I was. I slipped out of Bloom's office, checking to make sure no one was in the hall.

I realized I had been going the wrong way and double backed

around to the first interrogation room and moved in the opposite direction from where I started. I found the fourth room. Still, I needed to be careful. I leaned against the door expecting to hear voices, but there was only silence. I opened the door slowly, carefully, and peeked in. Sara sat silently in a metal chair reading the back of a pack of matches. She wasn't cuffed, but she was cold, and unable to move. I could tell she was scared, maybe of the thought of going to jail. The detectives were hard on me, but would they really have pressed Sara the same way? Bloom didn't seem like the type to bully a lady. Maybe he'd lay a little pressure on her, but the full-blown treatment?

I whistled as if she was a dame walking in front of a construction site. Sara turned around and a huge grin came to her face when she realized who it was. Tears had been rolling down her cheeks and she tried to wipe them away. I didn't know she had been crying, but I shouldn't have been so surprised. She was about to speak when I put my finger to my mouth to indicate the dire need for silence. Sara took the hint, coming over and embracing me completely instead. She held out the pack of matches, but I didn't care if she wanted to smoke. We didn't have time for that now. We had to get away as soon as possible.

I led her back down the hall, past the interrogation rooms, taking her downstairs. I didn't realize it before, but it was actually rather simple to escape a police station. In the movies, at least one cop would hell, "Hey, they're getting away." But all the police were too busy to care. I told her to act casual and walk slow and steady. If we acted like we knew where we were going we wouldn't attract any attention.

We walked past the desk sergeant, while he did the day's crossword puzzle, which seemed to be more important to him than anything else. At the moment I was thrilled, but also a bit worried that the police were this incompetent. It was scary to think these guys were supposed to protect the city when they didn't even notice a girl and a cripple were busting out. When we got outside I grabbed Sara's arm and urged her to walk faster. She raised the pack of matches once more.

"Sara, I don't have any cigarettes. Can't you wait?" I said as the frustration came through my voice. Through all the drama she started to laugh at me.

"I don't want a smoke," she giggled. "I want you to read what's written on them."

I didn't understand what could be so important about a pack of matches. She was following right behind me as I flipped the matchbook over. I opened the cover and saw a dozen matches, the kind that could be lit on any hard surface. Then I saw what Sara had wanted me to see. I stopped so suddenly that Sara almost walked right into me. Instead she sidestepped and grabbed my arm.

"Keep going," she said, "I think that cop is looking at us."

I noticed a dough-faced police officer walking by. I nodded a friendly hello and he mimicked my camaraderie with the same. It was just a beat cop, no reason to worry yet. He wouldn't know anything was wrong until he went back to the station at the end of his shift. I looked down at the matches once again to look at the words on the cover. In black cursive letters, *Schenley Park Hotel* was written over a metallic silver background.

I looked back at Sara. "Please tell me you got these the last time you were there," I said to her slowly.

"One of the detectives was using them," Sara said.

"Which one?" I asked, but already knew which one had been smoking in the interrogation rooms.

"Detective Bloom," Sara responded.

He could have taken them at the crime scene. The detective was a smoker after all and would be looking for matches all the time. Maybe the matches were older than just a few days. He was a homicide detective, after all. A hotel that big could have multiple deaths or incidents a year.

We walked for several more blocks before I saw an available cab. I raised my hand signaling the driver across the street. As quickly as I lowered my hand, the cabby floored the pedal and pulled out into traffic almost hitting several cars on the way over. Luckily the overzealous taxi driver made it safely without a dent.

The cabby watched his rear view mirror at his new fare, "Where to lady and gent?" He was gruff, unshaven, and held a half-smoked cigar in between his curled lips.

I looked down at the address Dunn gave me. Sara looked over at it and knew exactly where it was. She called out, "The Zoo!" without another pause.

The cabby started the meter and pulled out into traffic at the same frantic speed he used to pick us up. The meter began to tick away as he slowed down, not in such a hurry as before.

"Excited?" I asked.

Sara revealed a childlike smile. "I haven't been to the zoo

since I was a little girl. Might as well walk around before we have to meet him, right?" She asked without taking a breath. A little relaxation might do us good, give us time to clear our heads.

I flipped the matchbook around in my hand. "Maybe the cop picked them up when he was investigating the murder," I said.

"You didn't see the numbers, did you?" Sara asked me in an all-out serious tone.

I shrugged, not sure what she was referring to. I pushed the cardboard away from the matches inside and written in pencil on the inside flap was the number 3125. The numbers were written lightly in pencil, barely visible unless you looked for them. No wonder I missed them before. It was almost too much to comprehend. That was Victor's room number at the hotel.

"There is no way that cop killed Victor," I blurted out. The cabby turned back over his shoulder in surprised confusion.

"Just saw 'High Noon'," Sara quickly said. "He gets all worked up when we talk about it."

The driver shrugged his shoulders, not aware of the film, but didn't care either way. We were silent as we crossed the Highland Park Bridge. The traffic was bad, and it seemed as if every trolley was stopping at every single passenger stop causing traffic on the bridge to slow to a sluggish crawl. We only had a mile until we would arrive at the zoo, but because of the traffic it would take at least ten more minutes.

We had to piece things together. Detective Bloom worked homicide and would have been called to the Schenley Park Hotel. He would have found Victor's body in hotel room 3125.

He could have taken the matches then, but why record the room number? It would be all over his own notes.

Maybe Bloom was working with Keith. He could have left it as a message to point Bloom in the right direction. It would tell him where to go and what room to find the man to kill. It was possible, but was it probable? *Evidence*, Alex would demand. *Where was the evidence?*

We arrived at the zoo and glanced at the meter on the dash. I was amazed at the rise in prices since I got back from the war. It seemed as if inflation was rising faster than normal in the past couple of years. I reluctantly handed the cabby the money and told him to keep the change.

He dropped us off at the zoo's front entrance and then drove away, taking his spot in the queue near the exit. I turned to Sara. I couldn't believe I was even thinking it, but I could tell she was thinking the same thing. I shook my head. A corrupt cop takes a bribe, maybe looks the other way, but a hired gun? This wasn't leading anywhere even remotely good.

I paid the general admission fee, which was three bucks for the two of us. I handed Sara her ticket, and she eagerly yanked it out of my hand. She seemed giddy as we walked into the zoo toward what could only be described as the world's steepest escalator. Being scared of heights, I was not thrilled about the ride up to the actual amusement park.

I wasn't overjoyed that Andrew wanted to meet us at the zoo either, but I let Sara lead us anywhere she wanted to go in the meantime. We had time to walk around before we had to meet the detective at the tiger exhibit. I disliked the whole concept of caged animals. Taking them out of their natural habitat and forcing them to live in captivity seemed downright morbid to me. I didn't want to upset Sara more than I already had so I tried to have a good time regardless of my feelings.

Groups of children were milling about following their teachers, each child holding his or her buddy's hand. How strange it must be for the children to come to the zoo for the first time, expecting to see wild animals they had only read about in textbooks, only to discover the zoo's docile bored creatures.

We came to a twenty by twenty foot mesh enclosure where the zoo's only gorilla was kept. Fake vines were tied to plaster trees to give the space a jungle feel. The animal would never be at home in this enclosure, no matter how close to real life the attraction appeared.

Through the bars I could see the ape's frustration. I could understand his annoyance at being locked up in a tiny space when he really belonged in the open forest, free to climb, swing and hunt. The ape sat in the corner of his cage, head down, and played with his toes. His primary instinct would be suppressed in his man-made habitat.

I tried to compare it to living in a small urban apartment, but couldn't make the connection compellingly enough. I had the option of leaving whenever I wanted, while the gorilla was a real prisoner, held against his will, once a king among animals, now only a sideshow attraction for kids.

I felt uncomfortable watching the spectacle, but Sara didn't seem to think of the cruelty. She didn't see the harm that I did. She didn't understand how people could stare and examine you the way I experienced it. Just as I thought about it, I realized how stupid it sounded in my head. I shook my head smiling at my own stupidity.

Sara turned to me with joy spreading along her face. Of course she understood the way people could stare. She was gorgeous for God's sake. Men were drawn by lust and physical desire constantly to her perfect features. Even women would fawn at Sara with admiration because of how beautiful and intelligent she was. I watched Sara as she watched the ape. It was like a young girl seeing a sunset for the first time. Her eyes obsessed with everything the ape did, longing to understand the animal's thoughts. Sara must have understood the pain it felt being in the zoo, but still could not ignore its beauty.

Those who saw me as a cripple were only projecting their fear of catching the affliction they could never catch. Their fear would never go away as long as they remained ignorant. I think all people shared the same fear of being perceived as useless. People needed a purpose in life. Without a purpose, most people were lost. We understand ourselves through the careers we pursue. We are carpenters, bankers and barbers. We are not like the bums, vagrants and drunks unemployed on the streets. A job or a clear direction in life is our driving force in society. Without it we are truly insignificant.

Sara took my hand in hers. She must have felt my pain, the misery I felt looking into the eyes of a caged animal. She gently squeezed my palm, increasing the pressure of her grip.

Was she crying again? I turned in time to see more tears rolling down her cheeks. I had been wrong. It wasn't my pain that worried her, it was her own. I pulled her in, trying to provide some level of comfort to her, trying to make her feel safe. I did what I could and held her in my arms. I kissed her neck, her cheeks, wherever the tears had fallen. I wanted to draw in her pain, feed on it, until it was gone for good. I laid my open lips onto hers, a gap allowing my tongue to gently touch hers. I held her, wrapped my arms around her body until I was sure she was all right. I peered down into her eyes, and Sara gave me a smile that said she was going to be okay.

When had this friendship turned into something more? Had Sara's own worry turned her attention to a much greater need? My mind raced as I thought Sara couldn't truly want me. We were friends and didn't they say strong friendships make better relationships? I didn't think the proverbial "they" knew what they were talking about. I tried to ignore my own thoughts of self-destruction and focused on the present moment.

"Jamie, sometimes I get the feeling that you are staring at me," Sara said with a grin. I couldn't help it, but I tried to brush it off.

"I have two options here. I could continue to watch the gorilla find his toes, or I can stare at the most beautiful creature in the world standing right next to me." Sara blushed, but grabbed my hand, pressing it into hers. I didn't know what made me say that, but I was glad I did. I knew then that our friendship had completely changed. We were no longer just friends, but something more intimate. I couldn't call her my girl just yet, but I knew that day would probably come soon enough.

We held hands as Sara led the way, while I followed at her

side. The other exhibits weren't as depressing as the gorilla's had been, but that didn't change how I felt about the zoo. I walked for Sara, and only for Sara. I pushed everything else aside, those other feelings would have to wait. Right now, it was Sara and nothing else. We walked around the zoo for the next hour, looking at the animals until we both became bored. We kept moving, knowing that would keep us safe.

When it was time to meet the detective, we made our way over to the tiger exhibit. It was one of the only areas you could actually call a habitat. The tigers had plenty of room to roam around, but still seemed to continuously pace around their enclosure. They were searching for a life they could only remember from when they were cubs in the wild.

Andrew waited for us as he watched the tigers from the habitat's fence. His eyes followed the felines as they continued pacing through their make-believe home. We made our approach, but Sara stopped pulling me with her.

"Can we trust him, Jamie?" Sara whispered in my ear.

He had helped us, but why? I wasn't sure of Dunn's motives, but I didn't feel he was dangerous, certainly not dangerous like Bloom. I nodded my head without saying anything else. I pulled Sara along closing the gap with the detective.

Fake trees surrounded the edges of the habitat on all three sides. There were multiple measures to keep the tigers from getting out of the habitat. At the edge was a stone cliff that gave way to a deep gully extending thirty feet across. A fifteen-foot incline from the cliff to the fence would make it almost impossible for the animals to reach us if they tried. They looked hungry and anyone of us could have satisfied their appetites.

The detective acknowledged us with a nod as we entered his line of sight. I nodded back and Sara slightly waved, aware of the tension but relieved to have someone who could help us.

"Were you followed?" Andrew asked keeping his focus on the animals. He didn't want to draw attention in our direction.

I leaned over the side rail, looked at the tigers and responded, "No" with certainty. We waited in silence watching several of the animals lay down in the sunlight.

"I know you were set up," Dunn explained without any prompting. "That much is obvious," He continued. He didn't waste any time with normal pleasantries. "What I can't figure out is why anyone would go through so much trouble to frame you for murder?"

I told the detective what I knew about the polio vaccine and what Sara and I knew about the pharmaceutical companies. Andrew listened intently as Sara and I told him everything we had discovered. When I finished the story, Sara handed the matchbook to Dunn. He opened the pack and read the inside.

"I took this when Bloom was questioning me," she explained. "We can't prove it, but we think your partner murdered Dr. Wheeling and possibly Alex, too."

"Mind if I hold on to this?" Andrew asked holding the matchbook.

"Sure," Sara replied as Andrew slid the matchbook into his pocket.

"Anything else?" Andrew asked.

"What can we do?" Sara blurted out.

"Not much, unfortunately. They trust Ontario too much. He can go in and out of the laboratory as he pleases. He's been able to infiltrate everyone there. You need to stay away from him."

"So, what do we do now?" I asked.

"Let me take care of stopping Ontario. You two should get out of town for the time being. Stay low until this all blows over."

Sara puffed her chest out, "There's no way we can do that." She looked up at me. "Jamie, we can't . . ."

Those tender blue eyes again. How could I not give her everything she wanted? Anyway, she was right, we had to stay and see this through. There were thousands of children's lives at stake if we failed. Alex had tried to expose everything, but he was murdered. I had to do this for him, if for no other reason.

"We're not going anywhere. I don't care if this guy is working with the Russians, we are going to help you." He wasn't pleased, but what else could he do than deal with it.

"At least do yourself a favor and stay out of sight. Don't stick your nose in anything that could get you killed right now. I'll try and sort this out my way first. It's too dangerous right now to play heroes."

"What about the FBI?" Sara suggested. It was a good idea and one I hadn't even considered yet.

"That's good thinking kid, but I've already flagged them on this."

Dunn left without another word. Sara and I watched as he disappeared over the hill. She seemed somehow braver than before like listening to Dunn had made her realize she wasn't helpless after all. We finally had someone on our side. We weren't alone anymore.

I grabbed her hand, checking to see if her courage was contagious. It wasn't, but I held on just the same. We had to find a place to rest for the night, and either way we looked at it, we needed the journal. Even if we cleared our names, we still wouldn't be able to stop the vaccine from being used. We needed the book for that. It had the evidence to shut the companies down for good.

I didn't want to run away so quickly from the fight. I showed Sara the address I found of the witness Bloom had said could identify me from night Alex was murdered. I wanted to pay the man a visit, try to find some truth in the details. Who had the witness actually seen that night?

"What if he calls the police when we show up on his door step?" Sara asked. It was a chance I was going to have to take.

"We have to take that chance. I have to know what he saw that night."

The man's name was Tim Murphy and his address was only a block away from the Cathedral of Learning. I knew we told Detective Dunn we would stay away for a while, but this was too important to ignore. Sara found the house before I did. It was a thin three-story home attached on both sides.

I began to climb the concrete steps up to the porch, but my cane slipped from under me. Sara caught me by the elbow and helped me up the rest of the way. It was an odd feeling to let someone help me, but I trusted Sara. I began to wonder how far my trust would go.

The front door was open and the screen was stopping insects and other critters from getting inside. I knocked on the screen's wooden frame. The door was painted white against a red brick wall.

A light feminine voice from inside called out, "Be right there."

I turned my attention to the house's exterior. There was a fresh coat of paint on the wood around the porch. The house must have been fifty years old, but looked brand new. Mr. Murphy must have had a sense of pride in his home most people didn't exhibit in the city. A middle-aged woman wearing a floral printed blouse and a long blue skirt came to open the screen. Her hair was curly, but short all around. She looked like Harriet Nelson from "The Adventures of Ozzie and Harriet."

"Yes, can I help you?" Mrs. Murphy asked.

"Ma'am, we are looking for Timothy Murphy."

"I'm Doris, Tim's wife. What is this concerning?"

"Mrs. Murphy, my name is Jamie Schmidt. Your husband witnessed a murder several nights ago and I was wondering if I could ask him some questions."

Doris became uneasy, in fact she looked frantic. Her body began to shake. "Tim told the police everything he knew already. Please just leave us alone. This has all been very hard on Tim."

"Mrs. Murphy, if we could just speak to your husband for several minutes. The man who was murdered was a good friend of mine."

"I don't think Tim . . ."

"Doris let them in!" A husky voice called out from inside the house. "You don't have to treat me like a child." I couldn't see where the voice had come from, but it seemed close by. Doris frowned turning back to the origin of the voice. I could only imagine that the voice belonged to her husband Tim, the sole witness to Alex's murder.

Doris opened the screen to let us in. She was upset with the idea, but waved us inside regardless. Inside a balding middle-aged man was resting in a large sofa chair drinking a can of beer. By his feet was a medium-sized German Shepherd. The dog began to wag its tail as Sara and I came closer.

Sara approached the dog with a small wonder. "May I?" she asked Tim, wanting to pet the dog.

"Her name is Dizzy," Tim smiled. "She's friendly enough. Please." He waved Sara on as she sat down near the dog petting her head and scratching behind her ears.

"We had a Shepherd just like Dizzy when I was a girl. Her name was Mindy. She was about the same size as Dizzy. Not as cute though." Dizzy seemed pleased with the attention and a new smell. "Good girl," Sara continued under her breath.

Tim's attention fell back to me. I took a seat on a couch that matched Doris's floral pattern blouse and made myself comfortable. I laid my cane down so Tim wouldn't be distracted.

"You say you were a friend of the man that fell out of the Cathedral?" Tim asked.

"He was a close friend. His name is . . . was Alex." I explained. I wanted to ask the question that needed to be asked first. "Mr. Murphy, have you ever seen me before?" Tim was quiet for a period of time to digest the question.

"No," Tim finally said, as a huge weight was lifted off my shoulders.

"Who did you see that night Mr. Murphy?" Sara asked moving her attention away from Dizzy.

Tim rubbed at the scruff growing on his face. He hadn't shaved in a few days it seemed. He was worried about something. I've seen the look before. It was fear. Tim was scared, but I wasn't sure what would scare him so much. I wondered if he had gone to work at all in the last two days. He clearly didn't want to answer.

"I'm not able to tell you that, Jamie." He was staring at the dog, but then shifted his attention to my eyes. We made eye contact. I could see the fear now. He was terrified. "I wish I could."

"Did you see who killed Alex?" I asked. Tim shook his head.

"I don't know," He responded. "It didn't matter though, he didn't know that."

"Who didn't know what?" What was he talking about? "Alex didn't know?" I tried to navigate the discussion. He became more fearful by the second. Sara moved from the ground to the couch next to me.

"Not your friend." Tim didn't want to continue, but I moved forward urging him to tell us. "He thought I saw who it was, but I didn't."

I was having trouble following. I was patient, waiting for Tim to finish.

"He said if I told anyone he would kill my wife. He said he would come back and kill us both. He even threatened Dizzy."

Tim looked back down at his dog. "You know what? . . . I believed him."

"Then why would you tell us now?" Sara asked.

"The guilt," Tim explained, "I can't take the guilt any longer."

"Why do you feel guilty, Mr. Murphy?"

"They showed me a picture. They told me to say that the man in the picture was the man I saw that night coming out of the Cathedral. I couldn't do that because I didn't see the man that night. All I saw was his grey fedora and matching coat." Tim started to laugh quietly to himself. "I had wanted that hat."

He turned toward his wife to ask for forgiveness. Doris came over and sat on the arm of the chair Tim was sitting in.

"Go on," she encouraged her husband. Tim held his wife's hand as he continued his story and she bent down and kissed him on his forehead.

"They told me they would kill us if I didn't identify the man that night as the man from the picture." Tim took a deep breath, afraid for his life. "I signed the statement they prepared and did what they wanted." He reached over and took a folded piece of paper from the side table. "The sick part is they made me take the picture so I would always remember."

Tim unfolded the piece of paper, which I realized was the picture he was referring too. "Jamie, it's true that I have never seen you before today."

He handed me the picture, which Sara and I looked at together. It was a photo from several years ago, a picture that Alex had kept hanging in his study. The photo was of me when I had just come back from the war still carrying my duffel bag over my shoulder. He had surprised me as I stepped off the train.

"I'm sorry, son," Tim said. It was a sincere apology, but it didn't help either of us. There was nothing left to say as Doris escorted us out of the house.

We decided to go back to the Hill District. We checked into a place called the Granville Hotel. It was a small three-story dive on a side street off of Wylie Avenue. By the time we arrived in the neighborhood, the Hill was already jumping with energy. Men in freshly pressed suits were strolling around, their dates in tow, going to clubs for their nightly fix of music and liquor. Bright-colored suits with big floppy hats engulfed the men, while the younger women wore sequenced dresses. They all had great style and knew how to have fun.

We checked into the hotel as a married couple named Mr. and Mrs. Stone in town to visit friends. The older man at the front desk didn't care who the hell we were, just as long as we paid with cold hard cash. I wondered how many shady characters and known criminals had checked in under the same conditions we had. Using false names and identities right from the beginning made a terrific first impression. How many did the old man call the police on? I had a feeling he didn't unless they caused enough trouble.

The man from the front desk showed us to our room, which turned out to be much smaller than Victor's room at the Hotel Schenley. The room was plain looking, nothing fancy, but came with a deluxe-sized bed so I couldn't complain. There was a shared bathroom down the hall, which every key in the hotel would open. We were told to make sure the deadbolt was on from inside when we went in. We were given a set of towels for the shower and then were left alone.

Sara sat on the bed, which was much larger than hers at home. I looked around, but didn't see a couch to sleep on. Sara blushed and patted the bed.

I sat beside her and leaned in for a kiss, brushing my lips against hers. I tried to push her back onto the bed, but a piece of paper fell out of my pocket and onto the floor. I wasn't worried about it, but Sara picked it up and unfolded it.

"What's this?" she asked.

I completely forgot about the piece of paper I had stolen from Keith's office. The cops hadn't noticed it was in my pockets when they frisked me either. She handed me the note, a small piece of paper with the name and a long-distance 202 area code number of someone named Scheele scratched onto it. She said the name Scheele silently to herself. The name didn't ring a bell for me, but maybe Sara would have some luck. She looked up at me, staring into my eyes with her radiant blues.

"Do you have any change?" I asked her.

She reached into her bag and pulled out several dimes and nickels. A pay phone hung on the wall near the bathroom. I slipped in a dime, dialed the number, and then waited for the operator.

"Please deposit fifteen more cents for your call to Washington, D.C.," the operator said.

"It's a number for Washington D,C.," I whispered to Sara.

I added the money and listened as the phone rang at the other end.

A female voice on the other end picked up the line. "Surgeon General Scheele's office. How can I help you?" I hung the phone up.

"Surgeon General Scheele?" I questioned Sara.

"Don't you ever read the paper Jamie?" She laughed as she walked down the hall to the room. "Why would the Surgeon General make a call to Ontario, it doesn't make any sense."

"A lot of calls, actually," I corrected her and explained that I had found a stack of messages from the same man in Keith's office. "Does that mean the Surgeon General is in on the conspiracy?" I asked in jest.

"Let's forget about the spy angle for a moment, Senator McCarthy."

"Touché," I replied.

"Let's assume Ontario wasn't working for Cutter. It's not that he was needed to watch Salk's research. The head of the Department of Health, Oveta Culp Hobby, would be doing that, making sure the vaccine was progressing smoothly. Hobby already had a direct link to Salk, so why send Keith at all. They didn't need an extra liaison to the government. That would be too sloppy."

"I'm not following, Sara."

"From reading the journal I gathered that Hobby was overseeing the manufacturing of the vaccine and gave out the licenses herself. The Surgeon General had to approve the vaccine and the overall procedures of how it was made commercially, but wouldn't have any power over the financials. That was also Hobby's job. Ontario would only be watching Salk because Scheele wanted him to watch him.

If Ontario directly answers to the Surgeon General, it's not about Salk's vaccine, but the companies making it. Scheele must not trust Hobby's office. Ontario must have been around because Scheele knew about the problems the drug companies were having all along."

"Ontario did try to kill us in a church," I added.

"I'm not defending him, but he did want the journal remember? Maybe he thought we were a threat?"

"So if the vaccine wasn't safe for mass production and the pharmaceuticals wouldn't report any problems to Hobby . . ."

"Not to Hobby's office," Sara corrected me. "Hobby must have known already. No one wanted to tell Scheele what they knew. Hobby included."

"Scheele discovers the problem, but it's too late," I continued, "He doesn't want to tell Congress to withdraw the vaccine because then he'd look like a fool who couldn't control his own department."

Sara took over. "He has too much at stake now. He approved Hobby's decision when she gave out the licenses. It all makes sense. All five companies, Cutter, Parke-Davis, Wyeth, Eli Lilly, and Pitman Moore all knew they were going to get the licenses even before it was announced. It never mattered about the safety procedures. Even after Salk wrote his report, they didn't care. It was all back office deals."

"It only took one day for each company to ship the vaccine

after they were given the licenses. They only could have had that large of a supply if they already knew what was going to happen. They all knew they were getting their own license. Hobby must have told them in advance."

"But what about Bloom?" I interjected. "Where does he fit in?"

Sara paused, "Maybe Bloom was taking money from Cutter or even Parke-Davis. They could have hired him to cover up their mess."

It was possible Bloom was setting me up and threatening Tim, his only witness, to do it. Regardless of who wanted us dead and was working with whom, we needed to get the journal back. If Sara were right it would be our only leverage.

"We could try Dunn again," I suggested.

Andrew helped us escape. He didn't have to, but he did. I trusted him for that. It could cost him much more than his job if anyone found out about what he did. We couldn't just walk into the police station and ask him to help us. It was possible he wouldn't ever stick his neck out again to help us. Stealing evidence wasn't something I thought a police officer would do. Although, I didn't think a police officer would have helped us in the first place, but he did.

Sara agreed. We needed to at least try. If Andrew said no, then we would have to start over. Either way, it wouldn't hurt.

I left Sara in the room and went down to a phone booth on the corner. She wanted to come with me, but I wouldn't let her. I didn't think it would be a good idea for both of us to go together.

Just in case the police were looking for us. I wanted to stay away from the hotel phone in case they were able to trace the call.

I tried not to walk with a limp, but overcompensating made it more pronounced. I abandoned the idea all together and decided to take my time instead. Being the only white guy on the street pretty much gave me away in the first place, but I had to make the phone call. It was too important not to.

I passed several well-dressed men as I got closer to the phone booth. I had to wait while one of their friends finished a call. He stormed out of the booth, slammed the glass open and rejoined his buddies.

"Can't believe that woman, man. Always riding me for some . . ." I entered the booth, closed the glass door behind me and the man's voice died off. I dialed the police station and asked for Detective Dunn. A moment later I was connected to a familiar voice.

"Detective Bloom, how can I help you?" said the voice on the other end of the phone.

I wasn't prepared to hear from Dunn's partner. I wasn't sure what to do next. I stayed on the phone but didn't answer. I must have sounded like a pervert as I breathed heavily into the phone.

"Hello?" Bloom asked. "I know you're there fella. I can hear ya' on the line."

"I'm looking for Detective Dunn, please," I said. I didn't know why I couldn't hang up. I wanted to, but it was too late, I'd made contact and couldn't back out now. I could faintly hear a police siren in the background. Maybe it was just paranoia. Bloom made me nervous.

"He's not here, but I'm his partner, Detective Lawrence Bloom. Maybe I could help? What seems to be the problem?"

"Ahhh . . ." I needed to hang up, why couldn't I hang up? "I'll just call back when . . ."

"Say, you sound familiar . . ." There was pause, but he knew. He was a detective after all. "Mr. Schmidt, is that you?"

I didn't want to say anything. I didn't want to let him know he was right, but what the hell, maybe he could help me after all. I took a deep breath and covered the phone clearing my throat.

"Yeah, Larry, It's me."

"We've been wondering where you went to."

"Sorry I had to leave so soon. I had another engagement I thought was more important. I wish I could have stayed longer, maybe we could have grabbed a malt, a piece of pie perhaps." I couldn't help myself. Something about Bloom's voice made me want to taunt him even more.

I thought the siren was becoming louder. Was I imagining things or was a siren getting closer? It wasn't my imagination. It was actually getting closer by the second. I don't know how they found us. Police sirens echoed from below the Hill as the cruisers approached.

"Whoops, the operator is telling me to pony up another dime, but I'm fresh out, well got to go. Say hi to the wife and kids, Detective Bloomy."

Shit. How did they find us? There was no way the old guy back at the hotel ratted us out. I could tell we weren't the only ones on the run staying at the Granville. I was pretty sure I saw some hookers and a pimp in the lobby.

There was no way Bloom could have known where we were that fast either. I forced the phone away from my ear and slammed it back onto the cradle. I slammed the doors open as I left the booth. I didn't know what was going on, which was a feeling I was beginning to get used to. I tried to hobble back to the hotel, but two police cars flew right past me, going toward the hotel, sirens blaring.

There was still a chance they weren't coming for us. They could just keep going, never stopping at the hotel. They could be after someone else. What were the chances of that, I wondered. Either way, Sara was still in the room, but I wouldn't be able to warn her in time.

The cars burned rubber screeching to a halt in front of the Granville Hotel. The loud sirens switched off and an eerie silence filled the air. My worst fear just materialized in front of my eyes. Someone sold us out and Sara was all alone in the room. They would arrest her and take her into custody with or without me. I was supposed to protect her. That was my job. I should have never dragged her into this in the first place.

I watched in horror, as four uniformed cops piled out, two from each cop car. There was a quick discussion between them, and then two went into the building drawing their guns on the way in. Another officer went down a side alley next to the hotel leaving the single remaining cop by himself in front.

I stopped behind the corner store, peaking around it. I watched the scene unfold completely cut off without any power to help

Sara. I could only hope that they were there for someone else. My mind considered the possibility, but my gut knew better.

A moment later I watched Sara run out of the hotel, colliding with the officer standing in the front. He immediately caught her. She tried struggling violently to get away, but there was no use. The other two cops came out of the hotel ready for a fight. A second later, the forth officer came scurrying out of the alley and met the other three.

Four grown men against one small woman wasn't much of a fair fight. Sara was putting up a great effort for such a petite girl, but was still no match for any one of the cops. They finally detained Sara and easily set her in the back of one of the police cruisers.

The scene dismantled just as fast as it materialized. The police cruisers pulled out one by one, while I looked on helplessly. The cars rode past the corner shop turning back onto Wylie Street. Sara stared out the back window as the cars went past. Our eyes made contact and I realized I had just ruined Sara's life. They would charge her with conspiracy to commit murder. They would throw her in jail, leaving her there to rot for life.

I couldn't keep quiet any longer, my voice shot out but the sirens drowned it out. I started to run towards the police cruisers, reaching for Sara, but she did something unexpected . . . she smiled. I stopped suddenly as her face became smaller and less clear as the cruisers began their decent off the Hill. I stood still until the cars completely disappeared from view.

I played the scenario over in my head. I could turn myself in. Tell them Sara had nothing to do with it. I could take the rap for everything. That wouldn't work though, would it? If I turned myself in, they would still find a way to ruin both our lives. Then Alex's death would be in vain. The other option was to break into the evidence room and take the journal myself. They would have to let Sara go if I figured out who really killed Alex . . . .

She was smiling. Did I miss something? Why would Sara be happy about being arrested? It occurred to me that no one knew we were at the hotel. We hadn't even told Dunn where we were staying. Could Sara have called the cops, tipping them off to where we were? Did she call them intending to get caught while I wasn't there? I ran back up to the room and looked around for anything she might have left for me.

I searched for anything, something that would tell me what Sara was thinking, but she hadn't left anything behind. Was I imagining it, had her smile been a figment of my imagination? I sat on the edge of the bed and slowly slid down landing on the floor. The door was still open and directly down the hall I could see the bathroom sink. I pulled myself back up onto the bed and pushed off onto my feet. I was a little wobbly at first, but was able to obtain my bearings soon enough.

I left the room and made my way down the hall. As I walked closer to the bathroom, the mirror above the sink appeared to be covered with red. At first I thought someone had flung blood onto the mirror, but realized what it really was. I had to give Sara credit for being resourceful. Written fast in bright red lipstick on the bathroom mirror were the words, *You would have said no.*

It wasn't subtle, but it wasn't supposed to be. She knew the cops wouldn't have bothered looking for it. Sara must have called them from the hall phone when I left. When I spoke to Bloom he already knew his men were on their way, but probably didn't have any idea who phoned in the tip.

I hated the idea. She was right about one thing. I wouldn't have let her do it. Turning herself in to get what we needed was too risky. We would have come up with some other way, but now it was too late. The plan was already set in motion. Unfortunately, Sara thought this all out on her own without telling me. I was by myself for the next step of the plan, but didn't know what it was. The whole police force would be looking for me now. I had to think of something, and fast. Besides that, I needed to find a phonebook.

Chapter 9

Pittsburgh was a much smaller city as compared to cities like Chicago or even Cleveland. We had mass public transportation, but nothing on the scale of the other metropolitan cities. Yet, our own system was in a league of its own. Pittsburgh had a small, yet complicated, trolley system. Once you figured out the basics of the trolley lines, finding what you needed around the city was a breeze. Even better, if you knew someone at City Hall, it was only a matter of time before you had your own private trolley stop directly in front of your front door. I wasn't that lucky yet.

I jumped a trolley near the hotel and after riding around a bit, I found Dunn's house easily enough. It was a two-story townhome in the South Side. Most of the houses around the city were set up the same way, a small parking pad in the back, and the illusion of a yard in front. The plot of land was typically twenty-five feet across, fifty feet deep, and the homes always looked smaller on the outside than they did on the inside. Anyone would be lucky to have a patch of grass in the front. The front lawns were big enough to plant some flowers or maybe a small shrub. Forget having one in the back, because the odds were your backyard was someone else's house.

Detective Dunn's home appeared to be neglected. Green paint had started to peel along the porch, while the white trim riding the exterior had turned grey with dirt. The neighborhood was calm and quiet. The street lights were lit every hundred feet, and only the occasional car drove by.

The lights were off in the house, and I knew he would be sleeping. I knocked on the front door beating my hand loud enough to wake the deepest sleeper. Moments later a light turned on. Dunn, wearing wrinkled slacks and a white undershirt, slowly came down the stairs. Half of the man's hair was plastered against the side of his head, while the other half was sticking straight up.

He leaned into the door looking through the peephole. A moment later I heard several latches being unlocked, and then the door slowly opened. Dunn motioned for me to come inside closing the door behind.

"Jamie, what the hell are you doing?" he asked, rubbing his eyes and fumbling around the table to find his smokes. "It's . . ." He picked his arm up checking the watch on his wrist. "It's almost two." He took a drag and let out a long grey cloud of toxic fumes. I didn't care if doctors said cigarettes were all right for you. They smelled like shit.

"I didn't have any other choice," I told him.

I sat down on an oversized chair, which in the dark appeared auburn or red. Clutter covered the coffee table. Beside an ashtray overflowing with burnt cigarette butts, a silver paper weight rested fittingly on the table. To the right was Dunn's pistol secured in its holster. For a police officer, Andrew did pretty well for himself. I looked around the front room. A large sound system was up against the wall. A bookshelf was lined with LPs, and four two-foot speakers were spread out around the room, giving a 360 degree surround sound. Behind my chair was a fireplace containing dried wooden logs. I wasn't sure if it was fake or the real thing. Dunn was trying to follow my gaze as he continued to smoke.

"It's real," Dunn said reading my mind. I realized a set of fireplace tools sat beside the fireplace. A stoker, a shovel, and a brush all made from black iron. I wanted to feel the coolness of the iron against my hand, but had more pressing concerns.

"I need your help again," I said, making each syllable clear and precise.

"I already gathered that from your surprise visit. Ever hear of a phone?" It was a rhetorical question, of course. Dunn leaned back, kicking his legs up on the table. "I figured if you found my address you could find my phone number."

I sat back trying to mimic his composure and shrugged my shoulders. A wave of exhaustion poured over me. I wanted to shut my eyes and fall asleep. I stared out into space and lost my train of thought. I blinked my eyes open and felt like I was looking at Dunn for the first time.

He leaned forward reaching for the ashtray and stubbed his smoke out at its filter. I thought he was contemplating the dilemma at hand, but I didn't know which conclusion he would arrive at. Dunn's wheels were turning, that much I was sure of. He pulled another smoke from his pack and took the silver lighter from the table.

I didn't want to waste any more valuable time so I jumped right in. "I have a plan, but I'm going to need a favor." I leaned forward. "Do you have access to the station's evidence room?"

Dunn took another drag from his newly lit smoke. He nodded yes.

"It's hard to believe," I continued to say. I began to tell him about Cutter. I explained about the Department of Health. I explained how the Surgeon General was using Ontario to cover everything up from the inside. Above all, I told him how Alex's journal had enough evidence in it to blow the lid off the whole damned conspiracy. I didn't know if he believed me. I didn't have time if he didn't. I just had to get the journal back before it was too late.

After I finished, Dunn sat back taking a long draw from his smoke. I looked back at the silver object on the table. It was familiar and I realized what it was. It was a small silver elephant. The same lighter I had brought back for Alex after the war. It was odd that he would have the same one. Unless it was Alex's lighter. Had Dunn taken it from Alex's office?

"Detective, did you serve in Korea?" I asked. I didn't want to offend him, so I couldn't come out and ask Dunn if he stole it.

"Too old for Korea, too young for World War II." Dunn shook his head. "Hell, I haven't even been out of the country before."

"That's an interesting lighter," I commented. "Where is it from?"

Dunn took a glance at the lighter on his coffee table across from where I was sitting. He shook his head, unable to come up with a lie. I felt a surge of distrust sweep across my face. Dunn noticed my reaction right away, but it was too late. I had been wrong about who the corrupt detective was. I had found the real killer. He was sitting in the same room with me and he knew his identity had just been compromised.

I stood up to leave. "You know, it's late. I'm asking too much here." I moved towards the door. "I'll just let myself out."

"Sit down, Jamie," Dunn commanded as he pulled his gun out of its holster extending it in my direction.

"Sorry to wake you," I said not letting the gun into my consciousness.

"Cut the crap and sit your ass down!" Andrew yelled with venom in his voice. I sat down staring down the barrel of his pistol. Even if I tried to get the gun away, there was a chance he'd get a shot off. I had to play this cool. I just needed him to get closer. He would be close enough for me to hook his leg and get him off center. Instead of moving toward me, he leaned back on the couch, as if we were having a friendly conversation.

"I completely forgot about that damn thing. I guess I need to thank you," Dunn said with an evil grin.

"For what?" I asked, knowing full well what I had given him. Information was the key, and I had just shown my hand to the enemy. I had told him everything he needed to know.

"All this time we didn't know what we were looking for and here you come and just give us everything we need."

"Did you kill Alex?" I needed to know the truth.

Dunn nodded his head in confirmation. "I did. Setting you up was an afterthought. You should have seen your face when the hotel maid found you."

"You were still in the room?" I asked.

"It was perfect, don't you think?"

"Doesn't it bother you, knowing how dirty you are?" I asked hoping to get Dunn to do something stupid. If I could get him to let down his guard there was a chance I could use it to my advantage. Instead he just smiled, not the least bit phased by my question. He just sat there puffing away on his little white smokes. If I was going to live through the next ten minutes I had to think of something fast. Dunn's conscience didn't seem to be fazed. How about the loyalty card?

"Who's paying you? The Russians? You finally get tired of democracy? How much are they paying you? Hope it was worth it."

"I'm not a stinking commie," Dunn said as he cocked the gun's hammer. "I'm a patriot!" There was the button I was looking for. Calling someone a communist was like telling a guy his mother was a bitch. It was low, but it was guaranteed to hit a nerve. Dunn walked over, placing the barrel of his gun against my temple.

"I'm doing this for my country!" He added.

"It might be a little suspicious if they find a dead man in your house, Detective."

"Oh, I don't think anyone will care. You broke in and tried to kill me after all. A suspected murderer already, I bet they won't even give it a second thought."

My eyes peered to the side as I stared at the gun. His index finger began to pull the lever back, setting pressure down against the trigger. It was now or never. I cautiously reached back and slowly grabbed hold of the fireplace stoker by my side. I made sure I was continuing to stare directly into Dunn's eyes. He was insulted and wanted to prove himself once and for all. I didn't want him to see it coming. I still needed the element of surprise.

With a snap, I whipped the metal rod out against the side of his leg. The sound of cracking bone filled the room. His arms swung wide and the gun fired, blowing a chunk of high fidelity off the stereo. Dunn buckled sideways toppling over the coffee table, breaking the table down the middle. His gun slid out of his grasp sliding past the living room into the kitchen. His body cleared the table, landing hard against the wood floor causing the entire room to shake around us. Dunn grabbed his knee in shear agony. His badge fell out from his pocket, which gave me an idea.

I raised the stoker over my head and chopped it down on Dunn chest, knocking the breath right out of him. He went rigid gasping for air. He would be able to breathe after the initial shock subsided, but the pain would last much longer. If I broke his ribs all the better. I bent down jabbing the handle of the stoker against his temple. Dunn's body went limp. He wouldn't be a problem until he woke up long after I was gone.

I took his badge off the floor and hobbled into the kitchen looking for his gun. After what seemed like an eternity, I found the firearm under the oven and tucked it into my waistband. I wanted to stay longer and continue to beat Dunn within inches of his life, but I knew revenge wouldn't help my mood. I really needed justice after all, not a cold-blooded kill.

I swiped Dunn's car keys from the foyer near the front door. Looking down at them on my way out, I noticed the Chrysler emblem on the bigger of the two. I stepped outside and found a brand new 1954 white Chrysler Windsor parked by the curb in front of the house. I hadn't driven a car in years, but my learning curve would have to be short and quick. The car was long in front, ending in large owl-like headlights. The rims on the wheels matched the white paint job. Even in the moonlight the chrome shown like it was midday.

The engine turned over on the first try and I slipped the clutch into drive, lurching forward. I rolled forward hitting a blue Ford truck in front of me. I slammed on the brakes and the car instantly stopped throwing me into the steering wheel. I put the car in reverse and rolled backwards and bumped into a black sedan behind me. I couldn't see the make of it, but it looked expensive.

This time I put the car into drive and turned the wheel hard to the left as far as it would go. I pulled out of the space without another problem, finally getting the car in motion down the road. Cars seemed to be getting bigger, flashier, and less drivable with each new model.

I was betting Dunn wouldn't call about the stolen car, but I wasn't going to speed around inviting the police to pull me over. Besides, I had enough trouble getting the car to go where I wanted it to in the first place. My learning curve was becoming an impediment as I swerved the car back and forth, trying to get in under control. As long as I didn't get into a car chase with the automobile I was going to be fine.

A foul burning smell came from somewhere in the car, stinging my nostrils with a horrid tarry scent. I looked around and saw a small brake rod pulled up. Without thinking, I flipped it down and the car suddenly became easier to drive and several moments later the burning smell disappeared altogether. I wondered why anyone would bother putting an emergency brake on a car if wasn't going to work anyway.

Even with all the adrenalin pumping through my veins, I was getting bored driving around. I flipped the radio on playing around with the knobs until I found something that was appealing. The Chordettes doing "Mr. Sandman" came on like a big can of square. I needed something a little faster for cruising around in a stolen car. I turned the knob once more and hit exactly what I was looking for. Bill Haley and His Comets' "Rock Around the Clock" pushed a rhythm and beat I could relate too. I tapped my hands against the steering wheel as Haley counted the time and danced all night long.

I slowed down and lowered the volume on the stereo as I

approached the police station. I didn't want to draw any attention, so I parked the car a block away. If Dunn did call the car in as stolen, the last place anyone would look would be outside the police station.

The building was almost deserted except for the desk sergeant, who was once again doing a crossword puzzle. I was pretty sure it was the same puzzle he had been doing earlier in the day. I knew he wouldn't recognize me, but I didn't want to make eye contact just the same. I pretended I belonged there and walked into the station. I flashed Dunn's badge as I grabbed random papers off a side desk, reading them intently as I walked past the officer.

"Hey buddy!" the desk sergeant called out in my direction.

I stopped in mid-stride ready to bolt at the first sign of trouble. He didn't get up, but was still looking down at the newspaper in front of him.

"What's a four letter word for *Secret Jargon?*"

I thought about the clue for an instant and answered, "Code."

"Thanks bucko." The officer wrote in the letters pleased as he went onto the next clue. I continued my trek, turning back toward the officer, making sure he wasn't just pulling my leg. I could imagine two bullets tearing me down once I turned away, but luckily nothing happened. He truly didn't care about me one way or the other.

The station was quiet. I didn't know if anyone was left at the precinct. The desk jockey could have been the only one left, waiting for emergencies this late at night. I slowly walked with the soft illumination from the overhead lights setting dark shadows around me. All the office doors were shut, the lights off. Only one door was cracked open. I moved towards it, wondering who would be working late on a night like this. The journal would be kept in the evidence room in a box labeled with the name and case number of the investigation. I had read enough pulp mysteries to know how it worked. In a small station like the one I was in I doubted the evidence room was even ever locked.

I peaked inside an opened door realizing it was the same I had snuck into earlier in the day. To my astonishment, the workaholic was Detective Bloom. He sat over his desk filling out paperwork. His attention was focused on the stack of papers he had been catching up on. It was only a matter of time before . . . *RING, RING.* Right on cue. Bloom picked up the phone and answered.

"Drew, . . . yeah, I'm here. He what? He did? Why do you . . . ? A hunch! Well, your hunch better be right. Why would he be here, we've moved the girl downtown. Yeah, all the evidence too."

Downtown! They moved Sara and the journal downtown? I was wasting too much time snooping around. I needed to get downtown as fast as humanly possible. I turned as quickly as I could, hitting my shoulder against the door jam. I had always been a klutz, especially at those rare times when I needed to be sneaky. In the army, I was not the first choice to go on a stealth mission.

Bloom looked up from his desk making eye contact with me as soon as he did. There was a pause and time stood still. He was surprised to see me, speechless, unable to move. I didn't feel quite the same way. He held the phone, powerless to let it go.

"Is this remedial English?" I asked before deciding to hightail it out of there. I pulled the door closed taking a chair and jamming it under the knob. It stuck, making an instant lock. I trapped Bloom, making sure he couldn't get out of his office. With him out of the way, I could focus on getting to Sara.

I limped away, grabbing the wall for support. I found my way to the lobby and realized someone else was at the front with the desk sergeant. It was a beat cop. He was questioning the old officer at his desk about the night. I turned back around with the intention of escaping through the back. As I tiptoed away, the chair against Bloom's door fell in, and the door opened into the office. Just my luck, I should have known the door didn't open out. My plan was backfiring faster than I could handle. I saw Bloom's shadow come through the door before he did. I tiptoed back to the front of the station, hoping the beat cop had left.

He was still there talking with the sergeant. Behind me, Detective Bloom came around the corner. "Jamie, give yourself up!" he yelled drawing the other cops' attention.

Without hesitation, the beat cop pulled his side arm and yelled, "Freeze!" I didn't stop and he opened fire before I even had the time to react. The first bullet missed and exploded against the sheetrock behind me with a burst of white powder. I dove behind the closest desk I saw. The older police officer looked up from his crossword puzzle with more annoyance than surprise. He clearly didn't want to get involved in a shootout.

The beat cop came around the desk as I was crawling to the

front. The sergeant got up from the desk, upset at the interruption from his puzzle. He made a grunting noise and walked back into the hall. He didn't seem to be any help with regard to the safety of my life. Detective Bloom came running down the hall, passing the sergeant, yelling obscenities. There was little I could do while cops cut me off from the two exiting options I had.

If I was going to make it, I needed to regain my advantage. As I thought about it I realized I hadn't had an advantage in the first place. Hell, I only had a delusion of one. With that thought in mind, I felt better about my chances. If I stayed where I was the beat cop would kill me on sight. If I went toward Bloom, he wouldn't shoot to kill, but he would shoot to wound, which I wasn't too keen on either.

I decided to go with a more extreme option. I needed a hostage. I could walk right out the door, making sure neither cop would follow. I didn't have a gun, but was trained in close combat, which had begun to surface from the depths of my memory. The detective was too far away, which would be no use for hand-to-hand fighting. The beat cop was my best bet as he inched closer to my position.

I thought the hell with it as he came around the corner. I swept my leg clear out at his ankles catching the right one dead on. He tried to bring his gun around but lost his balance, collapsing under his own weight.

Bloom came around ready with his own firearm pointing down at me, but I was too fast and had the beat cop's small revolver pressed against his head. It wasn't personal and I hated getting the officer involved, but he had been in the wrong place at the wrong time. I felt the tide turn in my favor as the detective lowered his gun and dropped it at his side.

"Mr. Schmidt, you're just making this worse for yourself."

He was worried. I could hear it in his voice. Unlike Dunn, I think deep down Bloom cared about human life. Sure, he might have taken a bribe once or twice. Maybe looked the other way on certain sensitive occasions, but when a human being's life was at stake he valued it like the good cop he should. I had been wrong about Detective Bloom. I had thought him to be the evil corrupt police officer, but now I knew better.

I pulled the beat cop up on his feet as I covered him with the gun. I knew I wouldn't be able to actually shoot the man, but I wasn't going to let either one of them know that. The detective knew my life. He had access to my army record. I had confirmed kills, not that I was proud of them, but they were there. They wouldn't underestimate what I was capable of. Well, capable of on paper that is.

"I'm just going to walk out of here with . . . .," I checked the officer's name tag, " . . . Officer Collins. I'm also going to have to ask you not to follow me, okay?" I had to sound desperate, but it came out as a little sheepish. I made a mental note to work on my tough guy voice. I needed to make Bloom think I really would pull the trigger. I just hoped my voice wouldn't give me away. If this didn't work I was toast. I pulled Collins with me as I backed out the lobby.

Bloom started to follow us out, so I had to put on a show. I had to make sure he knew I meant business. I pushed the gun into the back of the beat cop's head, a little worried about the pain it would cause.

"What did I just say copper?" I shouted out like a Jersey mobster. The cop jerked his head forward from the pressure of the gun. I withdrew some of the pressure, feeling sorry for the guy. Bloom got the hint and at last backed off. I knew he wouldn't jeopardize another officer's life. I knew I had taken the right hostage. I had no idea how the beat cop would have reacted if their roles were reversed.

I pushed the door open pulling Collins out with me. I wasn't sure what I was going to do with him. I contemplated taking him with me, but he would probably be much more trouble than I could handle. He helped me make my decision much more quickly when he tried to pull away when we were outside.

"You just signed your own death warrant, you know that? When I find you, I'm going to make you beg!" Collins yelled.

The pain in my leg was excruciating and every step made it worse.

I took the butt of his gun and brought it crashing down on the back of Collins' head without any warning. Like a rag doll, the cop collapsed. I felt terrible about hitting him, but I didn't have another choice. I was hoping Collins wouldn't wake up with a concussion. In the back of my mind, I wanted to go back to Dunn's and put a bullet in his head for killing Alex. When I thought about Alex, I wanted to do it, but didn't think I could with a clear conscious. I did worse in Korea of course, but that was war.

What did I think this was? I paused for a split second. It was not war by any means and I could not let revenge get in the way of helping Sara. If I acted out in cold blood I could forget about clearing either of our names.

I wouldn't try to kill Dunn, but that didn't stop me from thinking about how I could do it. I stepped over Collins and almost lost my balance, righting myself against the railing instead of falling on top of him. I shuffled away toward Dunn's car. I had a plan, well half a plan anyway. I couldn't trust the cops. I couldn't trust anyone really, except Sara. I needed to go downtown and get the journal. I wasn't sure where I would go from there. Going straight to the press with the book might work.

I cruised in front of the station, watching Bloom try to open the door, pushing it against the cop's limp body. It took several failed attempts before he realized that Collins was blocking the way.

I raced the Windsor down Fifth Avenue, pulling up in front of the county court house. I left the car at the yellow line, disregarding the law. I needed a new mode of transportation after this and wasn't worried about the car being impounded. By the time they even started to look for Dunn's car I would be long gone. Hopefully, it would be towed way before anyone figured out who owned it. I'd be happy with anything that would make Dunn's life that much more miserable.

I pulled up in front of the Allegheny Courthouse. The courthouse was a successful attempt at recreating the original Fort Pitt in downtown Pittsburgh. In the middle 1700s, Fort Pitt was a central headquarters for the British troops, while they defended the region against the French. Soon after the British took complete control of the area, the city of Pittsburgh slowly took root around the fort where the Ohio, Allegheny, and Monongahela Rivers all joined together to form the Point, a small triangular land mass now housing an urban park and large water fountain.

The stone monstrosity wasn't a prison for long-term inmates, but it still housed hardened criminals. They would stay until they were moved to a permanent facility. The judges' chambers occupied one side of the complex and were surrounded by the representing lawyer's offices. Trials, arraignments and dispositions would take place in the many courtrooms spread throughout the complex's wing.

The actual jail was on the opposite side of the complex. A foot bridge connected the two wings over the streets oncoming traffic. It was a perfect marriage of crime and punishment. The guilty were simply escorted to the other side of the brown-walled fortress to be incarcerated. Individuals could rot in jail for months or years until they were completely processed through the system and said to have time served if their crime didn't outweigh their often long stay.

I walked in through the side gates where a guard waited to pat me down. I pulled the badge from my pocket when he found the gun hiding at my waist line. He waved me through without a fuss. I limped my way through the lobby, where round red marble pillars sat under larger beige stones. I'd only been in the courthouse once before, and that was as an elementary student years ago. I knew Sara would be kept in a general holding cell near the bottom, at least for the next couple of days. The judicial system was slow, and Pittsburgh's was no exception to the rule.

Sara would be fine for the night, but I would need to help get her out as soon as possible. I wasn't planning on breaking her out, but I needed to get word to her about Dunn.

I climbed the first flight of stairs, and then a second. Lucky for me no one was around. It was too late, but also too early for anyone to be at work yet. I was betting on there being several more cops further down near the holding cells, but I wouldn't be worried about running into anyone on this side of the complex.

As I stepped up on to the landing, my leg decided to buckle giving out from under me. I grabbed the marble railing to keep from falling down the stairs. I needed to slow down, but if I didn't hurry two men would have lost their lives for nothing. On top of that, the love of my life would end up in prison for a crime she didn't commit. Old wounds that hadn't completely healed were being torn back open. The events of the last couple of days have been forcing me to reevaluate my entire life. I had to get under control. My head began to spin and a wave of nausea crept up from my stomach into my chest.

I paused to brace myself. I closed my eyes, taking deep breaths. After I was sure I wouldn't make a mess, I took an assessment of my appendages. I wanted to make sure my leg wouldn't completely fail me again when I needed to make a quick getaway. After I was sure I wouldn't fall for a second time, I continued in search of the evidence room.

Large windows looked out over a courtyard in the middle of the five-story complex. On a warm sunny day the courtyard would make a great place to sit and relax, taking in a good book.

Light wooden benches lined a paved walkway surrounded by greenery.

The evidence room wasn't on the second floor, so I climbed another flight of stairs continuing my search. I was relieved to discover the room directly across from the main staircase I had just climbed. Sleeping behind a wide metal cage was an aging police officer alone in an office chair. I limped closer to get a better look at the cop behind the chain link. I gazed through a small rectangular opening cut into the cage. A small lamp provided enough illumination to examine the sleeping officer. His face was etched with wrinkles and his skin had an elastic quality to it. The hair on his head was all salt, but no hint of pepper in sight. Most likely he had been a cop longer than I had been alive. I thought the man's age could be the reason he was given such a low position after so many years on the force. The officer's head seemed to hang lower than his shoulders. His chest raised and then lowered with every deep breath he took. Judging by the volume of his snoring, he had been asleep a long time. I poked my head through the hole, checking out how I would get in.

"Excuse me?" I quietly said in the officer's direction, making sure he wasn't a light sleeper. The cop didn't move or stir at all. He was definitely out and wouldn't wake that easily.

On the cop's belt, close to his gun, was a key ring. It was risky but I thought I could reach far enough to get it. I didn't have Sara to cause a distraction this time, but I thought I could get the keys without any help. It would take some effort, but I didn't have a choice.

I tried to reach down through the opening to grab the keys. I reached my arm in through the cage window, but couldn't reach from my position. I leaned further in, placing my body against the cage, but I still couldn't reach. I had misjudged the distance I needed to recover them. I would have to think of something else. When I pulled my arm back, I heard a ripping sound and felt a slight tug at my arm. I twisted my body, extending my head to see inside the cage. My shirt had caught on a loose wire sticking out from the chain link. The fabric was pulling awkwardly as half of my upper body extended into the cage.

I tried to pull my arm out again, but the wire held strong, ripping my shirt further. I was stuck, but couldn't wait any longer. I needed to get that journal. I pulled hard, ripping my shirt's sleeve completely down to the wrist. I was free, but the noise was loud and caused gramps to get one last snort out before popping his eyes open. I jumped back as he bobbed his head around, blinking away his slumber. When he was sure he wasn't stuck in a dream and realized where he was, he cleared his throat.

"Hope I didn't make you wait long, son," he said with a smile. "I tend to do a lot of dozing off back here."

"It must get boring up here. I don't blame you for getting a little shut eye."

"Boring is how I like it. Seen too much action in my time to want anything else. You rookies today run into a fight. You don't want to take it slow or nothing." He nodded his head agreeing with himself. "Take it from an old hand, slow down and wait for back up when you need it."

He was giving me advice like he thought I was a new officer on the force. I couldn't ask for a better scenario. "I was just telling my partner the same thing." I wondered how far I needed to take it to sound convincing. A little more maybe. "I said to Larry, you need to relax every now and then. He's a real workaholic you know." The old man nodded in understanding. "As a matter of fact my partner is still at the station pulling an all nighter."

The old officer's head bobbed back slightly tipping to unconsciousness. I thought he was going to dose off again if I didn't start to entertain him in some way. I wondered if he liked juggling. Without help, his eyes widened and his head popped back up.

"Well, what can I do for you today?" the old cop said. "Or is it tonight?"

"As a matter of fact, earlier tonight my partner dropped off some evidence for a case we were working on. He didn't know I was in the middle of something big."

"What did he bring in?" he asked.

My heart started to speed up. I was never good at lying, but he actually believed me. If only Sara could see me now.

"It was a brown leather journal. Should have come in with the girl they transferred with it." I gave the officer a moment to register what I was looking for.

"Sure, I know the one. I was here when it came in."

"Great." Thank God. "I'm going to need to take it out for a bit. Something came up that could be really useful in the case." I thought I was beginning to sweat, but not in any place I wanted to admit too.

"Be right back," he said.

"Thanks," I replied as the old man shuffled away, happy for

a deviation from his nightly routine. He moved with some pep, but still at the speed of a turtle. He disappeared in the back and walking through to an attached room. A light switched on filling the front office with bright yellow.

Several minutes passed with no sign of the old officer coming back. I thought he might have fallen asleep back there, or worse, had a heart attack. He wouldn't have any way of calling for help. I was about to jump inside the cage when I finally heard his shoes tap against the linoleum floor as he made his way back out. I was relieved when he slipped back to the front, carrying a cardboard file box. He placed it down on the counter directly in front of me and pulled over a ledger.

"Name?" he asked.

Catching me off guard I almost read the name right off his chest intending to use it as my own. I was glad I caught myself in time because I didn't think I looked like an O'Riley.

I almost said Jamie, but caught myself again. "Andrew Dunn," I finally said, and added, "Detective Andrew Dunn." I almost lost it as I said the name a second time, but was able to hold back laughter. I flashed the police badge in front of Officer O'Riley as he pushed the evidence box toward me without looking.

"It's all yours detective. Just take what you want and I'll sign it out."

I opened the box and found several research notebooks from Salk's lab. Under those I found Alex's brown leather journal. I took the book and set the lid back in place. It was all I needed to get Sara out of jail. Going to the press was probably the only chance I had left.

"Thanks for the help," I said as I walked away with the journal.

"Excuse me Detective Dunn?" Gramps called out.

I stopped in my tracks. I expected Officer O'Riley to have his gun pulled and pointed directly at me. Was he able to see through my lies after all, giving him something to do? One last bust for old-time's sake? I was about to go to prison for the murder of two people and they would add impersonating a police officer to the list of charges. I slowly turned around, ready to face the barrel of the old man's gun. It would be the most action the dinosaur would have in his final days.

In the officer's hand was Dunn's badge. "You forgot this," O'Riley said.

I had forgotten the police badge on the counter and he was just giving it back. My heart raced as I walked over to the cage and took the shield from his hand.

"Thanks a lot. Don't know where my head is tonight."

"I won't tell if you won't."

"Huh?" I sounded.

"That I was sleeping on the job," the old man said with a light cackle.

"Deal!" I almost shouted as I walked away, hopefully for good this time.

I walked across the bridge to the jail and continued to the lower levels where the holding cells would be. I didn't know if this was going to work twice, but I didn't have another plan. I thought about how scared Sara must be, alone, surrounded by hardened criminals. Real lowlifes who would attack a wholesome girl like her.

I couldn't bring myself to think about the horrors she could face in a place like this. I entered the building and began descending the stairs. The lower I got, the drearier it became. My surroundings reminded me of medieval dungeons, where kings and queens would torture prisoners to get valuable information, all in the name of decency. Men would lie on the rack as their flesh was burned away from their bodies. The further I descended, the more I realized how my thoughts raced to Sara's unavoidable doom if I left her to this fate.

I reached the bottom floor, stepping off the last grey marble step into a dimly lit waiting area. I expected to encounter at least some police officers, but the whole area was empty. I found double metal doors that led into the holding area. My mind began to play tricks on me. What if the police were waiting in the next room for me? I thought it could be a trap. I had given them enough time to set everything up while I played buddy-buddy with Officer O'Riley.

I was being paranoid. I knew they didn't know where I was yet. They would still be scratching their heads searching everywhere for me. I was in the last place anyone would think to look.

I instantly wanted to turn around and run away when I entered the room. My instincts had been right, it was a set up. Two officers were down here waiting for me. I was done for. I wouldn't be able to save Sara or clear our names. Worse, the vaccine would continue to be used without any knowledge of its problems. Thousands of children would die at the hands of the disease they thought the vaccine was going to save them from. I stood by the doors waiting to be arrested. I closed my eyes preparing for the handcuffs to slap down onto my wrists.

I waited, and then I waited longer, but nothing happened. I opened my eyes and realized no one was there to arrest me. The two officers were supposed to be down here, stationed to guard the holding area and its occupants. They also appeared to be as bored as Officer O'Riley had been upstairs. I didn't think that these two cops would be as happy about the boredom as the old man was. These two were younger, both it seemed in their early twenties.

The older of the two was sitting at a command station behind a glass enclosure. He watched a screen intently that lit his face in a warm glow. The other stood in front of a small rectangular cabinet preoccupied, reaching into the cabinet and moving objects around. I watched as the younger officer took his time, rearranging guns on what appeared to be a small gun rack. He decided to grab a large shotgun from the minimal, but dangerous inventory, checking it for malfunctions. Neither of the cops seemed to care that I was there. On the side of the room was a large metal door with a heavy looking locking mechanism. I assumed that the guard at the desk had a remote somewhere at his station that he could use to unlock the door at will.

I counted to three. My palms were sweaty and I felt like I needed a change of underwear.

I was relieved that my plan wasn't to physically rescue Sara from jail. I understood that part could wait and no matter how hard I tried, I didn't think I'd be able to get her out of there anyway. I had the journal, but I was still risking everything just to talk to her. I needed her to know that I was going to go to the press. If it was a good idea, she'd agree with my plan. I just wanted her to know I would never give up. I knew I had to do it no matter the consequences. My feelings for Sara were growing rapidly, and I was beginning to believe that she was starting to feel the same way about me. There was a chance that I wouldn't see her ever again if this didn't work. I wanted to make sure she knew that I was thinking about her.

I took a step forward, realizing my feet were making a squishy sound every time they hit the marble floor. It was too late to back down now. I tried to shut out my physical limitations. I needed to be Detective Andrew Dunn, a hard-boiled cop not afraid of the consequences of his actions.

The officer at the gun cabinet acknowledged my presence, turning in my direction with the shotgun in tow, and gave me a friendly head nod. Despite the gun, and my screaming instincts to run, I moved toward the younger officer holding the shotgun.

"Can I help you?" the police officer said while he intentionally blocked my path. The officer's size was intimidating enough, and the shotgun firmly in his hands was just an added bonus.

I needed to answer, but my mouth wouldn't move and words stuck in my throat. Shit, I knew this wasn't going to work. I wanted to turn around and get the hell out while I still could. Instead, I reached inside my pocket, not realizing what it must have looked like as the officer clenched the shotgun willing it to be loaded.

My thoughts recovered before someone was shot without reason.

"Hey there fella, just getting my shield out," I said pulling Dunn's badge out from my pocket. The cop relaxed, moving the shotgun back down toward the ground. I flashed the badge quickly in the big guy's direction, just long enough for him to see it. I couldn't risk the cop reading it and I shoved it back into my pocket.

"Detective Dunn, homicide." I jumped into character without any more hesitation. My body and mind locked into character. The older officer, but only by several years, walked out from his command center and nodded at both the young officer and me. I didn't want them to ask any more questions, which would make me have to think. I needed to be clearheaded as I let Dunn's words slip from my mouth.

"Let me cut the fat here officers. One of the girls we brought in today has some explaining to do. We found this book outlining how she did her old man in." I was trying to channel Bogart, but I felt more like George Burns instead.

The smaller guard at the desk wrote out a form and placed it in front of me. "Sign here please detective," he said. "Must be a long night for you, coming down here at this hour?"

I laughed, "You know I've been at this damned case all night. I didn't even realize what time it was." I started to fill in the form, mostly with gibberish. I had to hope neither of the cops actually read what was on the sheet of paper. I barely looked at the form as I wrote out Dunn's name. I made up a badge number. I knew it was on the badge, but if I took it out to copy, they would know it wasn't mine. Every cop remembered his badge number. I had watched enough "Dragnet" episodes to know that. "This broad has been driving us crazy over at headquarters since we brought her down." Did I just say headquarters? What the hell was I talking about? "She giving you two any problems tonight?"

The bigger guy started to talk. "That little thing? No way, detective. I actually feel bad for her. We had to put her in her own cell. Didn't want any of the other ladies messing with that pretty face of hers."

I was on a roll and couldn't let up. "Don't let those blue eyes fool you, boys. She's a killer, a blood thirsty, cold-hearted killer." I signed the papers, scratching more gibberish, and began to walk to the metal doors behind the officers. "See you later fellas."

"Hey wait. Dunn was it?" The older cop said. He looked down at the form in front of him.

I stopped in my tracks. The gig was up. I was cooked. End of the line. I turned around, ready to stand my ground. Unfortunately, my voice cracked when I did. "Yes . . .?"

"You forgot to fill out the inmate's name," the smaller cop said. He pushed the form back in my direction.

I almost started to cry as I wrote Sara's name on the printed line. I wanted to scream at the two cops for nearly causing me to have a heart attack. I placed the pen down and continued toward the door.

"Have a nice day, detective," the older cop said as he reached under the desk, pressing the button to unlock the door. I heard the door unlock with a large metal to metal clank.

"You do the same," I responded as I walked through. I was

ready to curl up into a ball and lay on the ground like a small child deprived of his favorite toy.

As the door closed behind me, I felt my entire body relax. On reflex I gasped for air. I hadn't realized I wasn't breathing. Finally, I let out a long overdue breath. Once again the urge to empty my stomach passed and I slowly regained all my senses.

I followed the sign that pointed toward the women's side and continued down a wide hall, looking into mostly empty cells. The ones that were filled had faceless inhabitants quietly snoring on their bunks. After wondering around for the better part of ten minutes, I found Sara's cell. She was curled up on a cot, wrapped in a wool blanket. Her diary lay open by her side. Even in jail, she looked peaceful. A window in the corner let the light from the moon shine down, producing a glow upon her exposed skin.

I wondered how long I could get away with standing there, watching her without her knowledge. Would I get caught if I waited until morning watching her sleep? I didn't have too much time to wonder because Sara's eyes fluttered open. She instantly saw me and an overwhelmingly beautiful smile appeared on her face. Her brilliantly white teeth sparkled, until she saw the cell's metal bars between us and remembered where she was.

Her smile slowly faded as she climbed out of the bunk, walking slowly toward me. She clutched the blanket around her shoulders, keeping the cold air away from her fragile figure. I reached through the bars and held out my hand. She quickly snatched it into her own and squeezed it with her entire being. Sara pushed her head against the bars finding my lips with her own. We stood there for what seemed like forever, but she broke away once she noticed the journal under my arm.

"You found it!" she said with as much excitement as one could have after spending the night in jail.

I brought the book up into the open. "Yeah, now I just have to figure out what to do with it. I'm thinking of taking it to the paper," I paused and stepped back. "I just remembered I'm mad at you."

"You wouldn't have gone with the plan if I told you."

"I was so worried about you," I said. Sara placed her hands on mine and pulled me back into her.

"Jamie, you did it. You got the journal. All we have to do is get the book to Dunn . . ." I turned away when she said his name. "What?"

"It wasn't Detective Bloom, Sara. Bloom didn't kill anyone. Dunn did." She shook her head.

"But he was helping us!"

"He was playing us the whole time," I said in anger. "He needed us so he could get to this." I held the journal up in front of her. She took it and began to flip through the pages once again. I leaned over and put my arms through the bars. "I always wanted to know what it felt like to be in one of these."

"Not as much fun as you might think, tiger," she said without looking away from the page. She paused. "Jamie . . ." Sara turned back toward me. "How did you get in here?"

Just as I was going to answer her question, I heard the door burst open and at least two sets of feet started to sprint toward Sara's cell.

"He went in this way," the police officer yelled, his words echoing off the walls.

I thought I would have more time. Damn it. I locked lips with Sara one more time and then pulled away ready to run.

"Jamie!" Sara yelled.

I turned back. Sara was holding up the journal in her hand. This just wasn't my day. She held the book outside the cell. I took it from her and kissed her on the mouth once more, this time a little harder and with more passion than before. I didn't have any more time to waste as I pulled away taking the journal with me.

"How dumb can you two be?" Dunn screamed at the other cops. He was running with the other two officers. I could hear their quick steps coming closer. I ran the opposite way, but had no idea where I was going. I turned a corner and came to another row of cells.

"Is there any other way out of here?" Dunn questioned the guard, yelling, his words echoing all around me. The acoustics in this place were amazing.

"There's an emergency exit," the guard responded quickly. Their steps increased in rhythm as all three men sped up.

Another way out? It was my only chance. I had to find it. My sense of direction was completely discombobulated as I hit a dead end and doubled back hoping I wouldn't run directly into the three of them.

Before they could catch up to me, I finally found it. The door was to the right and I slammed into it, pushing the bar with what should have been enough force, but it wouldn't budge. They were closing in and I only had a matter of seconds before they caught me. I stepped back, looking for a way to open it.

"Press the red button," a voice called out from the inside of the cell closest to me. I turned to see a middle-aged man sitting up on his bunk, rubbing his bare chest and wearing blue jeans. Several days of not shaving gave the man a thick black beard that covered his face. I paused, not sure how to thank the man. "Better hurry, they're almost here," he said.

Thank you was all I could manage. I wanted to help the lost soul who had helped me. He didn't have to help, but he did. Their steps were growing louder with every breath and I knew I had to leave. I pushed the red button several feet away from the door and the door unlocked with the same metal to metal clank as before.

An alarm signaling my escape sounded as soon as I had the door open. It was piercingly loud. Over it I could still hear Dunn's footsteps closing in right behind. I turned back as the real Detective Dunn and the other two cops sprinted around the corner. Dunn went for his sidearm, but I didn't wait any longer to hightail it out of there.

When I was outside, I looked around for something to block the door. I found a small piece of wood. I shoved it under the door jam and it fit snuggly making a small wedge. I wasn't sure how much time it would buy me, but as my only option it would have to do.

The sun was beginning to rise. Commuters were already filling the streets, driving to work to start their normal day. I used the side rail as leverage to pull myself up a flight of stairs to the street. My timing was impeccable as a trolley rolled to a stop directly in front of the jail. The doors opened and I jumped on the rail car.

As the doors closed, the car began to move gliding along on its tracks. I watched as Dunn ran out onto the street followed soon after by the other police officers. The guards stopped when they got to the top of the stairs, slumping over in exhaustion. Dunn ran into the street attempting to race down the trolley, but I already had too much of a lead. He disappeared altogether when the trolley picked up speed going downhill onto a straightaway. I kept watching, waiting for the detective to catch up and find a way to jump onto the trolley. After a minute or two I realized I had lost him for the time being.

I sat down, taking a seat close to the back and let out a huge sigh of relief. My muscles were incredibly tense as I made an effort to relax. I held the journal tight to my chest. A moment later I realized the driver was staring at me in his rearview mirror. I tried to come up with something to shift his attention away from me, but I said the first thing that popped into my head.

"I didn't know she was married," I said loud enough for the driver to hear me.

The driver laughed and returned his eyes to the road, forgetting the whole fiasco. In his line of work he saw much weirder events than what I could offer. I sat back wondering where I was going to go now. I could go straight to the press, but thought about whether the journal would be enough. Would they want more than I could offer? I watched the houses zoom by as I stared out the windows. I zoned out, feeling my eyelids becoming heavier.

Listening to the hum of the car, I felt my head bob back, but I couldn't stop it from hitting against the window, jolting me wide awake. In a matter of seconds my head bobbed back once again, but sleep took its hold without any more interruptions.

Chapter 10

At first I thought I was completely numb, but slowly I realized just how much pain my body was in. The pain was there in full force, driving me to bite down on my lip in shock. The taste of iron filled my mouth, completely waking me from my slumber. For a moment I couldn't remember where I was. I was on a rail car, but not sure why. I wiped the blood away from my mouth and looked outside as the front of the Cathedral of Learning came into view.

For a split second I thought the whole last three days had been a nightmare. Everything --the murders of Dr. Wheeling and my mentor Dr. Gerlach, the vaccine, the drug companies, and the knowledge that Detective Dunn was to blame -- could have been imagined or dreamed. Then a rush of realization flooded into my conscious mind, filling my chest with pressure. The sense of dread washed over me, completely engulfing me, clutching my throat as I struggled to gasp for air. My chest burned and I realized that I was having a panic attack for the first time in my life.

I placed my head between my legs and tried to breathe deeply, opening my airways, expanding my lungs. I felt my whole body buckle from the sheer exhaustion of the last few days. I felt my face, going over the long stubble growing over my chin and upper lip. I forced my breathing to slow, hoping my heart would stop beating uncontrollably. I found my groove and felt my chest relax.

I got up from my seat and walked slowly up to the front door, waiting for the car too stop. My vision was still a little blurry from sleep, but I was aware of several of the other passengers staring at me. I smiled and nodded at a white-haired woman close by. She averted her eyes, refusing to make eye contact. Instead she turned to her husband trying to restart up a conversation he wasn't sure he was a part of in the first place. I smiled again, understanding the absurdity of it all.

The doors slid open and I waved at the driver on my way down the stairs. I lost my balance at the bottom step and almost tumbled out onto the sidewalk. I was able to regain my balance on a cute brunette co-ed waiting patiently to board the trolley.

I quickly apologized as I hurried past the girl, but her middle finger seemed to suggest that I wasn't forgiven. I stumbled toward the Cathedral across the street.

The sky was brightening as the sun slowly made its long journey over the world. Normal people were just getting up, ready to take a shower to fully wake from a long night's sleep.

I stepped off the curb, walking absentmindedly. Without warning, a large brown delivery truck swung out in front of me, coming so close I could feel my hair bounce off its side. I spun around to see a man in the back of the truck dropping a large stack of newspapers onto the sidewalk for the newsstand stall behind me.

"Watch where you're going, kid!" the man in the truck yelled out. I watched as the large newspaper truck drove away to make its next delivery.

The vendor from the stall stepped in front of me, taking a stack of papers from the pile and carrying them back to his stall. I found myself focused on the front page, not able to turn away. The vendor came back over, but I grabbed a paper from the pile.

It was the morning's *Post-Gazette*. The headlines were about the baseball game the night before. The Pirates had beaten the Cubs 4 to 1, but it wasn't the headline that had attracted my attention. It was another article, one further down on the front page.

One Firm's Vaccine Barred; 6 Polio Cases Are Studied

By Bess Tunnal

WASHINGTON, April 27- *The United States Public Health Service today ordered temporary withdrawal of its authorization to distribute and use the Salk vaccine made by Cutter Laboratories of Berkeley, Calif.*

after receiving reports of six cases of paralytic polio in children who received the vaccine.

Surgeon General Leonard A. Scheele, recalling Cutter's vaccine, has initiated an investigation, calling the measures safety precautions while voicing "complete faith" in the Salk vaccine.

"These actions do not indicate that the vaccine is in any way faulty," said Dr. Scheele. According to the doctor, "The children may have already been infected with the polio virus when they received their inoculations, but we felt the safest course of action . . . ."

He said that in all other respects the national inoculation program should proceed as planned . . . .

In New York, sales of the Cutter product have been halted. Health Department inspectors have seized all unused packages of the drug pending completion of the investigation.

The vaccine was being recalled, but only from the Cutter stock! What about the rest? How was it that Cutter was the only one being blamed?

"Hey buddy. This ain't no li'bary. Yins' gonna pay for that?" the vendor queried in his thick Pittsburghize accent as he waited for me to pay for the paper. I turned to the balding man whose stomach hung out from his belt. I found a quarter in my pocket and tossed it to the overweight vendor.

I read the article again, making sure I understood what was going on. Only one company had the vaccine recalled. The government knew there were infected vaccines, but Cutter was being held solely responsible for everybody's oversight. Health Services didn't know what it was doing. None of the vaccines were safe.

Sara was in jail and I was being set up for two murders I didn't commit. Would they call off the dogs now? Were we in the clear or was it going to be all or nothing? I still had evidence to prove where the blame should be placed. I knew about the murders and the cover up. Would Dunn let me go with what I knew? I highly doubted it.

I crossed the street, moving away from the Cathedral, and began my walk up the hill to the municipal hospital.

I approached Salk's lab, which was already buzzing with energy. At least thirty men and women in white lab coats were conducting different complex experiments. Rubber tubes entered then exited different glass cylinders and beakers. Bunsen burners were at full flame. Hundreds of stacks of Petri dishes filled the remaining table space in the room.

I slipped in, trying not to bring any attention to myself. I took out the journal from under my arm pretending to read it. On the opposite wall I found a rack with several white lab coats. I grabbed one, slipping it over my wrinkled rags, as if I had done it a hundred times before.

"Can I help you?" a female voice said from behind me.

I twisted around meeting the gaze of a young female lab technician. She was tall, taller than me, thin, and had perfect olive skin. The woman could have been a model except for the glasses and a white hair net she wore covering thick black hair curled into a bun.

"Ummm . . . ," I choked back. "Could I . . . please . . ." For some reason the words wouldn't come out. I didn't know what I was doing or who could help me. I had come this far on a whim, but was unsure of my next step.

"Are you looking for Dr. Salk?" she asked patiently realizing the effect she had on me.

"Yes. I am," I said.

Salk could help me. I could give him the book and he would know exactly what do to with it. "Do you know where I can find the good doctor?" Did I just say *the good doctor*?

"He's in his office. I can take you there if you follow me please." She led as I followed very closely behind. "We've had a couple other journalists come by this morning already, but I believe you are the first to try to impersonate a researcher to gain access."

She thought I was a reporter.

"You know us, always trying to get the big scoop."

I looked down at my clothes. A little dirt and grime all over my shirt. I guess I did look like a sleazy writer after all. I followed her to Salk's office. The door was open and a thin man with black horn-rimmed glasses sat intently reading a report on his desk.

"Dr. Salk?" the girl said, "Here's another one to see you."

Doctor Jonas Salk extended his hand to a chair in front of his desk. "Of course, please have a seat. Thank you, Phyllis." Phyllis smiled and left the room. "I don't mind being interviewed again," he said as he continued to write. "You will have to excuse me though because I don't think I can come up with anything original. I'm afraid I've given the same report to several papers already, so if you want something original I'm afraid I can't . . ."

I gripped the journal in my hands. "Dr. Salk, I'm not a reporter," I interrupted.

Salk leaned back in his chair and rested his hands on the table. "Oh, I'm sorry. I just assumed . . ." He paused, not sure of himself. He repositioned himself in his chair and continued, "Then what is it I could do for you? Mister . . .?"

I took a deep breath. "My name is Jamie Schmidt. Not long ago a very good friend of mine, Dr. Alex Gerlach, discovered very sensitive information concerning your vaccine, specifically the way in which it was being produced commercially."

Salk sat forward. "I've been away for the last week working with the Health Department and now this problem with Cutter has been brought to our attention. I heard about it this morning with the rest of the country." Salk wasn't mad, just a bit annoyed that he had to go through this conversation again.

I extended Alex's leather journal to Dr. Salk. "Please doctor, everything is explained in this book. I just ask you to please . . ."

"I must say this is a very pleasant surprise, Mr. Schmidt." I pulled the book back, turning to the doorway where the familiar voice of Dr. Longmont was echoing. Salk stood up and extended a hand to Longmont. They were shaking hands as if they had been friends for years.

"Jonas, I didn't know you were acquainted with young Mr. Schmidt," Dr. Longmont said as he let go of Salk's hand.

"Mark, good to see you. To what do I owe the pleasure of having Parke-Davis's director of operations in my humble laboratory?"

Mark Longmont gave me a smile that could kill the devil himself, a smile so mischievous that even Satan would quiver at his hooves. He extended his hand toward me, but I shifted my weight backwards, but caught myself before I went tumbling over in the chair. The two men didn't take their eyes off of me as I stood up.

Salk began again, "Maybe you could answer some questions for this young man. I'm not sure if I can be of any help to him at all. Now what was it? Something about the vaccine I imagine?"

"Jonas, I would be happy to help."

I clutched the journal, noticing Longmont's eyes repeatedly darting to it. I couldn't tell Salk now what I knew, not with Longmont here. There was a chance Salk knew about the murders too. What if he knew everything already? I was giving away my whole hand.

If Longmont also worked for Parke-Davis, he must have either known or come into contact with Dr. Wheeling. According to Alex's notes it wasn't a big company. Longmont might have known where Dr. Wheeling was staying and for how long. I guessed that Longmont had been Wheeling's superior and maybe very recently he developed some misgivings about their working relationship. Was Dunn the only one to blame for the murders?

I shook off the stares. "It can wait Dr. Salk, really. It's not important. Sorry to have taken up your time, sir." I walked out of Salk's office, leaving the two men. I could feel Dr. Longmont's stare as I exited the laboratory.

I left the hospital, looking over my shoulder every few steps. It felt as if I was being watched, followed by hundred of eyes all out to get me. I didn't understand the extent of what was going on. I was missing something critical. If Cutter was going to take the blame for all the problems with the vaccine, the other companies would never be implicated. Why would Cutter take the fall when the others were having the same problems? Each company was to blame. Would the Health Department really let the others continue to manufacture a bad vaccine?

I scanned the article once more for good measure, but nothing new jumped out at me. Six children who had been inoculated with the vaccine had contracted polio soon after. Sources said they weren't sure if the vaccine was harmful or if children caught the polio virus prior to the vaccine's use. The other five companies making the vaccine were in the clear as long as Cutter took the blame. That was it, Cutter was just a patsy. Parke-Davis, Pitman Moore, Wyeth, and Eli Lilly all must have had been forcing Cutter to take the fall. My mind raced, but I couldn't think of how they managed to pull something like that off.

Longmont would want the journal because it implicated Parke-Davis in a conspiracy. Would he really have helped kill two men to protect the company's reputation?

Alex had told me about a room in the Cathedral, which only several other people in the world knew existed. Eventually the room would be discovered by the masses, but for the time being no one else would be looking for it. It was rarely used, and only by the school's board of trustees, and only on special occasions. Alex had told me that the last time it was used was to vote out Chancellor Fitzgerald.

I left the hospital and walked over to the Cathedral of Learning. I took the elevator up to the thirty-sixth floor and found the cramped hallway and a narrow door at the end of it. The door was locked, and even if I had a key it would be useless. The door had a brass keypad perched over the handle. The pad was a simple five-button lock, like the one Alex had on his office door.

When Alex was drunk he would tell funny stories, some true, some impossible to prove. I would listen intently, drinking in every word, waiting for a hint of truth to pour from my mentor's mouth. Alex had hundreds of stories, but right now the only one that mattered concerned the sequence of numbers that would open the door in front of me.

He claimed the man responsible for the Cathedral's existence, Chancellor Bowman, chose the door's combination based on the easiest sequence he could remember. Alex had joked that any curious individual would be able to open the door by pressing the five digits in descending order. He would remind whoever was listening that Bowman's tenure as Chancellor at the University of Pittsburgh was short lived because of the man's lack of mental prowess. Alex had always been civil to the men in higher positions at the University, but respect was a completely different animal.

I entered in the code, wondering if the story was a charade. I heard a clicking sound from within the lock. I turned the handle, pushing in, but the door wouldn't budge. It didn't work. Maybe Alex was just trying to make fun of what he considered simple-minded administrators. I tried once more, harder than before, and thrust all my weight against the door. I felt the handle give way and the door flew open, causing the piercing sound of metal against metal to echo up into the steep staircase and into the darkness.

I extended my arm, finding the light switch and flipped it on, but nothing happened. The light bulbs seemed to have all burned out. I took a step up and closed the door behind me. I stood still in the dark, waiting for my eyes to adjust. I could begin to make out the railing, the walls, and then finally the stairs. I pulled myself along the railing, continuing to climb as I reached the forty-first floor.

An explosion from the base of the stairs echoed through the vertical space. I lost my balance, as the echo crept up, but I was able to catch the rail before I slipped and fell to my death. I leaned over the rail toward the noise, but couldn't tell what was going on. Five levels down, the door slammed open and a figure appeared in the bright frame of the lights. A gun in the figure's hand was still smoking from shooting out the lock. Then a beam of light flickered. A small handheld flashlight was pointed up the stairwell.

"Jamie," Andrew Dunn called out, "You up there?" I knew he couldn't really see me, but he still knew I was up here.

I wasn't sure how he had done it, but he had followed me without my knowing. I was up against a dead end. I closed my eyes and finished climbing the stairs to the forty-second floor. Dunn began moving up the stairs as his flashlight swung from side to side looking for the next step.

"I can hear you up there!" Dunn yelled.

I found the exit's metal bar and pressed it in. Dunn shot the beam of light toward the center of the stairwell, lighting the rest of my way. As I opened the door, Dunn's steps quickened, scrapping against the concrete with each lunge.

The entire forty-second floor was made up of just one room surrounded by a series of windows wrapping around the entire floor. Light poured in making it hard for my eyes to adjust to the sunlight. I fumbled forward knowing what I was looking for, but not sure where it was exactly. In the center of the room, a long dark cherry conference table stood. Its dark stain matched the ten dark brown leather chairs around it. I pulled out one of the large chairs to barricade the door. I limped around the conference table heading for the window on the other side of the room. There were at least twelve just like it, four foot windows with clear plates of glass, each with a unique view out over the city. I checked each window, one by one, unable to find what it was I was looking for.

The real secret to the room didn't have anything to do with the board of trustees or any secret compartment for hiding valuable articles. The actual secret was out on a window's ledge.

I finally found what I was looking for outside the last window. The secret was hiding in plain sight for anyone who came up to this conference room. Anyone could reach out and touch the falcon nest at top of the Cathedral. Everyone had known there was a falcon that flew around campus, but only a handful of people had known it had built its nest on top of the Cathedral of Learning years ago. I had heard stories claiming that it was real, but until now I always thought that those stories were just stories told for fun with no truth to them.

Set outside the window, on the ledge rested the falcon's nest. It was bigger than I could have ever imagined, at least three feet in diameter and half a foot high. I wondered how big the falcon must have been that built it. I was also thankful the bird wasn't there to peck out my eyes for doing what I was about to do. I unhooked the window lock and pushed the panel open. I slid the journal down into the nest, hiding the book from plain sight. As I began to pull my arm in, the door burst open and the chair rolled away. Shit, I didn't even realize the chair had wheels.

Detective Dunn stepped into the conference room, his gun already extended in my direction. Sweat dripped down into his eyes and down his beard, but he was hardly out of breath from the journey. He wiped his face with the sleeve of his shirt. I moved forward, getting ready for the chance to overpower the detective while he was distracted, but Dunn cocked his sidearm ready for my advance. So I decided to stay where I was. A moment later, Dunn opened his eyes and set them on me.

"Give me the professor's journal, Mr. Schmidt. I'm tired of playing these games. I'll give you to the count of three, and then

I'm going to try another approach, one that requires an itchy trigger finger."

"I know a great lotion for that itch, detective." I tried to stall him, but I didn't think my jokes would work this time.

"One."

"How about a backrub?"

"Two."

"If you kill me, you'll never find it."

Dunn lowered his gun thinking about my insight. A second later, he raised his gun once more. "I'll take my chances." He said disregarding my plea.

Dunn began to pull the trigger. Setting pressure for the release, but before he fired, he let his grasp loosen. He had decided he needed me after all.

"You're right, Mr. Schmidt. I'm going about this all wrong. I bet I could persuade your friend Ms. Thompson to help. I could be very persuasive alone with that young lady."

"You bastard!" I moved forward wanting to strangle the life out of this dirty cop. I knew I'd be able to. He'd get one or two shots out, but my momentum would give me the power I needed to get my hands around his neck.

I was overcome with rage by his threat. I was too exhausted to think straight. My body was disregarded all rational thought my brain could provide. I lunged at Dunn without even thinking. He took a shot, but his aim was completely off and he missed, leaving him unprepared for my abrasive move. I was able to catch the detective off guard. He expected that I would back down and cooperate with him because of his threat, but instead I surprised him with my attack. I was lucky the bullet missed, only hitting a window, shattering it behind me. I didn't waste time as I thrust my shoulder forward, following through with the full force of a trained jarhead. I collided fully with his sternum. My force and momentum sent both of us crashing into the closed door behind him. I didn't wait for the cop to recover as I took a swing, but Dunn was ready for it. He blocked and countered with his other fist. I took the full force of the impact to my jaw, which sent a jolt of electricity up the side of my head. I noted the need for a dentist if I survived.

I shot back with an elbow to his neck, but it wasn't hard enough. He pushed me off, flipping a knee into my back. I fell to the floor coughing up red fluid. I knew it was my blood, but didn't want to see it. Dunn leaned over me once more, his gun pointed executioner style down toward my head. I wasn't going to win this way, not in a physical fight. I closed my eyes showing defeat.

"I'll give you the journal," I whispered.

"Where is it?"

"Outside the window. In the bird's nest." I pointed with a shaking limp hand.

"Get it," he said.

"I can't.... I can't get up." He pushed the gun to my forehead. It was still hot from the last round. "You're going to have to shoot me!" I yelled and then lowered my voice in a calm patient tone. "I can't get up."

Dunn took some time to consider the situation. He pulled back, not letting the gun wonder away from my direction. I took the time to make an inventory of my wounds. My leg was searing with exhaustion from overuse, but that was nothing new. My jaw was throbbing, but wouldn't dampen my movements. All that was left were a few cracked ribs and a tender *medium-rare* kidney. The last two would cause a problem, but I wasn't going for full contact now, just an escape plan.

Dunn's curiosity got the better of him as I knew it would. He pushed the window open and looked down. He tried glancing at me and then back to the nest, but was having trouble doing both. He kept his eyes on me as he leaned over reaching for the nest the best he could with his free hand.

Dunn couldn't see the falcon soaring down out of the sky toward the Cathedral and its nest. It hovered in the air and made an arc around. I lost sight of the bird, not sure where it went. I caught it again as its two wings spread wide, swooping in, and closing down on its prey. Dunn was too preoccupied to notice the bird's razor sharp claws soaring toward him. He had grabbed onto the journal, but by the time he realized the large grey falcon was upon him it was already too late.

"Tweet, tweet," I said quietly under my breath.

"Huh?" Dunn said turning his face back towards me with a look of confusion. Before he could utter another word the falcon landed on his outstretched arm digging its dangerously sharp talons into Dunn's flesh. Dunn instinctively pulled his arm back into his body, flipping the journal onto the floor and bringing the falcon into the conference room with it. The bird flapped its wings and used the razor-sharp beak God gave it. Instead of only attacking his arm, the bird was now going for Dunn's face.

I saw my chance and took it with haste. I snatched the journal from the floor and got to my feet. I lied to Dunn. I could walk, just not well. My limp now in both legs turned into a hobble. I left the detective to deal with his new friend and made my way down into the dark stairwell, eventually fumbling out onto the thirty-sixth floor. I clutched the book with one hand and grabbed my ribs with the other.

I was stupid to come all this way just to hide the journal. I was being sentimental and it almost got me killed. I couldn't afford to be that pathetic now. I was getting lucky, despite the mistakes I was making, but if I kept it up my luck would soon dry up. I would eventually hit bottom.

The detective found me too easily to be working alone. I'd had too many people try to kill me recently to make this out to be a mere coincidence. There would be more cops coming for me and I had to be prepared. I needed rest, but I didn't have that luxury.

I barely noticed the elevator doors open, but I managed to walk in without much trouble. I thought of my poor tender kidney and was glad I had two. If God were real, he did an amazing job designing our bodies. Break one, use the other. That alone might make me a believer again.

The sun shot into my eyes as I left the Cathedral. I stopped by the concrete fountain in front of the stairs. A small child's face, made of concrete, spit continuously into a pool of water. The water was continuously filtering back up only to be spit out into the pool once again. I plunked my head in, dunking my entire upper body into the pool of gloriously clear liquid, using the chill to wake my pulverized flesh. The refreshing water woke me up into a state of near hypothermia. I wiped the water from my face and shook my head from side to side like an oversized dog.

I knew when I was being watched. I knew the other detective was there before I turned around. I could smell his overpowering cologne from a mile away. Detective Lawrence Bloom leaned against the concrete wall next to the fountain. There was no point in running. I wouldn't be able to outrun a bullet. Besides, Bloom didn't know what was really going on. He really did think that I killed Alex and Dr. Wheeling. He was acting only on a good cop's instinct. I was sure he was probably dirty when it came to a random bribe, but Dunn was lying about the real corruption. Dunn's partner was a good guy. I could trust a good guy, but only if he knew who the real bad guy was. Unfortunately, Bloom wouldn't believe his partner was a charlatan any more than he'd believe his own mother was stealing money from him. This was when the good guy could be just as dangerous as the bad guy.

"Get on the ground and put your hands behind your head," Bloom calmly demanded. "I'm not going to ask you again, Mr. Schmidt."

I wasn't going to put up a fight. I couldn't do it any longer. I dropped to my knees and did what I was told. Bloom slapped cuffs on my wrists and started to read me my rights. It's funny how it's called *reading your rights* when they never actually read them or meant a word of what they said. When he was done, Bloom pulled me up, forcing me to stand.

The detective's attention shifted as Dunn came running

down the stairs, landing on the pavement behind me. I expected the crooked cop to back off now that I was in Bloom's custody, but I wasn't sure he was going to, not after the torment I had just delivered.

Giant gashes pouring with thick blood covered Dunn's arms. His face was a crisscross of red scratches, dripping with red ooze. The worst was a missing chuck of flesh at the tip of his ear. The falcon had done hurt, but I realized it was only topical and not nearly enough to cause any permanent damage. I had wished for a miracle, but instead had gotten a small dose of reality. This was my fate. This is how it would end.

"What the hell happened to you?" Bloom asked his partner.

"A big fucking bird." Dunn moved to take position of me. "I'll take it from here, Larry."

Bloom brought me closer, pulling me around to his opposite side. Dunn stepped closer to his partner. "Larry, don't do this."

Bloom knew his partner too well and understood what was happening. He knew this anger and the actions his partner would take in the name of revenge. It appeared I had a protector after all.

"I'll be back at the station after I deal with this piece of shit," Dunn said as he moved forward, disregarding his partner's protective measures.

"I'll take care of this one, Drew. You go to the hospital. Those cuts look bad."

Dunn was getting angrier. He wanted to take me somewhere, but it wasn't to the police station. He didn't want to book me or put me behind bars.

"It's over Drew. We've got him! Stand down!"

Bloom's face went white when his partner pulled his .357 Magnum out of his holster. "I can't let you take him Larry. He's coming with me." Dunn aimed the gun at his partner. "I don't want to do this." Dunn held his gun firmly aimed at Bloom, not wavering on his demands. "Step away and let me take it from here."

Bloom must have seen the signs, the anger, the sense of insanity, because he wasn't as fazed as I thought he should have been. He turned toward Dunn, pushing me behind his body, setting an actual barrier between Dunn and me.

"I don't know what you're up too Drew, but you need to let it go. I'm taking the suspect in. Leave it be."

When two men with guns are in the middle of a standoff, it's my policy not to interfere. I wanted to duck down, but I didn't think it would do me any good. I would be collateral damage now. Bloom might protect me, but I wasn't sure in place of himself. The two men stood still waiting for the other to make a move.

Without warning Dunn lowered his gun and clicked back the hammer. The tension was cut and my breathing started again.

"Go get cleaned up," Bloom said to his partner. "I'll need your help with the report back at the station."

Bloom turned to go, pulling me along as he turned his back on Dunn. It was a mistake he would never be able to regret. I tried to pull away, tried to yell, but it was too late. Dunn fired and shot Bloom square in the head. Blood exploded from the exit wound, splashing everywhere. Bloom dropped to the ground without a word. The dead detective's blood had splattered over my face and pieces of his skull and brain matter clung to my clothes. Dunn didn't waste any time as he retrained his firearm on me.

I felt like collapsing. If Dunn simply killed his partner like that in broad daylight, I didn't have a chance. I was ready to vomit again, this time on the dead police officer at my feet. Dunn pulled my cuffs hard enough for the metal to dig into my wrists, and pulled me along. I wanted to scream, yell for someone to help, but there wasn't a soul around, no one to help me anymore. Where had all the students gone too? Where were all the people? Then it hit me. Everyone was watching the baseball game today. The Pirates were playing the Cubs today. No one would be able to hear the gunshots over the crowd's cheering at Forbes Field.

I didn't know Detective Bloom well. What I did know, I didn't particular care for. But seeing him murdered in cold blood gave me chills that would never go away. If nothing else, I could add another nightmare to my long list of painful memories. Dunn had killed my last hope, and now I was going to meet the same fate once he had what he wanted.

Chapter 11

I drove as Dunn sat in the passenger seat of his car pointing his gun in my direction. Once he had me behind the wheel he had removed the cuffs, making me drive to wherever he was going to finish me off. I tried carefully not to hit any deep potholes. I didn't want him to accidently pull the trigger. A trickle of blood dripped from my mouth. I quickly glanced down at my wrists. They were red and swollen, but besides a small cut along the left exterior of one, they were fine. My slacks were covered in blood most of which wasn't even mine.

I didn't know where we were going, but I knew it wouldn't be pleasant when we got there. We traveled east, away from town, taking the main roads. Tall slender oak trees lined the street, providing an overhang that shaded the commuters from the harsh morning sun. I waited for the breaks in the canopy above, trying to get the rays to warm my face.

Dunn wasn't wearing a seatbelt and I thought about crashing the car. I could slam it into a tree by the side of the road or maybe drive right off the many cliffs I curved around. I knew I wouldn't. I couldn't take my own life in the process. I'd wait for the easy way out.

I was tired of this whole mess. The truth about the vaccine was in the journal. Dunn had the journal now, so why did he still need me? My guess wasn't optimistic, and yet I felt relief. It was going to be over soon enough. He'd make me drive to a remote location, somewhere where no one would hear the shots -- two to the chest, one to the head, execution style.

Sara was still in lock up. I wondered if they would let her go after they threw my corpse into the river. Hopefully, they would once my name hit the papers. Unless they planned on pinning all the murders on her, in which case it would be a Spillane ending after all. The dame ends up the killer, and the reader never sees it coming . . . yeah right.

I glanced around the car. It was new two-door model, and nothing like the Windsor I had stolen earlier. The warm grey leather felt good against my sore muscles and I had more leg room than I knew what to do with. I knew it was a Ford, probably a Crown Victoria. It looked new too. Dunn must have been banked by some wealthy investors to sport a car like this.

Dunn told me to turn off the main road. I drove over a gravel path into a garbage dump. It wasn't garbage actually; it was a huge heap of black dirt. I couldn't believe Dunn was going to kill me in a slag heap, a place where the mills dumped their waste from the smelting of iron ore. No one would find my body, not ever. I would be lying beneath a mountain of slag waiting for a new housing development to come along. By then nothing would be left for them to find, my body and bones decayed by the foul smelling acids from the slag. Thinking about it gave me new respect for Dunn. He had thought this through. He wasn't a regular hired thug. He was smart. He knew how to get away with multiple murders.

He told me to stop and I turned the engine off. He motioned for me to get out of the car. I did what he wanted, all the time thinking about making a run for it. But I wouldn't run, not anymore, and he knew it. Dunn walked around to the front of the car. I wasn't going anywhere so he lowered the gun keeping it by his side, hammer cocked and ready just in case.

Slowly a black Ford pulled into the slag behind the detective. Dunn didn't bother to turn around. I could see the figure behind the wheel, but couldn't make out the man's face to identify him. The car pulled up beside us. The engine turned off and quieted in a low hum. The man opened his door and stepped out. It wasn't Keith Ontario, the other man who had tried to kill me. I had misjudged everything. My mind raced trying to piece everything together.

"You're late," Dunn said to Mark Longmont. "I was beginning to think you lost your nerve."

Dr. Longmont smiled and shook his head. "Detective, did you recover the journal like I asked you to do?"

Dunn threw Alex's journal to Longmont. "It's right there. Now I want my money."

"Take care of him and I'll get you . . . wait, is this a joke?" Longmont walked over to Dunn and pushed the journal into his chest. "What the hell is the meaning of this?"

Dunn looked down at the book. "I did what you asked, just give me the money." Dunn's face began to blotch. Big red spots appeared out of nowhere. He was nervous, and a bit angry. Dunn marched over and placed the barrel of his gun against the side of my head. He pushed the book under my chin. "Where is the journal?"

My eyes went wide. I looked down and noticed for the first time that the book under my nose wasn't Alex's journal. It was the same brown leather, but something was different. It was less used looking. I grabbed it and opened the cover.

The writing wasn't Alex's. It was cleaner, curvier, and more feminine like Sara's diary. She switched the books. I was speechless. Sara had saved my ass again. I wanted to cheer, but making a man angry as he held a loaded gun to your head might have been the worst scenario I could think of. I still had more time. I wasn't going to die, not yet anyway.

"I'm going to ask you one more time, Mr. Schmidt, and then I'm going to blow your head clear fucking off. Do I make myself clear?"

Longmont came closer and motioned for Dunn to lower the gun. "It's the girl. She must have switched the books. Let me have a moment with Jamie, Detective Dunn." Dunn lowered his gun and moved away, leaving us alone.

Longmont took a deep breath and let out a large lungful of air. The man took a cigarette out of his pocket and lit it with a match. He took a puff, letting out a cloud of white smoke.

"Jamie, I'm going to need you to cooperate with us this time. That journal is very important and I do not want you to jeopardize the safety of a certain loved one." He took the cigarette between his lips and inhaled once again. I understand you have endured an awful lot these past couple of days, but trust me when I say this whole mess will be over if you provide us with Alex's notes."

"Why do you want them so much? The entire world already knows Cutter is responsible for the infected vaccine. What difference will the journal make now?"

"Don't be coy, Mr. Schmidt. I know you've read the book quite extensively. That journal means quite a lot to all of us. It could jeopardize millions of American children, preventing them from receiving the polio inoculation. You see Jamie . . . oh, I'm sorry, I *can* call you Jamie, can't I?

"I prefer Mr. Schmidt actually," I answered.

"You see Jamie, if that journal gets into the wrong hands then there is a great possibility that the companies making everything from aspirin to the flu vaccine could be shut down. We can't have that now, can we?" Longmont took another puff. "If word spreads that the vaccine is not safe there will be a panic the magnitude you can't even begin to conceive."

"The polio vaccine isn't safe. You've already killed children with the activated virus in the vaccine," I shot back.

Longmont shook his head. "Look at the bigger picture. A few

children died, maybe a few more, but millions get to live because of their sacrifice." He nodded to the detective to continue.

Dunn stepped forward ready to restrain me. "Did Alex have to die over this? Just to save your job?" I shot back. Longmont motioned for Dunn to wait. "What about Dr. Wheeling, why did he have to die too?"

"That was an unfortunate necessary bit of collateral damage. Dr. Wheeling was a disloyal employee and was dealt with appropriately. Dr. Gerlach, on the other hand, could not see eye to eye with the greater good. Detective Dunn and I tried to persuade your friend, but with no success I'm afraid."

I turned toward Dunn, ready to rip his throat out. Longmont continued, watching as I killed Dunn with my eyes. "You can't blame Detective Dunn for doing what needed to be done. Your mentor had stumbled onto something that was beyond his understanding. The dear professor would have destroyed an industry that saves millions of lives every day."

"So Parke-Davis called you in to do its dirty work?" I asked.

"Consider me a type of insurance policy for the company if you will. They are only one of my employers. My skills are called upon to handle these types of, crises when a special interest needs protecting."

"You mean you kill to cover up the truth!" I yelled. "Your employers are killing children because of their own mistakes and you hide the truth. How very noble of you."

Dr. Longmont frowned as if he could possibly have feelings. "I'm afraid you do not see the entire picture and probably never will grasp it. Unfortunately for you, I do not have the time to persuade your opinion otherwise."

Longmont turned to Dunn. "We are moving to plan B. Get the girl and dispose of this one."

"Kneel boy!" Dunn commanded as Dr. Longmont turned to walk away. I refused to move, standing my ground. The cop punched me in my cracked ribs. The pain was intense as I buckled over. He kicked my knees in, causing me to drop to the gravel. It couldn't end out here, not like this. I had to get to Sara. Her plan wasn't working. They would find the book and she would disappear soon after. She was smart not to tell me about the switch, but now I was useless to her and disposable to Longmont. I had to think quickly. I waited for Dunn to extend the barrel of the gun toward my head for the final kill. I only had one more chance. I set my hand far into the slag, reaching in to my wrist.

"No more smart-ass remarks?" Dunn cackled. I answered back, but not loud enough for him to hear me.

"Speak up kid. This is your last request," Dunn said, while Longmont climbed into his car.

"You're looking a little anemic," I repeated loud enough for him to hear me.

"What does that even . . ." I flipped the iron slag up into Dunn's face as he pondered my words. I fell to my right, sweeping my left leg out with a snap. I knew this was going to hurt, but I didn't have an option. I needed to catch Dunn off guard and this was the only way I knew how. An intense sharp pain exploded from my foot and I heard the snap of bone as it connected with his lower leg. I was hoping that I only broke a toe, but the sound was too loud for just a toe.

Before Dunn toppled over, he fired his gun down where he thought my head was, but the bullet hit my shoulder instead. Dunn hit the ground hard, knocking his head against the black waste. I was hoping for the impact to knock him out, but wasn't that lucky. I kicked my other leg, the good one this time, out above me and brought it down hard onto Dunn's neck, catching his Adam's apple with a crunch. His eyes went wide as he began to gasp for air. He dropped his gun and pulled himself into a fetal position.

I rolled over onto my stomach and pushed myself up onto my feet. My leg was throbbing so hard I could feel the blood pumping through my veins. The impact from the shot was dreadful, but my shoulder quickly became numb as the blood flowed easily already covering my entire left side.

Getting shot was worse when you could still remember the last time it happened. I knew how the pain would increase as the numbness slowly faded, leaving only the intense burning of the wound. The first stage was easy to deal with. My body would numb around the wound, and adrenalin would pump through my veins so that the rest of the body wouldn't go into shock. The adrenalin would be enough to send a small child to the moon. It was the second stage I was worried about. That was when the pain would start to grow and the blood loss would start affecting my body. I would faint and then go into toxic shock from the lead in the bullet. Eventually, I would die painfully.

Longmont's car stopped when he heard the gunshot and

realized that his assassin was lying on the ground, out cold. I grabbed Dunn's gun and limped over to the car. The blood loss was already making me grow cold. I wondered if he had hit an artery. If that was the case, I would bleed out and die that much faster.

Longmont opened the car door, but as soon as he saw the firearm aimed in his direction he shut it in a hurry. I squeezed off a round, hitting the side mirror causing an explosion of glass. Longmont turned the engine over, but he didn't have enough time to put the car in gear. I opened the driver's side door giving him a sucker punch to his face. I reached over sending my elbow into his neck. Securing the keys, I pulled Longmont out onto his ass. I took a position behind the wheel, put the car into gear and slammed my foot down onto the gas. I pulled the car out sending a spray of gravel and dirt in my wake. In the rear view mirror, I saw Longmont trying to slap Dunn awake. Black slag engulfed my view, causing the whole scene to disappear behind me.

I was back on the road before I knew it. They were going to go after Sara and I had to get there first. I regretted not blowing out Dunn's tires. Dunn was a cop and would have a siren in his car. They wouldn't have to slow down or stop for red lights. That meant I couldn't either.

I was able to get to downtown in record time. I ditched the car at a department store on the corner and made my way up the street. I stood on the sidewalk looking up at the massive stone wall of the county jail. I couldn't just walk in the front door again. The whole police force would be looking for me. I was feeling dizzy and I didn't know how much longer I could stand.

I leaned against a wall for support. I needed to get to Sara before those two bastards could lay their hands on her.

I could hear Sara's voice in the back of my head calling out my name. I knew she needed me. I knew I needed to find her. The voice grew louder in my head until it actually was yelling my name. I closed my eyes to try to lower Sara's sweet voice in my head. When I closed my eyes, her voice changed. The pitch rose and her words changed. "How can you sleep at a time like this?"

The words were loud and clear enough to make me open my eyes. Sara's voice came again, but this time she said, "Jamie, will you hurry up, we don't have much more time. I can hear them coming."

Was I going crazy? Was Sara really having a complete conversation with me in my head? I dropped my head to the ground. As my focus adjusted, I saw a series of black bars below my feet, several feet below the ground. I looked further down the wall where there was a long walkway. Every couple of feet another series of black bars were set in the jail's brick wall. Sara's voice became clearer and I realized she was actually five feet below me. I was above her cell, right outside her window.

There wasn't an easy way down, so I lowered myself on the railing next to the sidewalk. My shoulder had started to burn, the numbness having faded. My grip on the railing had slipped and I'd fallen down, rolling to a stop right in front of Sara's cell. I peered through the black iron bars where Sara's face was peering out. A giant smile appeared on her face, her eyes grew wider, and her teeth began to show. In her arms was another book. I tried to push my face through the bars as far as I could.

"You could have told me you switched the books," I said without a hint of anger.

"I didn't have enough time."

"Giving me a heads up would have been nice. That's twice now."

Sara got onto her toes and pushed her lips against mine. The delicate softness of her mouth caused a shiver to radiate down my spine. It was easy to get lost in a kiss like that.

"Jamie, you're bleeding. Oh my God, there's so much blood." I looked down at my attire, realizing I must have looked like a walking corpse. I was covered in blood, most of which was not mine, except for near my shoulder.

"Just some scratches." I pulled at my shirt. "Not all my blood."

I heard Longmont from the other side of the cell. "Hurry up detective, the boy has already beaten us here."

I pulled the book out of Sara's arms and motioned for her to get out of the way.

"You want this doctor?" I held the book up. "Let's make a deal." Dunn came running into view, a ring of keys jangling, and proceeded to try them as I reached through the bars with the book stretched out in my hands. "I'll trade the journal for Sara."

Longmont motioned for Dunn to stop. "I'm listening," he said.

"You bring Sara to Clapp Hall in two hours. We make the trade. That's it. No tricks, no games. The book for the girl. You let both of us go once you have the book."

"How do I know you'll keep your promise this time?" Longmont asked.

I thought about the response, but Dunn beat me to it. "Because if he double-crosses us, we'll just kill the girl."

Dr. Longmont frowned, but didn't seem to be in all that much distress over the death of a girl he barely knew. "Fine." He spun around. "Detective, please do the appropriate paperwork to have her released."

For a fraction of a second Sara and I made eye contact as I pushed off the ground. A surge of understanding flew between us. I knew there was a good chance I wouldn't make it out of this alive. I pulled myself up onto the sidewalk, visualizing Sara's face. If that was the last time I was going to see her, I hoped to God her image would be burned into my corneas forever.

Twenty minutes later I was walking into the emergency room at Presbyterian Hospital. It was the closest hospital and I needed to take care of the bullet before I passed out. I placed each step down along the entrance floor, dragging my bad leg and leaving a trail of blood behind me.

"Could I have a little help please?" I called out. A nurse was sitting with a doctor behind the check-in desk. I moved over to the desk to check myself in. The doctor popped up from his seat and came over by my side. He shouted some orders to the nurse and she went flew to meet his demands. "My shoulder hurts." I thought I said as the world began to spin. My eyes became heavy as the nurse came toward me and the world turned sideways. Then everything went black.

I drifted into space, not sure where I was going, but happy to be there. I felt content and all my problems suddenly disappeared. I floated for eons, turning around in the dark mist, away from danger. I was empty, but filled with contentment. There was no pain and no worry. There was nothing, and then a white light filtered through my being. I drifted toward it as it called out my name.

"Jamie, Jamie," the voice called out. My body drifted toward the light.

". . . mie . . . Ja . . . mie . . . . Jamie . . . ." Light penetrated my eyes as my lids began to flutter open. I could see a dark figure towering over me, surrounded by a halo. My contentment had vanished faster than it had appeared. My body burned with the pain that sleep had covered. I had to close my eyes. The pain was too intense. I wanted to return to the dark place, go back to where I was safe. I tried to return, but a horrible smell made me open my eyes to officially acknowledge reality.

Keith Ontario was pulling away a small packet of smelling salts. I shifted in bed nervously, surprised by his presence. I tried to sit up, but the feel of sharp knives cutting through my shoulder sent me back down. I turned away.

"It's okay, Jamie. You're safe now," Ontario said with compassion in his voice. I was confused, but the fact that I was still alive was enough to get me to settle down. Besides I was in agony and it felt as if it would only get worse if I moved.

A nurse in all white took the packet and handed me a cup of water. I drank without a second thought. My body was on autopilot and it knew what it needed. I finished the water and held it out the cup. I needed more.

"You tried . . . to kill me . . . ," I struggled to get out.

Keith started to nod in agreement. "I acted in haste without certain information that I now possess." The nurse came back with another cup of water. I took it with eagerness, but decided to pace myself. I didn't want to throw it back up. I thanked the nurse. If felt good to have someone taking care of me, caring about my well-being. It wasn't much, but it didn't take much to make me happy. I thought I might be blushing.

"Jamie?"

I turned back to Keith. "Sorry, rough week."

The nurse took the cup, giving me an understanding nod. It wasn't the look of sympathy that I was used to, rather it was empathy and it caught me off guard. I turned to Keith, remembering what I had to do.

"Sara," I mumbled through a scratchy and horse voice. "They want . . . to trade the journal . . . for her." I went to grab for the journal, but it wasn't around me. I looked up into Keith's eyes. "Where?" I asked.

"The book is safe, Jamie. You lost a lot of blood and need some rest. I also owe you an apology."

Keith moved from my side to a chair close by. I realized I was on a hospital bed. I looked over at my shoulder, remembering the gunshot, but a clean white bandage was wrapped around it. A bag of blood hung over my head dripping through an intravenous tube into my arm. I decided to tell Keith everything. I needed help and he was my last chance. It didn't matter who he was or what his motives were in helping me. There was no one else.

When I finished my story, I looked down into the cup I was

still holding. It was empty. I had finished the water without even realizing it. The nurse took the cup, filling it without a second thought.

"First I should explain who I am," Keith said. "Hoover sent me."

I didn't understand, but Keith made it clear when he pulled out his FBI shield. "I've been working undercover in Salk's lab for months now, after we got a tip from the Surgeon General's office on a possible problem with the vaccine. At first we thought it might be a problem with Salk, but I quickly learned it was something much bigger."

"How did you find me?" I asked.

"All gunshot wounds are reported to the authorities," he said as if reading it from a book. "I intercepted the call and came as quickly as I could." He paused. "I also owe you an apology. We had no idea there was a leak in the police force. I promise you we will help get Sara back safely."

I accepted the apology and tried to get up from bed. I couldn't wait any longer. I needed to get to Sara. The nurse unhooked the IV from my arm.

The doctor yelled out from behind the nurse, "He is not in any condition to go anywhere!" Ontario moved toward the doctor and flashed his badge, pulling him out of the room to persuade him further.

The nurse placed a clean bandage on my shoulder where ten stitches closed the hole left by the .357 Magnum. After she was done, the nurse left the room, closing the door behind.

I waited a few moments before climbing off the hospital bed

onto the floor. I was barefoot and the linoleum was cold to the touch. I limped into the bathroom and relieved myself. While cleaning my hands in the sink, I looked up and checked myself in the mirror. I was wearing a small hospital gown that was open in the back. I realized my undershorts were not the pair I had been wearing earlier. I blushed at the thought of the nurse helping me out of my blood-soaked clothes.

Deep purple circles were clearly visible under both of my eyes. My upper lip was puffy, but not overly noticeable. I pulled off the gown to take a look at the rest of the damage. My right side was covered in a massive black and blue bruise from my armpit to my waist. Both my wrists were wrapped in gauze and my neck had several small cuts. My leg was covered in matching black and blue marks. I adjusted the bandages over my shoulder and was thankful the bullet didn't hit an artery after all. I took a quick shower, washing away some dirt and grime the nurse had failed to get. When I was done I felt much more wide awake. I knew I was exhausted, but I wouldn't let Sara become the nightly news.

I found a bag with my soiled clothes crumpled up inside. They were caked with blood, but I didn't have anything else and a hospital gown wasn't going to cut it. I got dressed and walked out of the hospital room, where Ontario was discussing something with a doctor.

"I'm going alone," I declared to the federal agent.

"I'm sorry?" Agent Ontario replied.

"I go in alone. If they see any of your men, they'll kill Sara on sight."

The doctor began to get agitated once more, but I could tell Ontario had already dealt with the technical aspects of my departure. The doctor wouldn't stop me from leaving now, but that didn't mean he was going to be happy about it. The doctor remained silent, until he walked away, yelling profanities to anyone who would listen. I could tell Ontario wasn't happy either, but if he wanted to get my cooperation in his case he had to let me go in alone.

I could tell Agent Ontario flirted with putting me in cuffs, but finally gave in. "Fine, you go in alone, but we do this my way. Understood?"

I nodded in agreement and I listened intently to his plan.

Chapter 12

The George Hubbard Clapp Hall was a long drawn-out work in progress. It was a blemish on the University of Pittsburgh's developing campus. The actual construction started over five months ago and still only had the beginnings of a steel skeleton. The rusty-red metal frame grew out of the ground, one day it would become a real building, like Pinocchio becoming a real boy. Trouble with the unions had caused the project to move at a snail's pace and because Pittsburgh was an industrial town, nothing happened without the union's approval. It was true legalized organized crime at its best.

Clapp Hall would one day be home to the school's science departments. The brightest students and world-renowned professors will one day work in the embryonic hold of Clapp Hall.

I had been at the construction site for only several minutes, but couldn't control my nerves. The sun was setting. A red glow beamed from the fiery ball in the sky, which was about to set behind the high hills of the city. Several large clouds were providing minimal shade, but it didn't matter. In another twenty minutes it would be dark, the sun gone, and the moon the only light in the sky. There were only a few places in the city where you could still see the open sky and rarely were stars actually visible at all. On Pitt's campus you were more likely to see Kirk Douglas than a cluster of stars in the night's sky.

I was standing on the third floor and wanted a good view of those bastards when they showed their faces. If they touched Sara in any way, all bets were off. I was counting on Longmont to be a gentleman, a monster of sizeable proportions, but a gentleman all the same. A cool breeze occasionally materialized in the air around me, sending chills down my spine. My shoulder was in minimal pain, the drugs the doctor gave me were working wonders. My hip was even bearable with the muscle relaxer they gave me.

Ontario was ready with a team of FBI agents as soon as we made the trade. They were far enough away not to attract any attention. Dunn and Longmont would be cornered, unable to make even an attempt at a getaway. My only job now was to make sure Sara and I stayed alive long enough for the agents to actually show up once the show began.

I was looking for a car to pull up, so I didn't expect to see Sara slowly stroll in alone from behind a fence into the construction site. Her arms were wrapped around her body as she tried to stay warm. Her hair was a mess and I could tell from this high up that her makeup was smeared. Mascara ran down her face making her look like a blond Egyptian. Sara stopped ten yards in, glancing at something behind her. She turned her head back and appeared to be talking with someone very close by. I was going to yell out her name, until I realized who she was talking to. Detective Dunn walked around the corner with his gun extended, giving Sara verbal commands. I checked the block quickly, but Longmont wasn't anywhere to be found. If he didn't show up soon, there would be a small miscalculation in the game plan.

Dunn barked orders and Sara stopped five yards from the metal frame. The detective stayed several feet back. He knew what he was doing. It was never a good idea to stand too close to your hostage -- too close and the hostage had a better chance of overtaking you in the case of the smallest of distractions.

"I brought the girl. Where's the book?" Dunn yelled from the ground. He was straight and to the point.

I stepped toward the edge, bracing myself against a side beam and looked down over the edge of the building. It was at least forty feet to the bottom if not more. Stacks of metal garters were piled high on the ground around the structure. If the fall wouldn't kill me, what I landed on would. I could count on splitting my head open without ever hitting the ground.

I held up Alex's journal and waved it in the air. "It's right here. Send Sara up and I'll throw it down to you."

"I don't think so! You first!" Dunn yelled. "When I have the book, I'll release the girl!"

Even if he did let Sara go, he would probably still shoot her in the back the moment he had what he wanted. I thought I could count on Longmont being a gentleman, but I saw Dunn as an animal not to be trifled with. He couldn't be trusted to keep his word.

"I guess we will just have to make the trade up here then." I pushed back. "I'll wait." I felt like my demand could push Dunn too far, but I had to find a balance or he would think he had the upper hand. If I didn't, then he would be able to use her against me, even after he had the book.

Dunn pushed Sara forward and they disappeared into the first floor. The initial concrete floor was finished on each level. The stairs had been erected, but without any of the railings. Sara was the first one up. Dunn followed, never shifting the gun away from his captive.

Sara's appearance startled me even more as she appeared from the stairs. Her eyes were puffy and red, clearly she had been crying again. I could kill Dunn just for that alone, but I had a long list of other reasons for wanting to kill him. I felt justified in wanting him dead, thinking about what the dirty cop had taken already.

I didn't want Sara to be harmed if Dunn got jumpy, so I didn't move from where I was. Sara was just a means for him to get the book and he wouldn't think twice about pulling the trigger if she got in the way. I didn't think it would matter one way or the other to him. Dunn would try to kill both of us as soon as he got what he wanted.

"Is this what you want?" I asked holding up the journal. "Where's your employer?" I added. If Longmont was hiding there was a possibility he knew the feds were on to him.

"He's around," Dunn responded. I thought I could hear a hint of uncertainly in the cop's voice.

I needed to stall Dunn for as long as I could, but sooner or later the games would have to end. I hadn't seen Longmont, but that didn't mean he wasn't within arm's reach. I wondered how far I could push Dunn, without sending him over the edge.

"Did he even tell you why they want it?" I asked.

"I don't give a rat's ass as long as I'm paid." Dunn set the gun against Sara's head. "Let's get this over with. Set the book down and walk away."

"Let her go first," I said as I slowly inched forward. Dunn paused to think and then pushed Sara out of the way aiming his gun on me instead. She fell to the ground, landing on her backside. Around her were some random tools, which didn't help in padding her landing. I knew she would be fine, probably a little black and blue, but nothing worse than that.

"Now it's your turn," He began. "Book on the ground, then back away," He demanded, unable to keep his patience any longer.

I needed to put on a show to make sure Dunn didn't suspect anything out of the ordinary. I didn't want him to open fire, which he'd do if he knew he'd been caught. I pretended to hesitate, but finally decided to set the journal down on the ground and back away in frustration. Dunn walked toward the book, occasionally looking over at Sara on the ground. Dunn crouched down keeping his arm extended, never intending to take the gun off me. Just a few more seconds and the G-men would step in. He held onto the book as he began to stand up.

I noticed Sara too late as she brought the wrench down on the back of Dunn's head. Neither of us had been paying any attention to her and hadn't thought she would do something so foolish. This time it was me who hadn't filled her in on the plan. The impact caught Dunn off guard, causing him to discharge his firearm in my direction. I dropped down without a second thought, not realizing how close I was to the ledge when I lost my balance.

As I fell I saw Sara bringing the wrench down a second time, hitting Dunn's gun away and sending it arching over my head. Instinct saved me as I reached out my hands, grabbing onto whatever I could.

The newly poured floor was slippery and I didn't have a good hold. My fingers were slowly losing their grip. I wouldn't be able to hold on much longer. Concentrating on my death, I barely noticed as Sara brought the wrench up once more ready to give Dunn a final blow. Her muscles tensed as she brought the tool down as hard as she could. But Dunn surprised her, grabbing the wrench in midair, pulling it out of Sara's grasp and tossing it over the side.

Dunn was able to stand, a line of blood streaking down his cheek. Head wounds always looked worse than they actually were. Sara barely made a dent in the detective's egocentric head. He reached back and slapped Sara across the face, knocking her off her feet. She hit the ground with a thud that sent a vibration through the concrete floor, not helping my cause to hold on.

I tried to pull myself up, first with my arms, but even with the muscle relaxers my shoulder flared. I didn't have the energy I needed and was about to lose my grip. I tried to kick my leg up to get some leverage, but I my entire body was having trouble doing what I needed it to do. I pulled myself with everything I had. My stitches must have popped open because blood was running down my arm once again soaking my new shirt.

I was able to peek my head over the edge, but the next thing I saw was a brown polished leather shoe coming down swiftly over my head. Dunn's foot made contact with my face, forcing me back down. I hung off the side of the building by only my fingertips. Already I could feel my fingers slipping off the flat surface. I couldn't keep a strong hold. Dunn stood over the ledge, looking down at me. His hair fluttered in the wind. I knew what he was going to do next. He smiled as he was about to finish the job. His foot moved to my left hand. I couldn't hang on much longer. His heel began to dig into my fingers. The pain was excruciating. I fought the urge to pull my hand away, knowing that if I let go I would fall to my death.

I heard a gunshot from above. The pressure on my hand withdrew the pain with it. Dunn stood still, confused. A second gunshot rang out and Dunn's forehead exploded as a bullet ripped through him, making his frown all the more appropriate. The pressure on my hand completely vanished.

Dunn's body went limp and I watched him fall forward. His body missed me completely, plummeting to the ground below. I didn't bother to look down. He was already dead before he took the fall. I couldn't hold on any longer. My fingertips, the only part gripping the edge, were about to slip off. I was about fall to my death below where I would join Detective Dunn. My left hand slipped off completely, but a hand reached down and grabbed it, saving me from a certain death. Agent Ontario knelt down on the concrete directly in front of me. He grabbed my other arm and slowly pulled me back onto solid ground. When I was safe he left my side and walked over to the middle of the floor.

"What took you so long?" I said between heavy breaths.

"No need for thanks, kid," Keith said as he bent down retrieving the journal.

I crawled to Sara's side, placing her head on my shoulder. I pressed my lips against hers and whispered into her ear that everything was going to be fine.

"We won," I whispered in her ear. Her eyes opened and she kissed me back without another word. I picked my head up long enough to question Ontario. "Longmont?" I asked.

Ontario shook his head while other FBI agents swarmed though the stairwell. They approached and surrounded us. He began barking orders to the unit of men, while I kept Sara safely in my arms. They soon disbursed all with different objectives. The paramedics were called. When they arrived they cleaned some of my cuts on my hands and applied more bandages. My bullet wound was re-stitched and bandaged once again. I felt like a mummy with the amount of gauze I currently had wrapped around my body. Sara only had some black and blue marks along her face, which she was given an ice pack for.

Keith advised us to go home and get some sleep before we were bombarded with questions. We would need to be debriefed later and would have to give statements to the FBI as the details of the past few days were sorted out.

311

I didn't want to return to my apartment. Instead I asked to be taken to Alex's house. Keith gave his okay and said he would send a police detail later in the night to make sure everything was all right. When we got to Alex's house, one of the agents swept through the house to make sure it was clear and then let me in. I kissed Sara goodbye and went inside. The agents took Sara back to her place leaving me to pass out from sheer exhaustion.

I woke up hours later with an unbearable thirst. I crept downstairs, but hadn't remembered the mess that was left in the kitchen. I wanted to clean up the kitchen, but just didn't have the energy. I hadn't seen the police yet, and wondered if they had got themselves lost looking for Alex's house.

I drank glass after glass of water, not sure where I was storing it all. I realized I was starving and searched the kitchen for anything edible. I found some rotten fruit, which I tossed out, but was able to salvage some cookies and applesauce. I loaded up on snack foods until I was contentedly full.

I wanted to return to bed and sleep for another day. I tried to climb the stairs to the bedroom, but didn't have the energy to finish. I decided I would sleep on the couch in the living room for the rest of the night. A creaking of floorboards above made me stop in my tracks. Someone was walking around on the second floor. Their steps became closer and I realized they were about to come downstairs. I hid behind the side wall and peaked out around the corner.

Longmont quickly strolled down the stairs, carrying a black briefcase. His rim of his Gahan hat was pulled low over his eyes. He was in a hurry judging from the way the case was carelessly packed. Papers were sticking out all over the place and it didn't look like he had the briefcase closed all the way. He stopped at the bottom of the stairs and stared straight ahead. I looked to the side and realized a mirror by the foyer was reflecting my position. From the stairs you could see me clear as day behind the wall. I could see him directly across from me at the bottom of the stairs. Neither of us moved, both unsure of how to proceed.

"Mr. Schmidt, how nice to see you alive," he spoke to the mirror.

"I could say the same thing to you, but it would be a lie," I called out.

"We seem to have a small dilemma here," he said as he slowly reached inside his jacket.

"I wouldn't do that if I were you, Mark. I can call you Mark, right?" I began reaching behind my back, knowing full well I didn't have a gun, but needing some leverage. "And call me Jamie. We've gotten to know each other too well for formalities."

I kept my hand behind my back, trying to make the bluff work to my advantage. If he thought I was packing heat, maybe he would think twice about pulling his gun out so soon.

"Mark would be fine, Jamie," he said as he held his position, keeping his gun at bay. My bluff was working. "It's only fair," he added.

I slowly inched out from behind the wall, keeping my eyes on the mirror, and then turned to face Longmont on the stairs. I kept my arm behind my body and hoped he wouldn't catch on to my ruse. He flashed a glance in the direction of the mirror and then smiled.

I glanced at the mirror behind me as well. I could see myself directly in its reflection, so that meant he could see my back in the mirror and knew I didn't have a gun. Shit, I hadn't thought that through well enough. I jumped out of the way as he pulled his gun out of its holster. I dove back behind the wall as he opened fire on me, blowing holes through the plaster walls.

A cloud of white dust collected in the air around me. I stayed low, trying to find anything I could use to defend myself. Alex was a pacifist, and didn't believe in owning a gun. The closest thing to a weapon would be a butter knife from the kitchen.

I waited for a pause in the shooting to make my break. Longmont came down the stairs gun blazing. I had to make it to the basement's back door and after four more shots, he stopped. I took advantage of his pause and raced to the basement.

Before I could descend the stairs, Longmont came around the wall and opened fire once again. Without hesitation, I leaped down the flight of steps missing every one. I was too high and caught the only light bulb in room, shattering it with my extended hand. I made contact with the floor, and rolled to the left, trying to blunt the trauma to my body.

I couldn't think about the abuse I was inflicting on myself. I realized the stitches on my shoulder had popped open yet again as my shirt got sticky with blood. Longmont followed quickly going down the stairs as I regained my bearings. He set his briefcase down and stepped out into the darkened room.

If I ran for the door the outside light would make my silhouette a giant target, so I had to be careful getting out. I couldn't make it to the back door without giving him a clear shot. I needed another way out.

I began to crawl behind the stacks of newspaper in the corner, trying not to make any noise that would give away my position. I crawled along the floor, eager to get through the maze before Longmont found me. Longmont's wingtips continued to click against the concrete floor as he moved around the room trying to figure out where I was.

"Jamie, where are you hiding?" he asked, waiting for a sign of where I was. "Why don't we talk about this like adults? We can sit down and have some tea, maybe coffee if you prefer."

He wanted to flush me out, but I wouldn't give up my position that easily. I slowly started to crawl as he spoke, trying to move with his words. If he realized I was directly in front of him I wouldn't stand a chance if he started shooting. I was dragging my bad leg behind me, pulling myself along with my upper body. I kept quiet as the pain seared through my shoulder. I positioned an elbow in front, maneuvering a few inches ahead, and then repeated again with the other elbow. I tried to provide momentum with my good leg.

Longmont turned in a hundred and eighty degree arc, searching around the room for me. "This could have been much easier, you know. I didn't want to hurt anyone. Dr. Gerlach wouldn't move on the subject though. If only he would have dropped it, there wouldn't have been a need to kill him. I'm sad to say it, but he was a stubborn fool."

He was provoking me and doing a good job at it. I was trying to ignore him as I continued my planned escape.

"Dr. Wheeling had only a matter of time, unfortunately. I was given an order to dispose of him a long time ago. I guess I'm to blame for letting this go on for as long as it did." He paused and then continued, "I'm beginning to think you don't want to talk." He stopped then and listened for my movements. He started moving again. "It seems a shame really. I mean, once I dispose of you, I'm going to have to do the same to Sara."

Longmont turned around aiming his gun in different directions, ready to shoot at the first sign of movement. I was passing the white ceramic toilet when he walked into a stack of papers, knocking it over. The tower fell forward directly in front of my path. I tried to back up, but my leg was getting caught making it hard to move without a struggle to turn around.

"Mr. Schmidt, I do not have time for this." I heard the match strike against flint, and then the match head igniting. An orange glow appeared from above and then descended, falling directly in front of me onto the newspapers. The papers were dry and caught fast. The flames quickly began to spread, rising fast, and spreading with a fierceness that surprised even Longmont. The man stood over me with a look of surprise. "There you are!" he said, pointing his gun at me.

Before he was able to get a round off, the flames rose higher making a wall between us. He jumped backwards and away from the growing fire. I jumped up to avoid the flames around me. I backtracked along my path getting out of the center of the inferno. Longmont extended his gun. He waited for me to comprehend my predicament. The fire was on one side blocking the door while Longmont was on the other blocking the stairs.

Neither of us moved as the fire grew larger creating a smoke screen around us. I began to cough waiting for Longmont to kill me, but nothing happened.

"Isn't this convenient?" He backed up and retrieved his briefcase. "Jamie, say hello to Alex for me."

He was going to try to trap me in the basement, killing me without actually pulling the trigger himself. Longmont disappeared from my view, exiting the basement at the top of the stairs. I ran back up the stairs only to find the door locked from the other side. I ran back down, coughing as the smoke burned my lungs. I pulled my shirt off and covered my nose and mouth, tying it around me head, making a knot at the back. The fire had reached the ceiling and the flames were catching onto the rest of the house. I had only one option left.

I squatted down low and breathed in a lung full of air, which I held as I stood up. I took a running start and jumped through the wall of flames. An orange and red glow engulfed my entire body as I dropped to the other side and slammed against the back door. It took all the strength left in my body to break the door down. I ran outside, tearing the shirt from my face, and fell to the ground recalling my fire safety training from the army. I stopped and dropped, rolling around on the grass until I was sure I wasn't on fire.

When I was sure the flames had gone out, I sprinted, running up to the front of the house. Longmont had just come out of the front door and was heading for his parked car. I could feel the harsh pain in my shoulder, the sting of cuts, my cracked ribs, and my fresh burns, but the adrenaline pumping through my veins was enough to help me keep my focus. I trotted toward Longmont, arms in, like a Steelers' linebacker. He was surprised when he saw me coming just as I flew my entire body into his, knocking him against the gleaming new automobile causing a dent in the side of the car.

We both landed on the ground, Longmont below me breaking my fall. I flung his gun away, throwing it as far as I could. He was unconscious when we hit the ground. I tried to stand up, but my head started to spin and I fell backwards and the world disappeared.

Epilogue

I sat next to Sara at a booth in the back of Haden's diner. We drank from mugs of hot coffee and waited. We held hands under the table, our fingers interlocking. It had only been a week since the fire department was called to Alex's house. The blaze had engulfed everything, leaving nothing in its wake.

Over the past couple of days, Cutter had been in the news more often than the communist scare. Its entire inventory of polio vaccine was destroyed, along with any evidence linking Parke-Davis to any wrongdoing. Murder had been covered up, and there was no mention to Mark Longmont anywhere in the news.

Lawsuits had been filed against Cutter, but it would take months for trial dates to be set. It seemed that blind faith in corporate America was finally coming to an end. Cutter wouldn't go out of business, not that easily. A deal with the devil was made and Cutter would take a fall, but the industry would support its own, making sure everyone in the corporation was well taken care of. The press would follow the scandal until sales demanded a focus on some other newsworthy topic. Cutter Laboratories would fall from sight, and the American public would lose interest soon enough.

Detective Dunn's body was found at the construction site. The news reported that the detective had murdered his own partner in cold blood and had then committed suicide. A note was found in his pants pocket explaining why he didn't want to live anymore. Alex's death was kept a suicide, and Dr. Wheeling's unfortunate death was made to look like an accident. In retrospect, I had to give the FBI credit. They knew how to clean up one hell of a mess.

Tim Murphy and his wife, Doris, decided to move to the suburbs after all. Even with the threat of Detective Andrew Dunn gone, they still felt uncomfortable so close to where Tim found Alex's body. Doris finally got to leave the city, and Tim decided he didn't mind the extra thirty minute drive back and forth from the steel mill. Tim had only been to the Cathedral of Learning once in his life and I had the feeling he would never return after what he found there.

The bell over the door rang as Agent Ontario strolled into the diner. The downpour outside had soaked his beige trench coat. He pulled off his grey fedora and placed it on the rack with his coat. He made eye contact with us, but didn't give any other indication of acknowledgement. He casually strolled over, taking a seat on the bench directly across from Sara and myself. Ontario ordered a cup of coffee and the waitress filled all three of our cups. He took a long sip, making sure not to burn himself on the hot liquid.

After a moment of silence, I filled the void. "You asked us to come here and talk, so what was it you wanted to talk about?"

"I'm leaving tomorrow," Keith said as he took out a cigarette, lighting it without another thought.

"Where are you going?" Sara asked, actually taking interest.

"I've been reassigned, but I can't tell you where. It's classified," he somberly informed her.

"You could have told us that on the phone," I called out with impatience.

"I thought you two deserved to know that the Bureau is going to deny that it ever had any knowledge of Dr. Alex Gerlach's journal."

Sara was about to shout, but Ontario put a hand up. "Before you say anything, let me finish." Sara shook her head in anger settling down for the time being. "The bureau is going to deny the existence of the journal altogether."

I cut in, "Is this a joke? Is Steve Allen standing outside waiting to tell me I'm on 'Candid Camera'?" The FBI was covering up everything, leaving no loose ends to unravel, and no one was watching close enough to see through the bullshit. "I can't believe you would let this happen."

"Jamie, the FBI doesn't have a sense of humor. I'm sorry, but as far as anyone knows, the journal never existed." He held his composure never changing his speech pattern, retaining an unemotionally boring tone.

I began to get angry, not able to contain the rage growing inside of me. "My best friend was murdered for what was in that book and now you're telling me it was all for nothing?" I couldn't believe any of this was happening. Sara continued to sit in silence, her hand gripping mine more tightly.

"Jamie, you don't have to agree with any of this. But I want you to understand that if that book were to find its way into the public's eye, the whole pharmaceutical industry would be destroyed. No more vaccines for diseases and no more aspirin for a minor headache. This goes far beyond the polio vaccine. It is much more important to the safety of the United States than you can possibly understand.

"We heard all this before from Longmont!" I angrily raised my voice.

"He was right, but wrong in his approach. We live in a world where our enemies are growing stronger every day. What would happen to our defenses if we lost the ability to protect our own people from illness? The information in that book might save a hundred lives, but are you willing to risk the lives of a 150 million at the same time?"

"After everything that's happened, you want us to simply forget?" I questioned.

"As far as the safety of the United States is concerned, yes." Keith paused. He wanted to make us understand, but no amount of information would change my mind. "This information could possibly bring the whole economy to a standstill. The country as we know it today would be no more. Are you willing to let that happen, Jamie?"

I shook my head in frustration. He was wrong about everything. Alex would have been responsible with the information. He wouldn't have destroyed an industry. Alex would have made sure that people knew the truth. He would have made sure the wrong were punished. The industry as a whole would have learned from its mistakes, righting wrongs it had let happen. The American people were smarter than our government gave them credit for. They would understand. They would understand the problems presented.

"Let the people make those decisions," I declared.

"He's right, Jamie," Sara's quiet voice piped in. She surprised me with her agreement. I paused, turning to the love of my life. "I hate to say it, but he's right."

How could she agree with Ontario? Hadn't she just been through the same horrible experience I suffered through? She had seen the blood left at the bottom of the Cathedral, but could still say for certain that a man like Agent Ontario was right.

"You know deep down he's right about this," Sara said as she let go of my hand.

She stood up and I watched as she walked away from the table unable to confront her own realization. I knew she was upset and ready to burst into tears any second. I wanted to run out and hold her, but there was still one last thing I needed to know before I could let this rest -- one last bit of information that would help me sleep again.

"Does Salk know anything about this?" I asked in the middle of a sip of coffee. I needed him to answer me truthfully. There was only one answer I wanted to hear, only one response I knew I could stomach. He set his mug down and shook his head.

"No, he doesn't," Keith said. The words echoed in and around my head. "We kept everything from him. He didn't even know I was working for the Bureau."

I was happy to hear that, but sad because I had lost so much. I could still keep my heroes, even though they lived in their glorious ignorance. That much I deserved.

"I guess you want to keep it that way?" I asked. Keith nodded in agreement. I stood from the booth, throwing down several dimes onto the table.

I reached out and shook the man's hand, giving the agent a nod goodbye. "I hope everything works out for the country," I said.

He looked up at me and gave a low sigh. "Don't worry, Jamie. It will."

I met Sara at the front of the diner and pushed the door open. She walked out, but before I left I turned back to Agent Ontario. He sat at the table, finishing his coffee. He was calm and collected and certain his agency had made the right decision. Deep down I hoped they had too. I turned away and followed Sara out into the mid-afternoon showers, hoping I would never see Agent Ontario again.

Todd L. Schachter
July 7, 2009

LaVergne, TN USA
08 September 2009
157159LV00002B/10/P